Pretty Dangerous

Lynn Emery

Other Triple Trouble Mysteries:

BEST ENEMIES

DEVILISH DETAILS

Chapter 1

MiMi strolled into the stuffy visiting room of Najayo Prison in San Cristobal, Dominican Republic. She gave the female guard a quick smile. The woman stared back at her with a bored expression. MiMi almost had her usual upper-class hip swaying confident stride. Almost. She tugged at the green prison t-shirt she wore over borrowed cheap blue jeans. Her hair pulled back into a pony-tail against the heat, she got tearful when she spotted her friends. Willa and Jazz waited wearing twin anxious expressions. When MiMi glanced over her shoulder at the guard, the woman nodded and gestured. At the signal, a second male guard let Willa and Jazz enter the room. Once they were all seated, both guards wandered off.

"I'm so glad to see y'all," MiMi blurted out. She leaned over and hugged Willa around the neck, and then Jazz. "Now tell me you're going to get me out of here. *Preferably today.*"

"How are you holding up?" Willa grabbed MiMi's right hand. Her maternal instinct turned up on high as she examined MiMi with a critical eye.

"Shit, girl. We ain't visiting her at the hospital. How

the hell you think she's doin'? Foreign prison's are like the worse place you can be and, ouch," Jazz stopped abruptly and rubbed her shin. "Do that again, Willa, and they gonna lock me up for beating you."

"I've been living this nightmare for three hellish weeks, so I don't need a reminder," MiMi said through tight lips. Then she swiped away tears as fast as they fell. "They don't care if you're innocent or guilty. It's all the same to these people."

"I told you not to chase after Jack's stolen stash. Your late 'fiancé' would probably be in jail if somebody hadn't killed him over that dirty cash," Willa smoothly switched from concerned mama to "I told you so" mama.

"He was your ex-husband. What does that say about you?" MiMi shot back with heat.

"That I had the good sense to divorce him," Willa replied mildly.

"Yeah, pretty sure they frown on laundered drug money over here as much as in the states," Jazz said softly as she glanced around.

"Wonderful, Jazz. Give them another reason to give me a life sentence," MiMi hissed back.

"Calm down. This place ain't advanced enough to have listening devices around." Jazz waved a hand as if she knew all about Caribbean prison facilities.

"How comforting." MiMi lowered her head to the rough table top.

Willa glared at Jazz. "I'm starting to wish I'd left you at home."

"Hey, I'm doin' you a favor cause I speak Spanish. I'd just as soon be back in Baton Rouge runnin' my business. Okay?" Jazz snapped her gum as she sat back in the chair.

"Mama Ruby and Aunt Ametrine are looking after your club just fine. You might even do better with them helping," Willa said.

"For all I know your church lady aunt is having Bible study in my place by now," Jazz snapped.

"You might show a little gratitude for all they're doing for you. And by the way..."

MiMi sat straight. "Hey, stop working out your family issues. I'm stuck in a prison and you're here to get me out. Focus!"

"How you gonna come here with your boo carrying weed anyway? That was stupid," Jazz mumbled.

"I didn't know he was going to buy drugs. Anyway, Roddy thought the authorities didn't bother much about marijuana, just the hard stuff," MiMi whispered. She checked to make sure the guards weren't around.

"Yeah, Mr. Genius got that one real wrong. The local lawyer your parents hired said the Dominican Republic doesn't have the same view as other Caribbean governments about marijuana," Willa said.

"You've met with him already? Please tell me he's close to getting me released." MiMi squeezed Willa's hand hard.

Willa winced as she worked her had free and rubbed it. "Mr. Columba is on it, but you know the police and courts are not happy when foreigners assume they can break the law. Those were his exact words."

"But I didn't break the law, and you know that." MiMi pounded a fist on the table.

"Girl, you picked a high-classed loser. *Again.*" Jazz moved away sharply to avoid another kick or slap from Willa.

"No, she's right. Who doesn't know it's dangerous

to be caught with drugs in a foreign country?" MiMi groaned and rubbed her forehead to ward off another stress headache.

Roderick Jefferson worked in the family owned commercial real estate and construction company—when he wasn't driving between Baton Rouge and other cities to parties or nightclubs that is. Still, at least MiMi's parents approved of him. Well, they liked that at least four generations of his family had money.

MiMi snorted. "My only consolation is that his butt is sitting in the men's prison."

"Ahem." Jazz snapped her gum loudly.

MiMi glanced at her. She put a hand over her heart when Jazz and Willa exchanged a look. "Did something happen to Roddy? Oh Lord, I'm sorry about what I said. I hope they haven't hurt him."

"Nah, he's fine," Jazz muttered.

"And uh, he out of prison and..." Willa glanced at Jazz. Her sister wouldn't return her gaze, instead staring off in another direction.

"What?" MiMi demanded.

"Roderick's father has local connections. He's already had one court hearing." Willa's voice trailed off when MiMi hissed at her.

"Don't tell me Roderick has been released. *Do not* tell me that!" MiMi sprang to her feet.

A guard appeared at the door to stare at them through the bars. He snapped a series of questions in Spanish and Jazz walked over to answer him. After a few seconds of conversation, Jazz came back to the table. She waved to the man who stood watching the three women. His expression showed they were testing the limits with him.

"I told him we'd brought some distressing news

from home. I explained you had never been in jail before. He understands." Jazz looked over her shoulder. She waved at him again and the man nodded.

"Look, don't give them any excuses to make this worse. Breathe deep," Willa whispered.

MiMi struggled to keep from screaming her response. Instead she took Willa's advice, inhaled and exhaled several times. Then she sat down again. "What else?"

"The lawyer representing you said that was unusual, but not unheard of," Willa winced under MiMi's hard stare. "The good news is, that might help at your hearing. Plus the weed dealer has disappeared, so no witness."

"Let's hope so, cause these people don't play when it comes to crime. See, for at least the last ten or fifteen years, the government has been determined to crack down on drugs especially." Jazz nodded when MiMi and Jazz both gaped at her.

"Miss International Affairs," Willa blurted out.

"Hey, I did some homework. Like *you* should have done before you sashayed your ass down here with Roddy boy," Jazz retorted as she stabbed a forefinger at MiMi.

"We came for a relaxing, fun getaway. All I looked up was beaches and shopping," MiMi protested.

"Riii-ght. Except you didn't mention to him you were looking for your former man's missing money. You could have easily gotten Roderick in big trouble. Which by the way could be what happened." Jazz crossed her arms.

Willa turned to Jazz. "Damn, I hadn't thought of that angle. If she was running around asking questions, somebody could have set them up."

"Hell yeah, a perfect way to get rid of her. It's not like MiMi can tell the authorities why she's really here." Jazz shrugged.

"Exactly, and send a strong message not to mess with these people," Willa added.

"Okay, y'all are really stretching. There is no grand conspiracy. Roddy decided to get high and was careless. I'll choke him when I get out of here, but my daddy is first on the list."

"Mr. Landry paid for the lawyer, so you know." Willa stopped talking.

"He took his sweet time." MiMi swallowed against the acid sensation in her throat. Awkward silence hung between them for a few seconds. Her father had given them a choice, pay for the bond or the lawyer. Not both.

"At least you got a daddy with money. Me? I'd be rotting in here for years. Well, maybe I could get a friend to help me out." Jazz gave a sultry chuckle.

Willa rolled her eyes at her sister. "Your sister is taking good care of Sage, one less thing you have to worry about."

MiMi blinked as tears formed at the thought of her sweet two-year-old. Sage would be three in a few months. "How was she when you saw her?"

"Adrienne says she's fine. She loves her cousin." Willa's expression brightened as it always did on the subject of kids.

"Brayden loves being the big brother, has since the minute he laid eyes on her." MiMi smiled as she dabbed tears away with the tissue Willa handed her. "I hope Adrienne isn't being too difficult. I know how she is."

Willa cleared her throat. "No, it's fine."

MiMi nodded, but then realized Willa hadn't

answered her question. "When was the last time you saw Sage, Willa? And don't tap dance."

"Ha, she knows you," Jazz put in. At the dark look Willa gave her, she pressed her lips closed.

"Adrienne's been busy with the kids, and her husband has been out of town so everything is on her. Your mama was sick with the flu a couple of weeks ago, so she helped take care of her," Willa said.

"She shouldn't have exposed herself like that with my baby in the house," MiMi said with a frown.

"Oh, no. She was careful to visit her once Mrs. Landry wasn't contagious." Willa fidgeted with her purse, realized MiMi was staring at her and stopped.

"Mother has a housekeeper. Adrienne didn't need to take care of her." MiMi crossed her arms. "Adrienne won't let you see Sage."

"Like I said, she's been busy. Well so have I honestly. I mean with my two kids and the business. You know. But she's a devoted aunt. I can tell," Willa replied.

"In other words, Adrienne is being her usual snotty self. I'm going to get her on the phone and set her straight." MiMi tapped a fist on her thigh.

Willa leaned forward. "If I even thought she wasn't being good to Sage, nothing would keep me away from her house."

"And I'd be with her," Jazz added with an edge in her voice.

"Priority one is getting you out of here, which will happen soon," Willa added, forcing sunshine into her tone.

"When?" MiMi's voice trembled as more tears filled her eyes and finally spilled down her cheeks. She wiped her face again. "Damn, I have to stop being such a cry baby. I was doing good, but it's been three whole weeks."

Jazz sat up with an interested expression. "Find either the toughest or smartest woman on the cell block. Best if she's both, but that's rare. That way you won't have to watch your back twenty-four seven."

"I volunteered to help in what passes for a beauty salon. So I made some friends, if that's possible in prison. Alliances are made and broken in here like crazy. Takes a lot of energy to keep up with who is with who." MiMi heaved a deep sigh.

"You're lucky you didn't get sent to another prison," Willa added quickly when MiMi snorted. "Najayo is considered a model prison not just here, but in the Caribbean."

"I'm in a cell with two other women and a toilet. My bed is a mattress on a cement shelf attached to the wall. I don't care about reforms or friends. I want *out*," MiMi shouted. She didn't care that the guard appeared again. She'd gone from tearful to angry.

"Sure, sure. I was just saying..." Willa glanced at her sister for help.

Jazz took over. "We're meeting with the lawyer at two o'clock this afternoon. The warden says we can come back in the morning. We'll have answers. Okay?"

MiMi appreciated Jazz's no nonsense approach for once. Jazz had been in MiMi's place a few times. So she knew sugarcoated hand holding didn't go far, especially not in a foreign lock-up. Things could go bad real fast.

"Thank you. Now go make it be true." MiMi raised both eyebrows as she stared at each of them in turn. "Wait a minute. Everything closes for siesta hours from noon until two o'clock. Are you just saying stuff to make me feel better? What's really going on?"

"Prison has changed you, girl. All suspicious and stuff," Jazz retorted.

"Anybody tried to jump you or anything?" Willa leaned across the table. She scanned MiMi like a nurse examining a patient.

"I'm okay. Thank God I know about make-up, fashion and job interview skills. I even co-led a couple of the classes." MiMi sat straight and smoothed back her hair.

"You *are* wearing lip gloss," Willa blurted out and turned to her sister. "Jazz, I told you she looked stylish to say she's in prison."

"I met one of the best hairdressers in lock-up one time. She stabbed a couple of people," Jazz added and popped her gum. "Like I said, make friends with the baddest badass in here."

"Luz and Diana have been nice to me. I give them tips on life in the states. They both want to go to New York or Los Angeles one day." MiMi cocked her head to one side at the snort from Jazz. "Well?"

"Let me guess, they told you they want to be models. Girl, please. What they probably want is to run a game for their boyfriends. Don't tell them your business." Jazz pointed a forefinger at her.

"Y'all call me suspicious. They're not even here for drugs or anything. I don't think so I mean." MiMi bit her lip.

Jazz slid her chair close to MiMi. "Tell me you didn't try to play detective and ask these women about DR banking and transferring cash."

"No. I mean, I asked some very general questions about crime, and you know, my father might send me money," MiMi said and winced when Jazz groaned.

"We definitely got to get you outta here," Jazz said.

"What? They know my boyfriend effed up and got me arrested. Most of the women are in here because of a man," MiMi protested.

"Exactly, they're all hooked up with thugs. One of those dudes could be hooked up with Felipe or some other American gangsta. They've got the money and they don't want questions asked," Jazz replied.

Jazz's harsh whispered reality scraped over MiMi like hot barbed wire. "I wasn't specific. I swear, very vague like I was curious about them and they're experiences."

"We're pushing your lawyer into action. Your daddy better stop this tough love crap and use whatever influence he has." Willa stood and slung her leather hobo purse over a shoulder. "You stay out of trouble."

"I'm, I'm going to be okay." MiMi tried to sound sure, but the crack in her voice betrayed her.

Willa gave her a hug. "Sure you will. Jazz was just laying out theories why you should..."

"Gee, this visit has me feeling so much better," MiMi grumbled and folded her arms tight against her body.

"Hey, if your new buddies really like you then you're gold. Keep your head up and your mouth closed." Jazz planted both fists on her hips. Her purse swung from the crook of one elbow. "We got you on this. Right, sis?"

"We expect to get you out soon, and I'm not just saying that. Bye." Willa went to the door and tapped. "Sir, ma'am, whoever, we're ready."

"Bye, girl. Look, I talked to Tomàs, the cute tall guard. He's gonna look out for you, too. Him and me might have a date later." Jazz winked at MiMi.

"Lord, give me strength," Willa muttered.

The "cute" guard led them out. Jazz put a little extra sway in her hips as she walked behind Willa. She gave the guard a coy smile. MiMi nodded in approval and laughed. Jazz would never need coaching in the ways of handling men. The female guard appeared seconds later and motioned for MiMi to leave the small room. With a sigh, MiMi complied. This particular guard didn't like MiMi one bit. No amount of charm had softened her. It was Tuesday and Officer Alvardo had just started her five day shift. The next few days would pass slowly.

****

That evening MiMi, Luz and Diana relaxed outside after dinner on a small concrete patio. MiMi and Diana sat in plastic chairs, while Luz leaned against the cinderblock wall. They watched other female inmates play a lazy game of soccer on the grass portion of the prison yard. Even at six o'clock in the evening, the warmth and humidity still hung on. MiMI used a hand towel as a fan.

"Ugh, I can't wait to get out of here. A month seems so far away. Ah." Luz sucked in smoke from her cigarette and blew it out.

"Yeah, well you better get some patience. Stop messing with Lola. One more fight and that month will turn into six." Diana waved at another inmate.

"Tell her to leave me alone. She's from your town, one of your old friends," Luz retorted.

"Okay. Have it your way. Don't cry to me when you end up with a longer sentence." Diana shrugged and lit up her second cigarette. She offered a half smoked one to MiMi.

"Not even being in here makes me want to start that habit." MiMi made a sour face.

"Uh-huh, in America they're big on no smoking. I need to quit if I'm going to find a nice American husband." Luz looked at her cigarette and then took another puff.

"Yeah, I can see you're making a real effort," MiMi joked. She ducked when Luz took a playful swing at her head.

Diana watched them for a few seconds. "You want to smell all fresh for that rich boyfriend of yours when you get out, huh chamaca?"

"I don't even want to see that, that..." MiMi's temper flared hot as the image of his smiling face flashed in her mind. Luz let loose with a string of derogatory names in Spanish. "Yeah, whatever you said."

Luz laughed. "Ow, he should leave before you get out."

"So, you figure he's gonna take the money and run?" Diana's tone was conversational as she gazed off at the soccer game.

MiMi looked at her. "What?"

"You were asking a lot of questions about hiding money and how to move money. Your boyfriend, he's smart. They think he's a tourist that just got stupid." Diana shifted her gaze to MiMi.

"Roddy is exactly what he looks like, a stupid tourist who scored and got caught. I just asked because you both were talking about your old boyfriends and gang members." MiMi hoped her voice didn't reflect her sudden case of nerves.

"You seemed a little bit more interested than just

making conversation." Diana lifted a dark eyebrow. She pushed away from the wall and sat down next to MiMi. "I might be able to get a guy who can help, for a reasonable fee of course."

"No way, you're totally wrong. We're not... you know," MiMi whispered and glanced around. "Roderick wouldn't know the first thing about that sort of stuff. And I definitely don't."

"Diana, I could tell she was green the second they pushed her into the cell," Luz put in with a snort.

"Uh-huh." Diana gazed at MiMi for a few seconds.

"Hey, your pal Lola is tryin' ta get your attention," Luz said and pointed to the other woman standing a few feet away. "Tell the bitch I said hello."

Diana transferred her gaze to Luz. She gave a short laugh and shook her head. "You never learn. Three times inside and you never learn."

"Yeah, yeah. Makes two of us," Luz retorted and winked at her.

Diana threw down her cigarette, crushed it out and strolled off, still shaking her head. Moments later she joined a group of inmates. Soon they were engaged in conversation. Their exchange flew right over MiMi's head. Once again she regretted not paying attention in her high school Spanish class. She listened for her name or any word she might understand. Soon the women moved away.

"I have to get away from this place," MiMi mumbled.

Luz waved to a player on the field who raced along. "Watch what you say to Diana. Her man is big into one of the gangs."

MiMi looked at her sharply. "She never said..."

"She wouldn't. If he thinks you or your boyfriend

are operating without his permission? That would be a sign of disrespect. Hey, score already," Luz shouted. She kept up her pretense of concentrating on the game.

"Like I told her, Roddy is a dumb tourist. I'm dumb for even being interested in Roddy." MiMi forced herself to laugh, hoping it sounded genuine.

Luz didn't look at MiMi. Instead she waved at another clump of inmates seated on the grass watching the game. "I'll keep close to you, so will my cousin over there, the one with the ball."

"I thought you and Diana were good friends." MiMi swallowed against the lump of terror in her throat.

"It's smart for me to know what she's doin' and sayin', okay? We get along, but I know to watch her. You should, too." Luz glanced at MiMi briefly. Then she glanced at where Diana stood with a clump of other inmates.

"Why are you telling me this?" MiMi wiped beads of sweat from her forehead. Suddenly the heat came from inside her gut.

"Diana, Lola and some of their friends are getting way to cocky for their own good." Luz wore a serious expression for an instant before she smiled. "Hey, let's get a basketball game goin' next time."

The players finished the game when guards signaled they were to wrap it up. They called back to Luz playfully about what she could do with a basketball. Half of it was in English, half in Spanish. A few women yelled Creole. Luz let loose another string of Spanish as she stood up.

MiMi stood as well. She wore a smile, but whispered out of the side of her mouth. "I don't want to get caught in some kind of gang war, Luz. I mean just because I was making conversation? I didn't even bring up Diana's past. She did!"

Luz looped an arm through one of MiMi's. "Relax chica. You should be okay until your girlfriends get you out."

"Lord, let that be *real* soon," MiMi said. She repeated that prayer for the rest of the night.

Chapter 2

Two days later, MiMi entered the court room making her best effort to look innocent. The judge maintained a bland expression when her case was finally called. She wore the dove gray skirt, a white blouse, and sensible pumps Willa and Jazz had brought her. MiMi glanced down at herself. The plain clothes would have to go later, but today she strove to fit the bland outfit. The judge gave MiMi a critical stare as she walked in with Officer Alvarez close behind. The woman nodded that MiMi could proceed to the table. MiMi sat between her attorney and the court appointed interpreter. She was doing fine, calmly listening to the muted translation from the petite woman. Then Roderick came in.

MiMi stopped listening and turned to her attorney. "What's he doing here?"

"Your cases are linked." Mr. Columba replied.

"Our cases are not 'linked'. Roderick decided to buy weed without consulting me," MiMi said and huffed in outrage.

She felt a tap on her shoulder and looked back.

Willa frowned a warning from the front row. Jazz gave a slight shake of her head and mouthed, "Keep cool."

Mr. Columba looked past MiMi at the interpreter. He continued in Spanish. Apparently explaining in detail exhausted his limited English language skills. He spoke rapidly making discreet gestures toward the judge and then the prosecutor. The woman nodded, let him finish, and then placed a hand on MiMi's left arm as if to urge restraint.

"Mr. Columba says the judge wanted to save time because you were arrested together. Señor Jefferson also mentioned you several times in his statement," the woman said with a note of apology in her voice.

"I'll just bet he did, the slimy weasel," MiMi hissed.

"We're not sure yet what his lawyer will say," the interpreter continued. She paused as MiMi's attorney broke in with a few more sentences. "Mr. Columba says it may not be a bad sign. Hold your patience."

"You're definitely channeling Willa," MiMi murmured.

"Qué?" The interpreter blinked at her in puzzlement.

"Never mind." MiMi decided not to look at Roderick again. Her "patience" would be tested enough being in the same space with him.

For the next forty minutes, a lot of legal housekeeping went on interminably. The lawyers and others apparently found it all quite routine. The judge even left a few times. Papers got shuffled as the court reporter and others went through whatever procedures they needed to complete. MiMi scowled when Roderick's attorney got to go first. She listened as the interpreter recounted his version of the events, which included MiMi wanting to party as much as he did. In this case implying she wanted to buy weed, too. She twisted her hands together tightly, wishing Roderick's lying neck was between them. Finally the interpreter stopped. MiMi's hearted pounded.

"What's happening? Is he blaming me?" she whispered.

The woman shushed her, and when the judge paused, she and the lawyer nodded to one another before she spoke. "Mr. Jefferson had less than two ounces, so he will pay a fine and must leave the country. He admitted that you didn't go with him to buy the weed, and the police can't find the dealer."

"Hallelujah," MiMi burst out.

The judge squinted at her as his words came out in rapid fire, all in Spanish of course. He banged his gavel to punctuate his displeasure.

"Lo siento mucho, tu honor," MiMi said promptly. She'd practiced that phrase with coaching from Luz for two weeks at least.

The judge's frown eased. Her show of respect seemed to have helped. "No más de de que usted, señorita."

"Sí." MiMi looked down at the table.

"Very good, Miss Landry," Mr. Columba whispered.

Then he stood and began to speak to the judge in Spanish. For another twenty minutes, MiMi followed the exchange between the lawyers. She sat rigid while Roderick spoke with the aid of his own interpreter. MiMi's lips curled. Obviously scared spitless, Roderick went overboard groveling before the court. The judge's dark eyes sparkled as he exhaled heavily a few times as Roderick rambled on begging for mercy. He talked about his parents depending on him to run the family business his grandfathers had founded, and mentioning his maternal grandmother's poor health.

"He's got to be kidding," MiMi mumbled and got a gentle poke from the interpreter.

She pressed her lips together. She wanted to tell the court that Roderick rarely visited the grumpy widow. The old lady had threatened to disinherit him more than a few times. His father regularly called him worse than useless. Roderick made it sound like he was a valued son whose absence threatened the family business. In fact, his younger brother spent twice the time managing their commercial properties and construction projects than he did.

The judge finally cut him off. "Sí, sí, Mr. Jefferson. Your points are made."

Roderick stammered to a halt as his lawyer patted his shoulder. The man practically pushed Roderick down to his chair again. MiMi chuckled softly. When she looked back, Jazz grinned and rolled her eyes. Willa merely shook her head slowly. The judge gave a long speech during which the interpreter maintained a respectful silence. MiMi tried not to shake the woman to make her talk.

Mr. Columba thanked the judge. MiMi understood that part of what he said. The tension in her shoulders, neck and back eased at the smile her lawyer exchanged with the judge. When the prison guard came toward her, MiMi blinked as tears formed in her eyes.

"No, no. Is alright. You come with us, okay?" Mr. Columba gave her elbow a quick reassuring squeeze before he gathered up his files.

"This way, please," the interpreter said.

"Okay." MiMi sniffed a couple of times.

Willa, ever the maternal type, handed her a small package of tissues. "Can we come, too?"

The interpreter smiled at her. "Sí."

Another case was being called as they left. MiMi glanced around at the orderly chaos around them. She had to admit that this was not the rush-to-judgment-third-world nightmare she'd dreaded. The courthouse was modern and clean. Lovely murals depicting Dominican Republic history covered the walls. Leading the way, Mr. Columba took them to a small conference room down the hall from the courtroom.

"The hearing went quite well. Mr. Jefferson admitted you didn't go with him to buy the drugs. I also got his lawyer to admit that the drug dealer had no contact with you." The lawyer beamed at MiMi and everyone else. His smile seemed to say he was more impressed with his own skills than happy for his client.

"Trust me, the judge caught on that Roderick was trying to blame you without making it look too obvious." Jazz smiled when the interpreter blinked at her in surprise. "Yeah, I speak Spanish pretty good."

"As I was saying," Mr. Columba broke in before anymore talk strayed from his shining moment. "The judge takes into account you have no criminal record in America. You didn't have the marijuana on your person. So you pay fine and free to go."

"Yes!" MiMi stretched her arms over her head. "Praise Jesus! Okay, y'all, let's get the blip out of here. I hope you have my plane ticket. They can keep those few knick-knacks I had at the prison."

"Yeah, we got your suitcase from the resort hotel," Jazz said. Still,

she wore a slight frown.

"Then I'm ready. We can go straight to the airport right now." MiMi faced the prison guard. "Thanks and tell the girls bye for me."

"Wait up a minute," Willa said, a palm up like the school principal announcing the bell hadn't rung just yet. She turned to Mr. Columba. "You mentioned the fine?"

"Yes, you can pay right here. You have five thousand American dollars, yes?" He looked at Willa and then at Jazz. "Plus about five hundred dollars in court costs."

"Sure we do," Jazz retorted.

"Then there is the matter of my fee. The balance is two thousand US dollars." Mr. Columba raised a dark eyebrow when neither Willa nor Jazz spoke.

"I thought Mr. Landry paid you in full," Willa said as she waved at MiMi to be quiet.

"No, only the retainer." Mr. Columba spoke to the interpreter in Spanish.

"The lady cannot be released until the fine and legal fees are paid," the interpreter translated.

"Okay, okay. We've got to work on it," Willa replied. She rubbed her forehead and paced in a circle.

Officer Alvarez wore a smirk as she turned to MiMi. "So you come back with me after all, eh? You can tell everyone goodbye for yourself."

MiMi backed away from the woman. "Willa, get daddy on the phone and have him wire the money. Can't I wait here until then?"

"Um, I have to track him down at his office. It might take more than an hour or so, MiMi." Willa glanced at Jazz.

"We talking big money, closing in on ten thousand. We don't know how your daddy is gonna take the news," Jazz said bluntly.

Mr. Columba spoke again in Spanish to the interpreter. MiMi flinched as he talked and the guard's smile grew wider. When the interpreter took a deep breath and exhaled before speaking, MiMi knew the news was bad.

"If the fine is not paid the sentence could be up to eight months at least. Seven since you've almost been here a month. So that's something," the interpreter said. She tried a weak smile, but it faded as she gazed at the expression on MiMi's face.

"I can't stay in this place for seven months. I'll miss my baby's birthday and..." MiMi covered her face and cried.

"Don't freak out. Your father will need time to make the arrangements, that's all Jazz meant." Willa eased her into a chair and placed an arm around MiMi's shoulders.

"Uh, right, right. I'm just sayin' he'll need a minute to get over the shock. That's a lot of cash," Jazz said.

"He's going to say no," MiMi blurted out.

"Your mother will speak up if he acts crazy I'm sure," Willa said. She handed MiMi a hand full of tissues.

MiMi wiped her eyes and sniffed a few times. Despite the despair settling over her, MiMi sat straight in an effort to be brave. "You obviously don't know my parents. Guess I'll have to get used to prison life."

Jazz studied MiMi for a few moments longer. "Girl, you gotta tell us the story about the Landry family."

"I'll call your father the minute we leave here." Willa patted MiMi on the back as she spoke.

"Yeah, if we have to send somebody to help convince him, that's what we'll do," Jazz added.

"Qué?" Mr. Columba let loose with a string of Spanish.

"We don't want trouble or to be party to any kind

of threats. We're a country of laws," the interpreter's eyes went wide as she tried to keep up with him.

"No, no, we only meant that my parents would go over to appeal to him on MiMi's behalf," Willa said just as rapidly. She glared at Jazz. "You stay with MiMi and keep your mouth shut."

Jazz smacked her lips. "Fine."

Willa motioned to the lawyer and interpreter to speak with her privately. The prison guard chuckled, amused at the scene unfolding. MiMi tried to resign herself to the inevitable. She could almost see the image of her mother's cold expression of distaste.

Jazz looked at the guard. "Hey, can give us a few more feet of privacy."

"Take all the time you need. Your friend has plenty looks like." The guard went over to stand by the one window. She smiled at them as she leaned against the wall.

"What's up with your mama and daddy?" Jazz whispered close to MiMi's ear.

"We're not exactly a happy family. That's the short version." MiMi gave a bitter laugh at the understatement.

"Yeah, but they've got the money and their kid is in a third world prison. They gotta know this is some serious shit." Jazz poked MiMi's arm to get more information.

MiMi sighed. She hadn't talked to Willa or Jazz much about her family. They'd grown up in a very different world of poverty, foster homes, and abusive adults. MiMi by contrast had attended excellent private schools, had the best clothes, and went through all the Black upper-class rituals. Yes, they had money, status and respectability. And they were as dysfunctional as hell.

"We have our own unique issues," MiMi replied. "They care more about appearances for one thing."

"More than their kid? That's some dark shit. No wonder you don't talk about 'em much," Jazz murmured.

"I don't think about it that much," MiMi replied and sat straight. "I have an idea. Mention the longer this drags on, the more chances it will make the news."

"Damn, and I thought our parents were messed up." Jazz shook her head.

They sat in companionable silence for a few minutes, mulling over their mother issues. Willa strode back in with a determined smile. The lawyer and interpreter followed behind her.

"Mr. Columba and the judge have been most helpful. I also talked to Mr. Landry." Willa's smile stretched tighter when she referred to MiMi's father. "He understands our situation."

"Our situation? I'm sitting in prison," MiMi clipped. She was about to go on but stopped when Willa shot a sideways glance in the lawyer's direction. Something in Willa's expression implied subtext that begged for explanation. Yet MiMi could tell Willa didn't want to talk in front of the others. MiMi sighed. "I'm sorry."

Willa walked up to MiMi and took bother her hands. "I'm working on getting you out in the morning."

"Okay."

After saying their goodbyes, during which MiMi managed not to cry, she was taken back to the prison. She fell into the cell block routine with frightening ease. Three weeks locked up and she seemed to become an inmate in spirit as well as physically. The guards went through the procedure of searching her. Then she changed back into prison clothes, was searched again and taken to a mandatory class. Reforms at Najayo Prison included regular activities. Not only did prison officials want the women to learn skills, they knew inmates sitting around all day everyday only led to trouble.

The instructor let out a sharp sigh of relief when she saw MiMi. "Oh good, you're still here. I've told the assistant warden thirty students is too big a class. I have them in groups. You take those two."

"Yeah, Senorita Suarez. Thank heavens she's still locked up for you, huh?" Rosaria, a short inmate always poking fun, let out a gruff laugh. She grinned when others giggled at her joke.

Mrs. Suarez turned pink. "Of course I didn't mean... I'm sorry you weren't released, MiMi. Of course I am."

"Don't worry about it. I'll get started," MiMi said to cut off more stammering and apologizing.

They were reading a sweeping romance novel with plenty of family conflict. MiMi had suggested using commercial fiction as a way to get the women more engaged in discussions. They talked about family conflict, making the right life choices, and of course, men. As the class went on, MiMi worked to pay attention, but had trouble concentrating. Fortunately, the current chapter had so much drama, a lively discussion went on without prompting. Mrs. Suarez must have noticed MiMi's distracted mood. She didn't scold her. Instead, the older woman took control of most of the hour long class. When the bell signaled lunch time, Mrs. Suarez asked MiMi to stay behind. She nodded to the guard.

Luz separated from the other women jostling to leave. "I'll put up the books and stuff for you, Mrs. S."

Mrs. Suarez waved a hand at her without looking around. She turned to MiMi. "If you want to talk, I can stay a while."

"I'm good. I'll help Luz." MiMi started to walk off, but Mrs. Suarez grabbed her arm.

"Listen, I know you're not the typical inmate. I'm sure you can learn from one mistake and put this behind you," Mrs. Suarez said quietly.

MiMi was in no mood for a heart to heart. "Thanks. Do you want the pencils and note pads on the shelf or in the cabinet."

Mrs. Suarez took the hint and neatly switched gears. "Hmm, oh put them in the cabinet. Luz, could you take that cloth and dust a bit. This room stays locked, so they don't clean in here as often as they should."

"Sure thing," Luz called back. When MiMi got closer, Luz winked at her. "Hey, cheer up. We both know your girls gone get you out."

"It's not my girls I'm worried about. I don't want to talk about it," MiMi grumbled.

"Sure. I know how it feels comin' back from court." Luz gave her a sympathetic look. "But we need to talk."

"Luz, I really don't..."

Luz checked to make sure Mrs. Suarez was preoccupied across the room at her desk. "Not about that. Remember I told you to watch Diana?"

MiMi frowned. "Yeah."

"She's got a guy on the outside. I wouldn't call him a boyfriend. They hook-up whenever. You know how that goes." Luz pretended to concentrate on dusting chairs and desks, but stayed close to MiMI.

"Not really." MiMi glanced over at Mrs. Suarez as well.

"They do some business together, and party

whenever," Luz whispered.

"Uh-huh." MiMi nodded. What Luz meant was Diana and the man would get involved in mutually profitable criminal business. They also had casual sex when it suited them.

"This guy Bruno wants Diana to find out if your boyfriend is trying to move money, drugs and guns. He wants in. So we got to make sure you stay out of her way for a while.

"Exactly how am I supposed to pull off that miracle? She's in our cell. Besides, I'm not going to tell her anything because there's nothing to tell." MiMi's stomach tightened with anxiety.

"She got moved to another cell while you were in court," Luz whispered. She smiled when Mrs. Suarez looked up at them. "We're going to clean the tops of the bookcases and that file cabinet."

"Great idea. I'll bet there's enough dust up there to grow crops," Mrs. Suarez replied. She went back to grading assignments.

"Why did they move her?" MiMi kept her back to Mrs. Suarez. She looked down as though sorting through the workbooks used in class.

"I don't know. Anyway, my pals won't let her sit next to you at lunch. Just stay outta her way." Luz moved away humming as she dusted. Then a few minutes later, she moved back.

"With any luck, I'll be out and on a plane tomorrow," MiMi said. "And I'm not scared of Diana."

"The little college princess talking tough," Luz teased.

"I handled Carissa when she got in my face, didn't I?" MiMi shot back. Two days after she'd been on the cell block, the woman had tried to bully her.

"You held your own. Just remember the fight moves I taught you in the yard."

MiMi thought about her parents, Roderick and others who had tried to bring her down. "Screw being the 'princess' everybody thinks they can mess with. From now on, I'm going to be a warrior queen."

"You better save that for when you get outta here. This ain't your world," Luz said.

"It is now," MiMi said fiercely. When she slapped a stack of books on a shelf, Mrs. Suarez jumped. MiMi smoothed the angry expression from her face and smiled. "We're through, Mrs. Suarez."

Two hours later, MiMi sat perched on a table with her feet resting on the bench attached to it. She watched four other inmates play cards. The recreation room had two other tables and single plastic chairs scattered around. Guards observed from a command station a few yards away. One female guard walked the floor, alert for signs of trouble. Elise, a young Haitian woman, kept yawning.

"Hey, America," Elise said without looking up from her cards. She liked calling MiMi by the nickname some of the women had given her. "After this hand, I'm out."

"Okay, why you tryin' to get out now that you got most of my cigarettes? Nah, I'm gonna win them back." A tall woman from La Romana, a city near the Dominican Republic capital, frowned at Elise.

Elise grinned at her, head tilted to one side. "You can't win them back 'cuz I'm that good. Besides, there's always another game on another day."

"Humph," the woman grunted. She mumbled a few words, but said no more.

"Hey, you'll probably win from me. I'm terrible at cards," MiMi spoke up to defuse a possible problem.

"Rich America, you don't smoke. Hey, I bet you got some nice lipstick or mascara with my name on it," the woman replied. The disgruntled creases in her brow smoothed out as she smiled at MiMi.

MiMi was about to reply when she saw movement to her left. Diana strolled up with two other women. She sat on the other end of the table. Her two friends stood, arms crossed. The guard seemed to be busy making notes on a log. The card players were intent on the game. At least they acted like it. MiMi felt the atmosphere press in on her.

Chapter 3

"Yeah, she's got money. Why not just give it out to your friends and skip the game?" Diana spoke languidly.

"I'll decide who gets what when." MiMi kept her tone casual as well. She saw the card players tense. Several cleared their throats.

"I woulda asked you in private, but sense you got me moved, I had to come find you," Diana said softly. "What lie did you tell the assistant warden, rata?"

MiMi looked at her briefly then away. "You're delusional. I'm no rat."

"She says your loco, demente," one of the two women explained when Diana glanced at them.

"Big English words to insult me. You better watch yourself, rata," Diana spat.

To be called out as a snitch was dangerous in prison. Only a month ago MiMi would have tried to talk her way out of a confrontation. But that was before she'd been kicked around one too many times. Every disappointment and let down flashed through her like a hot stake pushing her to the edge.

MiMi stood to face Diana. "I'm not the rat, Diana. Tell everybody how you got special treatment before they cleaned this place up. We'd all love to hear the story of who you gave up."

"Perra," Diana growled.

"Yeah, I'm the bitch ready to take that hot man of yours. He's been sending me love notes since he saw me in court the other day."

"That's bullshit. Mateo doesn't even know you," Diana shot back, now on her feet with her hands balled into fist. Her irrational jealously about her lover was legendary.

MiMi smiled. "He's out with charges still pending, right? He managed to get close. I thought he was going to ask about you. I was looking good, so I guess he changed his mind."

Diana growled and took a swing at MiMi with an open hand. MiMi didn't run. Instead she caught the hand, twisted it hard and jerked Diana closer. A sharp kick to Diana's side made her scream. The other two women tried to join the fight, but three card players blocked them.

"Nah, Diana started it. Let her finish it," Elise said.

Diana rushed head first to tackle MiMi. Instead she ran into MiMi's foot. The tip of MiMi's sneaker clipped Diana's chin just as three guards ran up. Two grappled with the battling women to separate them. The third guard stood with a baton raised, a warning for the other inmates not join the fray. Three more guards raced to the lounge. They barked orders for the women to return to their cells.

"You must like it here, Señorita Landry," a guard shouted as she shoved MiMi away from Diana.

"I defended myself," MiMi said. She breathed heavily from the fight and the effort to speak coherently.

"She's tellin' the truth," an inmate being herded out shouted. "Take a look at the video."

More inmates joined in the chorus as everyone picked a side. The guards barked warnings at them. Reinforcements helped clear the lounge. MiMi and Diana were taken to be examined in the prison clinic. Aside from bruises, neither of them had been seriously hurt. Both were ordered to cool off in solitary confinement. After reviewing the video, the supervising guard and assistant warden let MiMi return to her cell. Her dinner arrived on a tray twenty minutes later. Luz came back from an evening group session and sat on the floor. She watched MiMi eat for a few minutes.

"They still letting you out tomorrow," Luz said finally.

"I cursed being watched all the time, but I'm loving those cameras now," MiMi said around chews. The beans and rice at least were still warm. "My first meal will be a shrimp po-boy when I get home."

"Or maybe they just want you outta here. The last thing the government wants is an American princess getting messed up in here." Luz grinned at MiMi.

MiMi paused with the spoon halfway to her mouth. "Sounds like you know a lot. You heard something?"

"Me? Nah, I ain't got no ears in here," Luz replied mildly. "The Americans get testy when one of their own gets hurt. US reporters would have a good time splashing the news all over."

"You pay attention." MiMi gazed at her. She developed a different assessment of the young woman.

Luz gave a gruff laugh as she flipped the pages of a graphic novel with a moral lesson. "What, I'm not the dumbass third world skank you thought I was? I may not have a college degree, but I know stuff."

"Like how Diana got moved to a different cell," MiMi said quietly.

Luz turned slowly on the bench to face her. "Some friends did us both a favor. Leave it at that."

MiMi put the plate on the bed. "What'd she do to you, Luz?"

Luz stood and walked to the front of their cell. She leaned against it casually for a few seconds, the graphic novel in one hand. After looking around she sat next to MiMi. Luz again turned pages of the graphic novel.

"Nothin' you want to know about. Unfinished business, she thinks it's over." Luz's soft voice sounded dangerous.

"Great, and now she thinks I jacked her instead." MiMi grabbed one of Luz's comic books. She stood and went to the bars to double check no one was nearby to listen.

"You'll be out of the country and out of reach by tomorrow. Diana got plenty of enemies anyway. She gonna look for somebody closer to home to blame anyway," Luz replied.

MiMi looked around at her. "Like you."

Luz flipped the book closed and drew her legs up to wrap her legs around her knees. "I can take care of me. Stop tryin' to be somethin' you ain't."

MiMi studied her for a few minutes. She crossed her arms. "I tell you who I am, a fed up former princess sick of being played."

****

True to her word, Willa showed up the next morning at ten thirty with Mr. Columba. They presented the release paperwork to the warden. MiMi watched in surprise as the process to set her free went smoothly. Her heart pounded each time the warden or officer in charge paused to scan a sheet of paper. Forty-five minutes later they were in the rented Toyota Rav 4. MiMi let out a gasp once the SUV cleared the heavy yellow gates.

"Get us the hell out of here," MiMi said, her voice shaking.

Willa turned around in the front passenger seat. She grabbed MiMi's hand, squeezed it hard, then let go. For the next few miles, no one spoke. The drive from San Cristobal to the airport in Santo Domingo was a short fifteen miles. Jazz drove as though she'd lived in San Cristobal. She even let out a few choice words in Spanish for bad drivers. When Willa turned around to stare at the bandage on her hand *and* the bruises, MiMi knew what was coming.

Willa raised both her dark salon contoured eyebrows at her. "You want to talk about it?"

"They told us you got into a fight with a tough girl, but you're okay," Jazz blurted out. She glanced at MiMi in the rearview mirror before looking at the road again.

"My former cell mate came at me. I'm gone and she's still locked up. End of story." MiMi looked out of the window.

"Something about you is different." Willa studied her. When MiMi didn't answer, she tapped her on the knee. "Hey, us three been through a few things together. We're on your side."

"Not like your high and mighty parents." Jazz spoke with her characteristic bluntness. "And don't shush me, Willa. I'm just speaking truth."

MiMi swallowed hard as a tear managed to escape

before she could wipe it away. "Obviously we're not the Cosbys."

"Humph." Jazz glanced at Willa and seemed to decide not to say more.

With a deep breath in and out, MiMi pushed aside her sadness. She'd long ago learned to live without warmth or true affection from her parents. They'd given her money, cars, and a nice private school education. She'd always managed to take advantage of the privileges that came with being Drexel James Landry's daughter. She'd looked for love elsewhere. At least now she had her friends. She looked at Willa.

"Diana thought I'd told the guards something to get her in trouble and out of my cell. I put my foot up her behind, convinced her she got it wrong." MiMi smiled when Willa's eyes went wide.

"You got into a fight, a fist flying real fight?" Willa's open mouth formed a wide circle. She glanced at her sister.

Jazz slapped the steering with one hand. "Give up the juicy details."

"I got in a lick upside her ugly head and kicked her in the kidneys." MiMi giggled when Jazz hooted.

"Oh hell naw." Jazz burst out laughing.

"Keep your eyes on the road," Willa said.

"Let's turn in the car, get checked in and hear the rest of this story." Jazz laughed as she pulled to the rental car parking lot.

Thirty minutes later they had their boarding passes and sat in the Delta Sky Lounge. With four hours until their flight, they had time to relax. All three took advantage of the ladies restrooms that included an attendant. MiMi changed into comfortable knit leggings, a long tunic and flats. Pulling her hair into a ponytail, she breathed even easier now. They were actually closer to being off the ground and away from her nightmare. Once they got settled with beverages, Jazz grinned at MiMi.

"Spill it all," she said.

"You would have been proud of me, Jazz. I cold cocked that heffa with this, and this." MiMi swung a fist and then kicked out with her black Ferragamo leather flat. She let out a genuine laugh for the first time in weeks.

"Oo-wee, I didn't teach you that." Jazz took a drink of beer.

"Nah, my friend Luz and some other girls showed me how to take care of myself. Of course, I had more practice than they thought. Those girls in the sororities could get rowdy, too." MiMi pointed at Jazz and giggled.

"I thought y'all was all sister love and stuff." Jazz sat forward eager to hear more.

"MiMi is exaggerating. We don't brawl like street women," Willa broke in with a scowl. She took a dainty sip of her wine.

"Sorority girls have issues with each other. We just don't air our dirty laundry," MiMi said.

"My old crew was sorta like that. We settled out disputes in private. That's why we got all this killin'. These street gangstas need to evolve like those old school mafia guys did back in the day." Jazz nodded and tossed peanuts in her mouth.

"Really? Comparing sororities to gang members?" Willa glared at both of them.

"The gangs do charity work, educate their members, and have their own colors. Just like the cute little Greek girls." Jazz winked at MiMi, who giggled even harder.

Willa smacked her lips. "I'm not going to let y'all push my buttons."

"Aw c'mon, give us some of that bourgie outrage," Jazz said to needle her.

"Yeah, Willa. We like it when you..." MiMi spotted a figure walking into the lounge. She stood slowly, eyes narrowed as her gaze fixed on Roderick like lasers from an automatic weapon. He took off his sunglasses as he looked back at her.

"Uh-oh," Jazz whispered. She put down her frosted mug and stood.

Willa sprang from her seat. "Look, we're trying to get out of this country."

"I'm not going to cause a scene," MiMi said softly. She continued to stare at Roderick for a few moments. Seconds later she sat on the sofa again, picked up her drink, and sipped.

Willa and Jazz heaved matching sighs of relief as they joined her. Roderick's lawyer strolled in. Both men went to the bar to order drinks. MiMi stared through a large window that gave them a view of one runway.

"I think you're showing a lot of maturity, MiMi. I have to congratulate... No, no. Please don't come over here," Willa whispered.

Roderick walked over to them holding his drink. His lawyer, Don Estrada, watched from the bar. MiMi gazed at him with a blank expression. She didn't have to wonder what she'd ever seen in him. Six feet one inches in his socks, Roderick had smooth clear skin the color of almonds. His full lips looked always moist and utterly kissable. He wore a designer white camp shirt with sky blue stripes, two hundred dollar blue jeans and tan leather slip on shoes. Everything about him said he had money. As he got closer, Roderick smiled. Female heads turned. A few glanced at MiMi then back at Roderick. MiMi read their thoughts. They were coming up with ways to pull his attention to them. Roderick had that effect on women. He'd certainly had that effect on MiMi.

"Afternoon ladies," Roderick said with a nod to Willa and Jazz.

"Hello," Willa murmured. She shot a worried sideways glance at MiMi.

"Whatever." Jazz sat back and crossed her legs.

Roderick merely smiled at her dismissal even as he gave Jazz's shapely legs an appreciative scan. Then he focused on MiMi again. "MiMi, can we talk?"

"Now's not a good time," Willa broke in quickly.

"I don't want us to go back to the states enemies." Roderick sat in a chair close to MiMi, which caused the other two women to gasp in unison.

"Man, you livin' dangerously," Jazz quipped.

"I'm fine. Give us a moment." MiMi continued to gaze at him.

"You sure?" Jazz squinted at Roderick.

"Our conversation will be short," MiMi replied and drained her glass.

A waitress came over with another glass on a tray. She smiled at Roderick briefly before looking at MiMi. "Another glass of Pinot Noir, ma'am."

"I knew what you'd be drinking," Roderick said.

"He's got style, gotta give him that." Jazz seemed to give him a second look of appraisal.

"Come on," Willa retorted as she pulled her sister by the arm.

Roderick gave a short laugh. "Your friends are very protective. I'm glad you had support through this awful situation."

"A situation totally *your* fault. I bet you didn't admit responsibility to your parents or mine. You definitely didn't volunteer that little detail to the police or the judge." MiMi kept her voice low and calm.

"I explained to the judge that you weren't with me when I arrange to meet... my friend," Roderick replied. He paused when the waitress brought his bottle of expensive dark beer. "Thank you."

"You're very welcome." The waitress beamed with pleasure at his attention and left.

MiMi let out a snort at the little tableau of seduction. "You mean when you met your local drug man. Did you already know him or did you get the hook up once we arrived?"

Roderick looked around to make sure no one was close by. Even though they were alone, he still got up and sat next to MiMi on the sofa. "A couple of buddies introduced us. Unfortunately, he was being watched by the police."

"Because of you I may not have a job when I get home. I have a baby to take care of..." MiMi breathed in and out to keep from crying.

"I have a lot of connections. You'll get a job, maybe even work for me." Roderick put a hand on MiMi's knee.

She shoved it away with a sharp motion. "I'll work at the dollar store first. One thing I don't need is more of your company."

"I made a stupid decision. Guess my parents have been telling me it's time to settle down with a good woman, raise a family." Roderick stretched an arm across the back of the sofa behind MiMi.

"Yeah, well good luck and God bless on your search for Ms. Right," MiMi muttered. She gulped some of the rich red wine.

Roderick turned slightly toward MiMi, but didn't move closer. "I don't have to search."

MiMi gagged. "You've got to be freaking kidding me. That greasy charm won't work, not after this hellish 'romantic trip'."

"Honey, come on. One mistake."

"Don't you even think about us as a couple. *Ever*." MiMi stood over him, hands on both hips.

Willa and Jazz made it across the room in record time. Estrada's long legged stride helped him reach Roderick and MiMi first. MiMi went into a profanity laced explanation of what she thought of Roderick. His eyes went wide with shock. Though MiMi spoke in a low tone, it didn't lessen the intensity of her verbal assault.

Willa stepped in front of MiMi. "Okay, chat time over. Let's just go our separate ways."

"I think it's best to let the lady finish her drink and calm down, Roderick," his lawyer added.

"I didn't know you had such fire," Roderick said in a husky voice. His gaze swept over MiMi as he licked his bottom lip.

"Damn, he's a freak," Jazz whispered over Willa's shoulder.

Willa got up in Roderick's face. "Go away."

"MiMi, no matter how it looks, I have deep feelings for you," Roderick spoke over Willa's head.

Willa pointed her forefinger at his nose until her French manicured nail almost touched it. "If you don't get your--"

"Cop at three o'clock," Jazz cut in sharply.

All of them froze and looked toward the entrance to the lounge. A tall man the color of brown sugar entered dressed smartly in a suit. Roderick's lawyer wore a frown as though trying to figure out the man's identity. Willa glanced at MiMi, who shrugged back at her. The man went to the bar.

"We don't know he's a cop. He could be a business traveler," MiMi offered.

Jazz turned her back to the man, who now spoke quietly to the lounge employee. "I have cop radar, and he's one. He's plains clothes, a detective so something serious has gone down."

The man nodded to the employee. He walked over to them, a hand in the inside of his jacket. He led with his police identification. They were cornered, at least that's how MiMi felt.

"Hello, I'm Detective Juan Aguilar. I would like to talk to Mr. Jefferson and Miss Landry."

"I'm Mr. Jefferson's attorney."

"Senor Estrada, your legal work representing defendants is well known to us," Det. Aguilar cut him off.

"Then you know I won't allow him to answers questions until we have more information," Estrada said smoothly.

"If he has nothing to hide then Mr. Jefferson should be eager to cooperate," Det. Aguilar replied mildly. "Miss Landry, I'll speak with you first."

"No, you'll tell us why you're here first," Willa said.

Det. Aguilar gazed at Willa for a few seconds. Then he turned to Roderick. "You are friends with Benito Herrera, yes?"

"Never heard of him," Roderick said promptly before Estrada could speak.

"You knew him as Benny, one of the three aliases he used. He's the drug dealer who sold you marijuana." The detective lifted a dark eyebrow at him and glanced at MiMi.

"Ah." Roderick shrugged. "Calling him a friend is a stretch. But yes, we met only once."

"My client has gone to court and the case is over, Detective Aguilar. I fail to see why you're here," Estrada put in before Roderick could keep talking. He shot Roderick a look of warning.

Aguilar noticed with a short grunt. He turned his attention to MiMi. "How many times did you meet Mr. Herrera, or Benny, Ms. Landry?"

"I'm not answering anymore questions because my lawyer isn't here." MiMi showed him a look of confidence she definitely didn't feel. Her heart thudded so hard she heard blood rushing through her arteries.

"If this man has gotten into more trouble, Mr. Jefferson doesn't know anything about it. My client is a respected businessman in his country," Estrada said firmly.

"Yes, a respected business man who likes to smoke marijuana when he travels to foreign countries," Det. Aguilar said dryly.

Estrada drew up to his full five feet eight inches, looking every bit the outraged attorney. "Unless you have a reason to delay his departure, Mr. Jefferson will be leaving in about two hours."

"Not unless he answers more questions. Same for you Miss Landry." Det. Aguilar seemed unimpressed by Estrada's performance.

"Then stop playing games. We established in court that my client doesn't have information about the drug trade in Santo Domingo, much less the country," Estrada snapped, keeping his voice low.

"This isn't about petty drug dealing by a tourist. Herrera is dead, murdered. His body was found on a country road near Cotui."

Det. Aguilar scanned their faces for reactions. He got plenty. They all started talking at once. MiMi stammered out incoherent sentences. Jazz cursed a few times. Willa grabbed MiMi and Jazz by the arms as though she needed support. Roderick stepped back as if he was about to run. Estrada glanced around at the attention from other travelers in the lounge.

"Please, everyone, calm yourselves. Let's go to that table in the corner for more privacy," Estrada said, raising his voice to be heard.

"An excellent idea," the detective said calmly.

Aguilar strode over to the large round table without looking to see if they followed, which of course they did. Once they were all seated, he took out a note pad. He studied it for a few seconds while they all squirmed.

"Benito Herrera, or Benny, disappeared five days ago according to his girlfriend." Det. Aguilar looked at Roderick. "About the time you were released from jail, Mr. Jefferson."

For the first time Roderick lost his cocky posture. "Now hold up a minute."

Estrada frowned at Det. Aguilar. "You say this girlfriend reported him missing. Did she give an exact date?"

"She hadn't heard from him in a while, so she asked some of his friends," Det. Aguilar replied.

"In other words you don't know when he disappeared. He's a petty street criminal, known for being transient. And by the way, his chosen profession means he led a dangerous life. You should be tracking down his drug supplier and other associates." Estrada gave him a pointed stare.

"Mr. Jefferson and Ms. Landry are associates, and we check *all* leads," Det. Aguilar replied promptly and pressed his lips together.

MiMi could tell the detective felt his advantage had evaporated. Maybe he didn't count on Roderick's lawyer being with him at the airport. Thank heavens for Roderick's fiercely protective mother. No doubt his parents had paid Estrada handsomely to babysit their troublesome son until he was safely out of the country.

"I appreciate you have to do a difficult job, Detective Aguilar. But my connection to Mr. Herrera is non-existent. Believe me, once I was arrested, the last person I wanted to see was him."

"I thought you never met him, Miss Landry." Det. Aguilar leaned both elbows on the table. He gazed at her with a "Gotcha!" expression.

"I saw him at a court hearing or maybe a police photo spread," MiMi replied, not missing a beat. She didn't look away from the detective's scrutiny.

Estrada looked at Aguilar. "Is that all, detective?"

Aguilar continued to eye Roderick for a few seconds before he slid the note pad back into his jacket pocket. "I believe so. We have your contact information in America should we have more questions."

"Of course. I hope you catch the killer, detective. I really do. His family needs closure." Roderick stood and glanced at his cell phone as he talked.

The detective wore a frown of contempt for a brief moment. Then his impassive mask dropped into place. He stood. "Thanks for your cooperation. Have a safe flight." He gave Estrada a curt nod and then strode out.

"We handled him alright," Roderick said and grinned at the others.

MiMi sprung from her chair toward him. "One

more word and I swear, Aguilar will be investigating another homicide."

Roderick raised both hands, palms out. He took a step back from MiMi. "You're under a huge strain, baby. I understand. I'll give you some space for a minute."

"Give me space? Give me space?" MiMi sputtered more sounds in speechless rage.

"We leave now," Estrada said quietly.

The lawyer pulled Roderick by the arm and they left. Fortunately, only three other people were in the lounge watching, and all of them were strangers. MiMi took in gulps of air to calm down as Willa continued to counsel her about self-control. Jazz left and came back with more drinks on a tray.

"We need these." Jazz drank half the beer in her mug and sighed.

"Damn, MiMi. Couldn't you just get the usual vacation trouble like everybody else? You know, lost luggage, insect bites, diarrhea." Willa drank a mouthful of white wine.

"I'm going to make Roddy pay," MiMi said through tight lips.

"Stay away from Mister Bad News That Gets Worse." Willa put down the wine glass and shook MiMi by the arm. "Hey, you better listen to me."

"I hafta agree with Willa, girl. Take a cooling off period before you hook up with him again." Jazz nodded. She hissed when Willa scowled at her.

"Cooling off period? Dump that chump," Willa shot back.

"I guess you missed the part about him being rich." Jazz waved a hand at her sister and looked at MiMi. "I say, don't write him off completely."

"Unbelievable," Willa muttered into her wine glass.

An hour later, they went through boarding and got on the plane. MiMi sat in the window seat. Jazz squirmed to get comfortable in the aisle seat. She made eye contact with a handsome man on the next row. Soon they were flirting in Spanish. Willa sighed deeply, but didn't say anything to her sister. Then she looked at MiMi.

"It's finally over, okay? I know you're disappointed Roderick turned out to be an asshole and all, but at least you found out. You can move on to somebody better." Willa gave her hand a pat.

MiMi smiled at her with a sigh. "You're absolutely right."

MiMi gazed at the clouds through the glass. She looked forward to the hours she'd spend with Sage. The happy mental images faded when she thought about work and her boss. Providing for Sage was her top priority. If only she found that missing cash, Sage's future would be secured. So MiMi decided on her to-do list. She would keep her job and find the money Jack had so carefully hidden away. Then she added another item; figuring out a way to deliver some much deserved payback to Roderick Conwell Jefferson.

Chapter 4

Willa and Jazz napped on the flight from the Dominican Republic to their stop at the Atlanta airport and again on the flight to Louisiana. During their stopover, MiMi called her sister to check on Sage and arrange to pick her up. Adrienne cheerily described how much Sage loved being with her cousins. Despite Adrienne's assurances, MiMi only felt more anxious to see Sage for herself. MiMi tried to release the tension by keeping her eyes open but couldn't. She gave in after the first fifteen minutes in the air. Instead she looked over her research on money laundering. Willa would probably flip out, and Jazz would call her crazy. MiMi didn't care. The more she dug, the more she became convinced her deceased lover had hidden almost one million dollars. She couldn't write off that kind of change. Sage deserved it, and MiMi felt she'd earned it.

MiMi sighed when they touched down at Armstrong International Airport in Kenner, outside of New Orleans. Irrational as it seemed, she expected an air marshal to pop up out of nowhere and take her away. Yet the end of their journey was blessedly uneventful. They caught a shuttle to the airport lot where Willa had left her SUV. An hour and half later they were in Baton Rouge. They pulled up to MiMi's house first. The afternoon April sun still beamed down just as hot as though it was midday. She gazed at the lovely landscaped front yard and tan brick three bedroom ranch with love.

"Thank you Lord!" MiMi breathed.

Willa got out and helped carry MiMi's three bags to the front door. "Yeah, now get some rest and figure out how to stay out of trouble for the next decade."

"Amen," Jazz called from her seat in the SUV. "I don't want to visit anymore jails or courtrooms. I've been in enough of those on my own shit. Don't need yours, too."

"What a sweet sentiment," MiMi retorted. She grinned when Jazz gave her the finger. "Seriously, I really owe y'all."

"Oh hell yes you do," Willa replied promptly, a hand on one hip. "Now look, I hope this little episode has convinced you to forget Jack's shady money. You have a child to think about."

"I was thinking about Sage, but you're right," MiMi said quickly when Willa started to speak again. "I have to let go of the past."

"Exactly. Not living the rich life isn't a death sentence. Work hard, do what you gotta do." Willa pointed a finger at MiMi for emphasis.

MiMi frowned. "Right. My job, if I still have one."

"Set a meeting with your boss as soon as possible."

"Yes, mother." MiMi gave Willa a quick hug. Then she blew a kiss at Jazz. "I love my two BFFs."

Jazz waved at her. She had ear buds in and was bobbing her head to an unheard beat from the playlist on her smartphone. "Whatever."

MiMi laughed and turned to Willa. "I'm going to pick up Sage before I do anything though."

"Give her a kiss for us." Willa yawned. "I'm going to the office for a minute after I drop off Jazz. See ya."

"Bye, and thanks again for everything," MiMi called as Willa walked back to the SUV.

After texting her sister again, MiMi put away the luggage without unpacking. She had a doll from the Dominican Republic sitting in Sage's car seat as a surprise. Twenty minutes later, she pulled up to Adrienne's two story home on Brister Boulevard. Arriving in her sister's circular driveway never ceased to impress MiMi. And that was exactly the effect Adrienne and her husband had gone for when they bought the seven hundred thousand dollar home. Never mind that they only had one child, her son Brayden. MiMi smiled at the thought of her eight year old nephew. Brayden smiled his way into female hearts easily. And Sage adored him. He laughed a lot, and accepted others without judgment. MiMi hoped he would hold onto his personality, and not become his parents. Or his grandparents for that matter.

MiMi parked her Lexus GX behind a sleek gray BMW 328i and tried not to have car envy. Her sister and brother-in-law also had a shiny new BMW X5 SUV. The front door swung open as she got out of her vehicle. Adrienne's husband, Christopher, strode out. He stood six feet tall with cafe au lait skin. Snatching him off the market had made a host of debutants depressed. As usual her big sister beat out the competition.

He didn't look up from his Blackberry. She watched with amusement as he kept going down the brick sidewalk without seeing her or the SUV. MiMi gave his wool and silk blend thousand dollar black suit an appreciative nod. Chris had his faults, but selecting his outfits wasn't one of them.

"Hi Chris." MiMi was about to tease him but stopped. Christopher Jameson Fortenberry, IV had little, if any, sense of humor.

"Hi MiMi. Adrienne's inside. I have to go back to the office. Hope you had a nice trip." Chris gave her a brief smile.

"I had a real bang up time." MiMi couldn't be mad at him because Chris had no sense of irony either. He always said exactly what he meant, or he kept quiet.

"Great."

"Yeah, great," MiMi said dryly."

"So I have to go. A group of Chinese shareholders are in town and we're having a business dinner." Chris smoothed down his expensive silk tie.

"I'm surprised Adrienne's not in one of her fabulous cocktail dresses and already in the car. She loves those international social affairs."

Adrienne missed no opportunity to hit up the well-heeled for her charities. Not to mention she'd make contacts for her private consulting business. Supporting her man was way down on the list. Chris knew it, too. As usual, her small arrow of sarcasm missed the target with Chris.

"Hmm, she claimed she couldn't find a babysitter. I think she didn't want to share Sage with anyone," Chris said as he looked at his Blackberry again.

MiMi felt a twinge of nerves at his observation. "Adrienne? She worked at home when Brayden was a newborn to stay in the game."

"Maybe having a little girl makes the difference. Brayden stopped wanting to be fussed over when he was four. He'd rather be out with me and my brothers, listening to us talk business and sports." Chris smiled in a way that actually lit up his hazel eyes.

MiMi smiled back at him. His chief redeeming quality in her eyes was his genuine devotion to his son. It probably helped that Brayden looked so much like his father. "Strong kid if he won't let Adrienne boss him around."

"Yeah, drove her nuts until she realized it was a losing battle. He's got her genes after all." Chris held up his Blackberry with a frown. "Wow, I have to go. Sorry to rush off, MiMi. You know how it is."

"Yes, I do," MiMi said and watched him rush off.

Chris glanced at one of the bay windows. His face lit up when he saw Brayden waving energetically at him through the glass. He waved back and then got in the BMW. MiMi blew a kiss at her nephew which got her a wide boyishly handsome grin. When she turned to the door, Adrienne stood staring past MiMI down the driveway.

"He's working late at least twice a week these days. Business is good." Adrienne gave a short laugh that contained no humor. Then she focused on MiMi. "Welcome back to freedom."

MiMi ignored the subtle dig about her time in jail. "You look well."

"This old thing? I'm taking it to our charity designer consignment shop next week." Adrienne smoothed a hand down one leg of the lovely blue cotton lounge jumpsuit. Pewter gray leather flats completed her look as the wealthy lady who does lunch. "Well come on in. Sage is still playing with her doll house. She's absolutely in love with the thing, and the set of dolls mother got her."

"I hope they don't have any small parts."

"Give me some credit. They're all organic cotton cloth dolls, the best by the way, from Children's Palace. It's a new store in Towne Center." Adrienne closed the door behind them once inside. She glanced at MiMi from head to toe as they stood in the spacious foyer. "You don't look the worse for wear being in the big house. Do they still call it that, or have I been watching too many vintage gangster movies?"

"I'm not in the mood to hear your attempts at humor about it either."

"Trust me, none of us were laughing," Adrienne replied mildly. "Daddy ranted on and on. Mother spent hours on the phone putting out feelers to make sure none of our friends knew. Thank God Roderick's parents have the sense to be discreet."

"Please. Your 'friends' have their own skeletons rattling around various closets. They should talk." MiMi crossed her arms.

"True, but another exciting tale about you being in trouble again would drown out the noise," Adrienne said. Her full lips lifted at one corner.

MiMi held her temper in check. Adrienne had a special skill of pushing MiMi's buttons until she exploded. Not today. "Chris didn't seem scandalized or eager to rub my face in it. At least he's showing some compassion."

"That's because he doesn't know. Only Roderick's parents, our parents and I know. We plan to keep it that way." Adrienne spun around and strolled into the large open plan living room. Just beyond was a formal dining room that flowed into a large kitchen. She sat down on a sofa.

"You're keeping secrets from Chris?" MiMi tried to

make it into a mocking tease, but something about her sister's behavior bothered her.

"He's mostly interested in work these days and getting the next big bonus." Adrienne's pretty face grew stony as she gazed ahead.

"You like those healthy shots of money. More fun shopping for you," MiMi quipped. She glanced around at perfect order. The room, like the outside of the house out front, looked ready for a model home design magazine.

Adrienne picked up a silver framed photo of her husband on a lovely teakwood table. "I'm a bit deeper than the next pair of two hundred dollar ballet flats."

MiMi glanced at her sister. The bitterness just beneath the surface of her statement came through clearly. "I doubt anyone considers you a lightweight, Adrienne."

"You'd think so wouldn't you." Adrienne put the photo down and looked at MiMi with a slight frown. "I'm sure you have to be exhausted. Why don't you get some rest for a couple of days? Sage is fine here."

"I got rest on the flight, so I'm good. Besides, I'm used to being a tired single mommy," MiMi said with a smile.

"But Sage loves her room. I'm paying my housekeeper extra to look after her while I work during the day. It's perfect really. I'm right down the hall in my home office if Estella needs me. Then when Brayden gets home we have quality time." Adrienne gave a contented sigh.

MiMi's smile faded. "I appreciate you looking after Sage for me. Honestly, I missed the little terror. I can't wait to give her a big hug, a warm bath and tuck her in like always."

Adrienne stood up abruptly. "I really don't see what's the rush, but since you insist."

Before MiMi could reply, her nephew called from upstairs. "Hello Aunt MiMi. Climb aboard my spaceship."

"On my way, captain," MiMi yelled back. She looked at Adrienne who shrugged.

"His father lets him read those science fiction comics for children. One Sunday they watched Star Trek movies all day." Adrienne wore a sour expression.

"You should be thrilled. He must not spend all his time working." MiMi wondered at the strange vibes her sister seemed to radiate.

"Humph." Adrienne brushed past MiMi as a signal she had no interest in expounding on the subject. "Like I said, Sage is in her room. She loves it in there. Brayden, have you been checking on your little cousin?"

"Yes, mommy. She's hugging those dumb dolls again. I tried to get her to hold my spaceship, but she just tossed it on the floor."

When they reached the top of the stairs, MiMi wrapped both arms around his slender frame. She kissed the top of his head. "She's a baby, sweetie."

"Nope, she's a *girl* like at school. They don't do cool stuff like boys. Except mygirlfriend Allison. She likes to watch space movies." Brayden grinned widely.

"Brayden, Allison is your *friend*. We talked about the meaning of the word girlfriend," Adrienne said crisply.

"Yes, mommy." Brayden's tone sounded obedient, but his eyes twinkled when MiMi winked at him.

"Mommy's here to take you home, Sage." MiMi couldn't wait any longer.

She strode past her sister and down the hall. Sage

was in a bedroom near the master suite. A white painted safety gate came up waist high to keep the toddler from wandering out and onto the stairs. Sage sat on the floor in front of a playhouse that she could crawl inside easily. MiMi gasped. Soft light green and pale pink decorated the room. The curtains matched the trundle bed coverlet. A lovely oriental carpet with jewel tones covered half the hardwood floor. Expensive toys had been artfully arranged around the room. Several large dolls sat in an open toy box. A voice startled MiMi out of her state of astonishment.

"Hello Miss Landry, so nice to see you." Estella, Adrienne's housekeeper, beamed at her. "Look, darling girl."

Sage looked up and gave a squeal before Estella could finish. "Mommy!"

Estella laughed as she lifted the gate. "She was just asking about you."

"Mommy." Sage raced across the room and into MiMi's arms.

"We're going home, sweet stuff," MiMi said. She dusted kisses all over the round soft face as tears rolled down her own. "Mommy missed you so much."

"Mommy home." Sage grabbed onto the front of MiMi's blouse tightly.

"Well I'm going home, Mrs. Fortenberry. Welcome back." Estella gave MiMi a maternal pat on the back.

"Thank you so much for helping take care of her, Estella. I know you had to work extra."

"It was a joy looking after her. Reminds me of when my children were young. My youngest is fourteen now." Estella sighed. "Thank goodness this is the fourth and last time I deal with a teenager."

"You're still young enough for another one." MiMi

kissed Sage's smooth cheek again.

"Ha! My husband knows better than to even suggest such a thing. Goodnight ladies. Bye Brayden." Estella waved to them as she headed for the stairs.

"Bye, Mrs. Estella," Brayden yelled back. He started to dash off to his room, then doubled back. He hugged MiMi and Sage at the same time. "Bye."

"Bye little man," MiMi said and kissed his cheek. She went into the room still holding Sage. "Aunt Adrienne says you've been such a good girl. Let's get you packed up."

Adrienne followed close behind. She started picking the few toys scattered around on the floor. "Like I said, you're rushing for no reason. Sage has a routine. She should be settling in for a story and winding down for bed. My Lord, it's almost eight o'clock at night."

"What time did she have her nap? I hope it wasn't too long after lunch. That does keep her up late." MiMi put Sage down in the play pen to free both hands.

"I know what time she needs a nap. Are you saying I can't care for her properly? I'm not the one who went off for a whole month," Adrienne muttered.

"I didn't leave for so long on purpose. And no, I wasn't criticizing you. I just asked a question. You sound more like mother every day." MiMi held a stack of Sage's underwear. "I don't see her overnight bag."

"Oh, that thing you brought wasn't big enough. I had to buy her more clothes, so I got a bigger one." Adrienne went to a closet, pulled out a fancy large pink bag with Sage's name on it.

"The bag I brought was just fine. You didn't have to spend so much money." MiMi marched to the closet. Sage's old bag, a green and yellow plaid cloth duffle, was stuffed into a corner. "What are you going to do with the room? I'm sure you won't have guest stay in here and sleep in a toddler bed."

Adrienne ignored MiMi's comment about the pink bag. She continued to stuff clothes and baby items into it. "I'll leave it as is. Sage will probably need a safe place again with the *friends* you hang out with."

MiMi stomped out of the closet. "My friends have given me more support in the last three years than anyone has in my life. They flew to the Dominican Republic. Now tell me, which one of my family members showed up?"

"Excuse me? You'd still be in jail if Daddy hadn't paid for your defense attorney and those hefty fines. What a silly mistake." Adrienne gave a huff of disapproval.

"Roderick is the one who made the damn mistake," MiMi hissed. She glanced over at Sage, who was preoccupied with her new favorite doll.

"So now you're using profanity in front of the baby," Adrienne said with a frown.

"My family's idea of 'Mr. Right' got me arrested, and I'm the one you criticize?" MiMi clapped a palm on her chest. Her sister only wanted to see MiMi as the problem.

"Your *friends* may find this kind of behavior just fine, but not in my house around my children," Adrienne shot back, pointing a manicured fingernail at MiMi.

"You mean your child. Sage is my daughter, and we're going home." MiMi spun around and grabbed the bag. With the shoulder strap on, she picked up Sage. "Come on, sweetie pie. Tonight you'll be in your own bed. All this pink is starting to look like stomach medicine."

"Mommy, mommy," Sage said in a toddler sing-song voice.

"Yes, mommy is here, and she's not going anywhere for a long, long time."

MiMi glared at her sister for full five seconds. Adrienne glared back but kept silent. With a last look around to make sure she hadn't missed anything, MiMi went down the stairs. Adrienne followed. She made baby talk to Sage, but kept her distance. Adrienne stopped at the last step of the stairs.

"Wait a minute. Take one of her new dolls. She'll probably fret without it. I can get it." Adrienne half turned.

"Don't bother. She has lots of toys at home." MiMi slid back the locks on the fancy front door.

"Okay, but slow down." Adrienne sighed as she came down to the foyer. "I'm sorry for saying those things to you a minute ago. I was out of my lane."

"Very much so." MiMi faced her sister. She didn't trust herself to say more.

"Let's get along for the sake of the children. Sage's toys can stay here for her next visit with Aunt Adrienne. Isn't that right precious?" Adrienne came close and smoothed Sage's thick soft curls. Sage yawned and put her head on MiMi's shoulder.

"I won't need a babysitter for a while, so you might consider donating that stuff to the children's unit at Our Lady of the Lake."

"Now you're being vindictive," Adrienne said. Her voice had the quiet, flat tone of suppressed anger.

"No, I'm being a mother. As you pointed out, I've been apart from my child too long. I appreciate the offer to help out though," MiMi added, her tone empty of warmth or gratitude.

"I see." Adrienne brushed her perfectly styled hair. "Goodnight."

MiMi was out the door and at her car before Adrienne could respond. She dropped the bag and opened the door. Her hands shook as she fumbled with the getting Sage properly secured into the car seat. MiMi rebuffed Adrienne's offers to help. Finally getting the now cranky toddler strapped in, MiMi closed the door and tossed the bag into the back of her SUV. Minutes later they were on the road away from the beautiful upscale neighborhood. MiMi took in deep breaths to stave off the anxiety attack building.

Chapter 5

Lucky for MiMi, the daycare hadn't filled Sage's slot. So she sat across from her boss the next day. Ten minutes in to her talk with the lanky blonde, and MiMi knew she had plenty to worry about.

Fashion Sense had grown from a string of specialty women's boutiques with only two stores to a major chain. Along the way they'd expanded to clothes and accessories for men and children. The merchandise at Fashion Sense was pricey enough to satisfy new money shoppers. The economy of Baton Rouge continued to go strong, attracting well paid white collar jobs. The people who filled them wanted to have distinctive everything. Fashion Sense catered to their mild sense of snobbery.

Kerry Newton stood six feet tall in stockings. A former model, she affected the same stylized movements from her days on the runway. She'd never become an international sensation. Still, she spun descriptions of her modeling fame as though she had. Now she was the regional manager of buyers at fifteen department stores in four states. She held a cordless phone against her left ear, and gazed through the window of the third floor office.

"Listen, honey, I'm so over hearing excuses from everyone. You tell the saleswoman that we don't want a substitute. We signed a contract for the Bellows line of home fashions. We've planned an entire marketing push around it. Now get it done." Kerry hit the button ending the call and thumped the phone onto her desk. "All I ask is for people to do the job I hired them to do. Is that too much?"

MiMi knew enough not to reply to her rhetorical question. Besides, under the circumstances, MiMi was sure Kerry included her in that complaint. Kerry's assistant, Tyler Grant, bustled in, swished papers in front of her, and waited. The young man avoided eye contact with MiMi, just as Kerry had done since MiMi stepped through her door. No doubt he, like other employees, wanted to know if MiMi was in or out first. None of them had the guts to risk being on Kerry's wrong side. So much for worker solidarity, MiMi thought sourly.

"Lilly wants you to call her," Tyler said. He cast a furtive glance at MiMi. Five minutes later he hustled out to implement Kerry's terse instructions.

"Now," Kerry said. She sighed and looked at MiMi as if she were one more hurdle she had to jump. "You know we're already heavy into preparing for the fall season. We're working like crazy to finish the store catalogs."

"I gave Tyler a full notebook on the hot colors and looks before I left," MiMi said.

Kerry went on as though MiMi hadn't spoken. "Even in this digital age a lot of our customer base of baby boomers still like the paper catalog. Our web team is putting in overtime to roll out the online version."

MiMi broke in before she could go on. "I met with

Elle and the team two weeks before my vacation. They have a complete list from the manufacturers. My contacts at Wilson's, Barberry's, and other houses sent me their fall fashions. Elle says y'all met on them."

After a few beats, Kerry leaned both elbows on her cluttered desk. "You were gone over a month when it was supposed to be just a few days. That's a problem."

"I couldn't control complications with my flight and then my friend getting sick. But Elle assures me all the stuff I left meant no hiccups in the planning."

"I thought your friend got sick first, which forced to you change flights and that's when you ran into problems," Kerry replied. One pencil thin, brow arched to within an inch of its life, lifted.

"Yeah, the point is I checked with the team before I made it home. Elle said they didn't miss a beat. I can pick right up because everything I did was spot on. The look this season will be earth tones mixed with bold colors." MiMi tapped the open workbook she'd spread on Kerry's desk.

"Right, but the thing is Tyler stepped in to help. He's been invaluable to me, doing way more than just being my go-fer. He's getting his degree in a few weeks." Kerry rocked her leatherette executive chair back and forth.

"Good for him. Now he can work his way up from the display floor just like I did for the past six years. That's after I got my *bachelor's*."

MiMi pushed down the growing anger threatening to explode into a tirade. She almost added that Kerry had been hired after her. For all her hard work, MiMi had been overlooked again. Kerry's expression tightened. She, too, had only an associate's degree. Rumors hinted she'd had a romance with one of the top executives when she was still a model.

"Naturally, you've made contributions since you've been here." Kerry affected a sympathetic expression that didn't look natural for her. "I'm sure you need to settle in with your little girl, catch up on loose ends at home, etc. Take another week or so. Then we can talk." Kerry closed the workbook.

"No," MiMi clipped before she could go on.

"Excuse me?" Kerry blinked eyelashes heavy with black mascara at MiMi.

"The rest of the week should be enough." MiMi picked up the workbook and stood. "I'll thank Tyler again for pitching in on my way out. He followed my blueprint pretty well considering his lack of experience."

"That wasn't exactly a suggestion, MiMi." Kerry looked up at MiMi stonily.

"I've spoken to Mr. Jenkins and Darcas. They're fine with me coming back Monday. In fact, Darcas said I could come in tomorrow if I wanted. Oh, and before I came for our meeting, Elle and the team brought me up to speed. Took less than five minutes. Like I said, the work I did before I left was quite thorough. Darcas agreed. See, I left her a detailed summary." MiMi held up the workbook.

Normally, MiMi didn't rub Kerry's nose in the fact that she was on great terms with the regional VP and the director of fashion merchandising. But MiMi needed leverage as Kerry circled like a shark tasting blood in the water.

"I see." Kerry's jaw muscle worked as she no doubt held in what she really wanted to say. She slowly stood, but looked down at her desk for several seconds before she raised her head. "Well played, Landry."

"Look, we both want Fashion Sense to be

profitable. My reputation is built on how well we sell. The minute I don't produce, I'm out. No amount of chitchat with the bosses about Mardi Gras and gumbo will matter. But they know I make money. The numbers don't lie." MiMi met her gaze without looking away.

"Right, of course," Kerry said. The words seemed to be forced through her lips. She tried to smile, but it ended up as more of a pirate's sneer.

"We're on the same team, Kerry. When I do my job, you look good. I think Tyler is talented. He's got a future in this business. I'm going to do all I can to help him." MiMi nodded as she tucked the workbook into her large leather tote bag.

"How nice of you." Kerry came around the desk. "This job means a lot to you, doesn't it?"

"My career with Zen Corporation means a lot to me," MiMi replied evenly. "I care about our company, and showing my daughter that women can balance family and business. Being a mother, I know you understand."

"I do, and I'm glad we had this talk." Kerry smiled and held out a hand. "Monday then."

"Monday, nine sharp as usual," MiMi replied and shook the cool dry hand.

****

Early Friday around noon MiMi sat in Jazz's apartment behind Candy Girls. Jazz ran a night club that also included a restaurant. Workers from the surrounding blue collar neighborhood streamed in to buy lunch. In another six to eight hours the party crowd would dominate. Then the cooks would put out free appetizers until midnight. Cheap finger food would go with the more expensive mixed drinks. The sound system belted out the throb of R&B music, the constant soundtrack of Jazz's business. Until the beat picked up, and rap lyrics were no longer G-Rated, families with kids in tow would stop to buy supper plate.

Jazz sat on the living room floor playing with Sage on a child's tablet computer. They were surrounded by a soft play pen gate since Jazz's place wasn't child proof. As they tapped flashing baby animals in bright primary colors, music played. Sage squealed as a rabbit hopped from one cupcake to another.

"This carpet is the boss," MiMi said, eyeing the jewel tones of green, red, blue and gold of the Oriental wool rug.

"Yeah, I had to redecorate." Jazz let out a whoop as baby fox chased the rabbit. Then she huffed. "Stupid game."

"In other words, you're letting a two year old beat you." MiMi laughed.

Jazz scowled. "This game doesn't even make sense. All they do is bounce around on cakes and gobble up candies."

"Ba-ba." Sage switched her attention to a large purple ball. Her cute chubby legs kicked the soft bouncy toy a few inches. She clapped as though she'd just achieved a winning score.

"Whoa, my leg fell asleep." Jazz got to her feet. She closed the gate to keep Sage safe and then staggered to the sofa.

"Getting kind of old to sit on the floor with kids, huh?" MiMi teased.

"Watch it or I'll throw you and your cheating crumb snatcher outta here," Jazz shot back. "You're older than me. Thirty-five your last birthday, right?"

"Thirty-one, and you d... darn well know it." MiMi kept her voice low. Not that Sage noticed. She carried her teddy bear by one leg as she kicked the ball again. They watched her for a few minutes as they sipped sodas.

"Your folks wouldn't approve of you bringing Sage to this part of town. The center of sin and depravity is only a breath away," Jazz said melodramatically.

MiMi laughed. "That's a direct quote from Aunt Ametrine. My mother would say 'Sage should be exposed to a more elevated social environment'. "

"Translation: 'Keep my grand baby out the hood, girl!'" Jazz started to light a cigarillo, glanced at Sage and put it away.

"They don't mind throwing hints that I won't inherit if I keep hanging with the wrong people. That's why I need my own." MiMi picked up dishes with the remains of their lunch from Jazz's café. She went to the kitchen and loaded the dishwasher. Then she started wiping the counters.

"Okay, but running around the world after Jack's stolen cash is a bad, not to mention dangerous, idea." Jazz propped her feet on the sofa cushion. She waved at Sage with a smile. The baby made squealing noises and continued to play.

MiMi carefully hung up the dish cloths to dry on a towel holder. She scanned the kitchen and dining area one last time. Then she joined Jazz on the sofa.

"I want something of my own, and for Sage. My parents like the use their money like a club."

"Nasty way to treat your own kids," Jazz agreed.

"Maybe, but I should be independent. Getting a rich husband isn't much better. I'd just trade one kind of economic prison for another." MiMi sighed and sank back against the cushions.

Jazz gave her the side-eye. "Then why did you chase Roderick so hard?"

"Insurance," MiMi replied bluntly. "I'd have my own money, and his would just give me more operating cash, a cushion. What?"

"Sorta sounds like something your family would do," Jazz said just as bluntly.

MiMi gave a short laugh. "I was attracted to Roderick, so it wasn't all cold and calculating. But trust me; he had status and my father's assets in mind when he asked me out. Plus our parents finessed our meeting."

"Those social events to make sure all the bourgie kids hang with the right crowd," Jazz said dryly.

"Yes, the debutant balls, coming out teas, dances, theater nights and parties all serve a purpose. People who have things in common are attracted to each other. Like you and Detective Addison." MiMi gave Jazz a sly look.

"Yes, we're still seeing each other. No, we're not going to live together. I like simple," Jazz said firmly.

"Oh please. Explain to me a simple relationship with a man. I've never seen one." MiMi gave a snort.

"We have a little fun conversation, lot of hot sex, and say see ya later. Simple." Jazz winked at MiMi.

MiMi hopped up to cross the room. Sage had escaped the baby play area they'd created. She'd become fascinated with the buttons on Jazz's expensive sound system. MiMi steered her back to her toys. Once Sage became distracted with her teddy bear and another toy, MiMi sat down again.

"Keep telling yourself that lie, okay? I've seen the

way you look at each other," MiMi retorted.

"Whatever. Back to you and this money. Willa is right. Concentrate on your career. Wow, can't believe I'm quoting her." Jazz shook her head.

"Says the woman who owns a business. Working for someone else isn't insurance. I'm tired of kissing butt and following someone else's agenda." MiMi picked up a throw pillow and tossed it around.

"Didn't sound like butt kissing the other day. I can't believe you went gangsta with the woman. You sure as hell have changed." Jazz studied her for a few seconds. "Look, I realize you've been through some stuff, but don't let it make you hard."

"Oh yeah? Look where being girly-girl has gotten me. Jack crapped on me. My parents and sister push me around. I don't want my daughter to think she has to be a doormat to get ahead."

"I get you, girl. So let's all clean up our acts. Well, Willa's pretty sanitized already." Jazz laughed. "So you and Roderick are through?"

"He tried to throw me under the bus. What do you think?" MiMi retorted.

"The guy did tell the judge you weren't in on the drug buy. If he was going to set you up, he could have put it all on you. You were taking a puff when the cops rolled up on y'all." Jazz shrugged when MiMi gave her a squinty-eyed look. "I'm just sayin'."

"I made a mistake, but I don't smoke weed on the regular," MiMi whispered. "Apparently Roderick does."

"Kinda hypocritical if you ask me. You drink wine and martinis. Weed is a recreational high like alcohol."

"Don't forget the part about weed being illegal," MiMi replied tartly.

"All I'm saying is, y'all were on vacation and he did

something stupid. It happens."

MiMi frowned. "Maybe if we were still teenagers on spring break, but not at our age. Roddy should have shown more judgment."

"Says the woman who used him to chase down laundered money in an offshore account." Jazz ducked when MiMi tossed the throw pillow at her.

"Shut up," was the best MiMi could say as a comeback.

"Okay, okay. Don't get violent. You've still got your job. That's something."

"For now. Kerry doesn't know the real story of my extended vacation." MiMi chewed her lower lip. "I don't know. Flight complications and saying Roderick got sick sounds thin even to me. What if..."

"Hey, what happens in the DR stays in the DR. She won't find out." Jazz patted her on the leg.

"Yeah, I guess. I've been doing Internet searches to make sure. So far I haven't found anything." MiMi let out a slow breath to release the tension that had suddenly tightened her muscles.

"See? And they haven't contacted y'all about the murder either," Jazz said casually.

MiMi sat straight. "Oh shit."

"I thought you said no cussing around the baby," Jazz scolded. Then her grin faded. "What's wrong?"

"I haven't searched for articles on the murder. What if the police told some reporter I was questioned?"

"Shit," Jazz whispered.

"Get your tablet. I'll look on my smartphone." MiMi grabbed her hobo bag to pull out her phone.

Both spend thirty minutes searching the Internet. MiMi held her breath when she put in her name.

Nothing. Then she used Roderick's name as keywords. All that came up were a few stories about his company. They found only one article about the murder on an obscure Caribbean news page. The article only identified the victim and said no suspects had been identified.

"So you can relax." Jazz poured soda in glasses for both of them.

"Yeah, right."

MiMi stared at the search results on Jazz's tablet. She still felt a sense of doom; like a hurricane that would rock her world was building in those beautiful Caribbean waters. Going to the Dominican Republic and asking about Jack's account at the bank there had stirred up... something. When Sage let out a yelp, MiMi looked up and smiled with affection. Sage yawned as she rubbed her eyes with chubby fists, fighting to stay awake. She scooped her up and kissed her cheek.

"You're right. It's over. Come on, baby girl. We're going home. It's time for your nap and for Auntie Jazz to get back to work."

****

In an hour they were home, and Sage was in her playpen sound asleep on her favorite blanket. MiMi enjoyed the quiet routine of putting the house in order. Maybe Willa was right. She should count her blessings, forget dreams of a big bank account, and just live. Then she sat down at the desk in a corner of the kitchen to pay bills. Economic reality slapped her upside the head repeatedly. After another hour of staring at figures that didn't change for the better, MiMi rubbed her eyes. The personal finance software was pretty efficient in showing her the bleak bottom line.

"Thank God I fought for my job, but it's not over," MiMi murmured as she tapped the keys of her laptop.

Kerry wouldn't give up. MiMi sighed at the prospect of a daily battle. At least Kerry would return to corporate headquarters in a village outside Milwaukee, Wisconsin. The frozen Midwest was the perfect place for that icy witch. She didn't have an empathetic bone in her body. The next two weeks would be touch and go, but once Kerry boarded that plane, MiMI would be golden. First thing Monday, she would go in and make nice to Kerry. MiMi doubted it would make a difference, but at least she could tell Darcas she made an effort. The doorbell chimed just as MiMi hit submit on the last electronic payment. She logged off the credit card website and sighed.

"I sure hope this is the prize patrol from that sweepstakes company." She looked through the window beside her ornate front door of thick beveled glass. "Damn it."

"Hi MiMi. Don't pretend you're not home. I saw the curtain move," Roderick said quickly.

"I don't have to. This is my house, and I don't have to open the door. I can just let you stand there looking stupid," MiMi yelled back.

"C'mon, honey. Remember what we had," Roderick called back.

"You're right to use the past tense, Roddy." MiMi glared at the door with her arms crossed.

"Listen, I talked to your parents and they understand. Your mother suggested we talk things out," Roderick said.

"I'll just bet she did," MiMi muttered. The phone rang. In no hurry, MiMi strolled to the kitchen to answer it.

"Don't make me yell through a closed door. Your neighbors will call the police."

"Bye Roderick," she called over her shoulder. She picked up the cordless handset, then regretted not checking the caller ID. MiMi hissed at the strong contralto voice on the other end of the line.

"Miliana Elise Landry, you let Roderick in. He deserves an apology for the way you've treated him," her mother said.

"Apologize?" MiMi sputtered. She held the phone away from her to gape at it. "I was in a third world prison because of him!"

"That's right, Miliana Elise. Tell the entire city at the top of your lungs."

"Mother..."

"Your father spent a fortune to settle the matter and keep the scandal from crossing borders. No one knows, and including your employer. If you still *have* an employer," Mrs. Landry said, her voice cut through the handset like a honed steak knife.

Trust her mother to score several points in one deft move. MiMi swallowed the string of curse words that bubbled up her throat. "I appreciate what daddy did for me, although he let me sit in jail for a long time. I do still have my job," MiMi replied tartly. She almost added "As if it's any of your business."

"Don't get an attitude with me," Mrs. Landry shot back. "Of course you had to wait. The authorities weren't going to simply let you go because he said so. Don't be ridiculous. Now I'm going to tell Roderick that you'll let him in."

"He called you? Are you kidding me? What a big baby."

"Stop being vindictive and let him in," Mrs. Landry said.

"You can't order me around like I'm a child." MiMi stomped one foot and pursed her lips at the phone.

"Of course you have a right to be upset. But at least give him a chance to explain and apologize. Your father did silly things when he was young. That didn't stop me from realizing he was the right man for me. Think of Sage's future." Her mother's voice softened to her "I'm on your side" tone.

"I can't believe you think Roderick is father material after the stunt he pulled."

"MiMi, I know you smoked marijuana several times in college. And was Jack Crown father material?" Mrs. Landry, her voice sharp again.

MiMi's mouth had opened wide to argue the comparison between Jack and Roderick. The defense froze on her tongue. Score another set of points for team Pauline. "I get it, mother. We all have faults; we all make mistakes."

"Precisely, now open that door and don't wake up Sage with silly theatrics."

"How did you know..." MiMi blinked at the phone.

"I'll call later. Goodbye." Mrs. Landry hung up as if confident her command would be obeyed.

"The woman knows what goes on in my house as well as I do," MiMi mumbled as she hit the off button.

She went back to the front door. Roderick's tall frame could be seen through the beveled glass, a dark shadow against the bright sunshine around him. He waited patiently, no doubt assured by her mother things were fine. MiMi huffed in frustration, but after a few seconds she snapped the locks and yanked opened the front door. Roderick looked too good dressed in a dark gray suit, soft blue dress shirt and silver tie.

"Progress," Roderick said with a grin. "Now the big question; will you let me cross the threshold?"

"The bigger question, will I knee you in the groin," MiMi snapped. "You've got a nerve, pleading your case to my parents and then coming over here."

"I owed them an apology, MiMi. They were worried sick, and it was all my fault. Totally." Roderick grew serious. "I can speak from right here. I don't blame you one bit for..."

"Oh just come in," MiMi cut him off. She stood aside as he walked past and then closed the door. Her charm school, sorority debutante manners kicked in. "Would you like some iced tea or coffee?"

"Decaf if you have it," Roderick replied. "I'm cutting back on caffeine. It's not good for you." He followed her and sat on a stool at the kitchen island, elbows resting on the black marble as if he belonged there.

MiMi loaded the coffee brewer with a pod of gourmet decaf. "Right, but taking a toke of weed from some Dominican street dealer is completely healthy and safe."

"Ouch." Roderick hunched his shoulders dramatically. "In my defense, I'd been drinking rum tiki cocktails on and off most of the evening. So had you."

"Yeah, well." MiMi sniffed. "I was on vacation after all."

"My judgment was a bit impaired, at least give me that much. We partied hard though, had a blast." Roderick cocked his handsome head to one side.

MiMi spun around to face him, hands on her hips. "Being in prison with hardened criminals cancelled out the fun part."

Roderick stood and came around the island. "Look, I effed up big time. But don't forget I told the police and the prosecutor you had no part of me buying the weed. It was just a tiny amount anyway."

"My attorney made you tell the truth."

"Our lawyers planned it as a strategy. They figured the prosecutor and judge wouldn't believe me swearing you didn't know right off. So they decided to make it look like I confessed after I was backed into a corner."

MiMi gave him a skeptical frown. "Mr. Columba didn't say anything to me about it."

"He didn't because they wanted you to have a genuine reaction. Nobody watching could doubt you wanted to strangle me." Roderick's full lips tilted into a sideways smile.

"I still might," MiMi retorted. She turned away to break the spell of his hazel-eyed gaze. "Come to the DR, you said. It'll be romantic, you said."

"I'll say I'm sorry as many times as it takes for you to forgive me," Roderick said softly. He sighed and went to sit on the stool again.

MiMi felt a shiver down her back at the sound of his voice, smooth and sincere. His willingness to give her physical space added an extra touch. The man could charm women into agreeing that the sun rose in the west and set in the east. Was she being a fool for him? She avoided looking at him as she put artificial sweetener in her coffee and stirred. Then she sipped from the mug and sat down. MiMi decided to change the subject to blunt the power of his magic touch.

"So, how much hell did your father give you when you got back?" MiMi said.

Roderick let out a groan. "He's docking my pay for the next three months to pay him back for the legal fees and bail. And I'm on probation at the company. He says I won't be made CEO if I make one more 'boneheaded move'."

"Three months to get back thousands? Wow." MiMi mulled that over as she drank another sip of the strong Louisiana brew. Obviously he was being well paid. Of course he was, she thought.

"Don't worry. I had enough left over for this." Roderick pulled a red leather box from his jacket pocket. He put it down on the granite countertop. "Open it."

MiMi blinked at the fancy gold logo embossed on the outside of it. He nodded when she looked at him. Then she lifted the lid. "Oh. My."

"Chocolate with no calories," Roderick said quietly.

"I, it's... my goodness." MiMi lifted the necklace from the midnight blue felt interior. A fourteen carat gold chain ended in an oval pendant set with chocolate and champagne diamonds.

"Let me put it on." Roderick got up, carefully draped it around her neck, and fastened it.

MiMi became mesmerized by sparkle. "It's gorgeous."

"The colors are perfect for your beautiful cinnamon brown complexion. I'll get Sage's present. Wasn't sure you'd let me in," he quipped. Roderick dashed for the kitchen door before MiMi could speak.

Not that she had words anyway. MiMi kept staring at the way the diamonds reflected light into a rainbow of colors. Roderick came back holding a huge chocolate brown teddy bear.

"Roderick, you didn't have to bring us such fabulous gifts," MiMi protested. She caressed the pendant even as she spoke. "Sage adores teddy bears. I was going to start a collection for her. She's going to be thrilled when she wakes from her nap. How did you know?"

"Every little princess deserves the very best. Why don't we take it upstairs? She'll see it when she opens her eyes."

MiMi gazed at him. "Oh Roderick, you're making it hard for me to hate your guts."

Chapter 6

For the next two weeks, Roderick's campaign to court MiMi had gradually chipped away her resistance. Small gifts arrived every few days, like her favorite flower- pink roses. One day he sent a lovely silk scarf. Then came a sterling silver charm bracelet that included Sage's birthstone set in one of the charms. She didn't have to guess how he knew what she liked. He had the blessing of her parents. She didn't protest when he left some of his things at her house, including in her home safe. They were like a family already. MiMi suspected their mothers had coached him on how to impress her.

On a Saturday afternoon, MiMi sat across from Willa in Mama Ruby's kitchen. She wore the necklace and the charm bracelet. Willa's adoptive mother stirred a large pot of her famous gumbo, but they both knew she was all ears to their conversation. Willa's eleven year old daughter, Mikayla, played with Sage in the den at the other end of the open floor plan. Willa's father had excused himself to "let the ladies have some girl talk". He really meant a basketball game was on and he didn't intend to miss it.

Willa leaned over, voice lowered to a whisper. "Let me get this straight. The guy who got you locked up in a Caribbean prison came over to your house. You two have a quickie while the baby was sound asleep. All is forgiven because he bought you an expensive piece of jewelry."

"Well don't make it sound cheap and slutty," MiMi mumbled.

"Uh, there's no way to *not* make it sound cheap and slutty. You literally rolled over for him. I thought you'd given up the gold digger game," Willa replied and sat back.

"He didn't buy me," MiMi snapped. "We talked about the *incident* and he apologized, plus he explained a few things. Some friend you are, thinking the worst of me."

"You accepted his gifts after he threw you to the wolves. The judge was perfectly willing to lock you up for years," Willa said.

"Lower your voice," Mama Ruby whispered sharply to her daughter. "And I agree with MiMi. That was a terrible thing to say, calling her cheap and slutty."

"Her words, not mine," Willa protested. "And why are you defending her behavior?"

"Ametrine always says the Lord wants us to have a forgiving heart. I don't think she should keep holding a grudge against the man if he's truly sorry."

"The voice of reason speaks up." MiMi gave Willa a frown of disapproval. "Roddy didn't 'throw me to the wolves'. He made it quite plain that I didn't know he was going to buy weed. Besides, we'd both been tipping back a few too many rum punches that day."

"In other words, you may have drunkenly agreed

to score," Willa muttered. She ignored her mother's sharp glance.

"Nobody's perfectly innocent. Besides, he's been so sweet since." MiMi turned her wrist to admire the shine of her bracelet. The tinkle of the pretty charms made her smile.

"Hmm. Your parents want y'all back together I guess." Willa sipped from a glass of diet cola.

"Mother and Daddy happen to approve, yes. What?" MiMi looked at Willa.

"Your parents are suddenly concerned about your love life. Sounds suspicious," Willa replied, her tone heavy with what she left unsaid.

"Of course they want the best for me and Sage. Daddy knows that Roddy comes from a good family. In fact, our fathers have worked together on several business deals. Daddy built three warehouses, and one housing development. Mr. Jefferson wrote the commercial insurance policies on the construction jobs."

"Uh-huh." Willa got up to help herself to a still warm hush puppy.

"Hey, save some of those for dinner. We'll be eating in less than thirty minutes," Mama Ruby scolded. She glared at her as she finished mixing the potato salad.

"Umm-hum," Willa said around chewing the buttery treat. "I don't mean to be cynical..."

"Oh no, not you," MiMi shot back and rolled her eyes. "Anyway, I know what you're going to say. Yes, my parents think we could form a pretty powerful business combination. You know how tough it is for minority owned businesses to get their share of contracts. All this backlash against set asides and affirmative action is to blame."

Mama Ruby lifted the large soup ladle "Yes, as if we're anywhere close to making up for over four hundred years of not owning property. You know, Elton's grandfather should have owned..."

"Over ninety acres in West Feliciana Parish, but the white sheriff and the white judge lied about the deed. I know, mama," Willa broke in.

"Don't forget what happened to my great grandfather. By rights our family should own another sixty acres in Pointe Coupee Parish." Mama Ruby went on again to tell the family story of her ancestor. He'd become so successful, that envious local whites threatened to lynch him. "He had to leave everything behind to keep his family safe. Granddaddy said if it had just been him, he would have fought. But he had a wife and children to think about."

"How awful," MiMi said, as if she hadn't heard the story at least three times before. She shook her head. "At least his son was able to go back and get some of the land returned."

"Yes, made history in this state. So I know how your daddy feels about building something for the future." Mama Ruby gave a sharp nod. She put the lid on the large gumbo pot.

Willa's daddy came into the kitchen. "Ruby telling y'all them old dusty family stories again." He grinned at them all.

"Children need to know our history, Elton. How else they gonna appreciate what we came from? I had a point, which is I understand why MiMi's daddy wants her to have a man who's got something."

Papa Elton's thick dark eyebrows pulled together. "Oh yeah, we all know about them Landrys."

"Elton," Mama Ruby said in a harsh whisper and jabbed him with an elbow.

"I mean, uh, how they worked so hard. Ahem, let me see what's going on with the game." He scurried out before anyone could comment.

Willa stared at her mother, a question on her smooth brown face. "Okay, so Mr. and Mrs. Landry are right to set MiMi up with this guy."

MiMi ignored the undercurrent. "Anyway, I don't exactly have a pristine track record myself."

"Yeah, like being my husband's mistress," Willa said dryly.

"*Ex-husband*," MiMi protested. "Well almost, and you were glad to be rid of him. You said so like a million times."

"It's the principle," Willa said with a grunt. "Anyway, whatever. Chase the money if you want."

"I happen to like Roddy," MiMi said with a scowl.

"Okay." Willa smirked when MiMi huffed with irritation.

The doorbell of the kitchen door rang, cutting off their impending spat. Mama Ruby went into the alcove that led to their back patio. She came back smiling with Jazz and Baton Rouge Police homicide Detective Don Addison.

"Look who showed up and brought company with her. We've got plenty so y'all come right on in."

"Hey everybody," Jazz said. "We ate a late lunch, but thanks anyway."

"Afternoon," Don nodded. He looked around as though expecting to find something to confiscate.

"I don't care what you say, Jazzmonetta. Y'all make a nice couple," Mama Ruby said in a stage whisper. She winked at Don. Then she bustled around getting bowls set out for servings of gumbo.

Willa smacked her lips. "Very subtle, mama."

"Elton will probably eat in front of the television despite my nagging. So the children can eat in the den, and the grown folks can sit right here. That way y'all can talk." Mama Ruby made it plain she would stick around to hear every word.

"Sage can't eat the gumbo, too spicy," MiMi said.

"I put aside a little pot for her and Mikayla before I added the pepper. Oh and no hot sausage for them either. I was raising children when you were in diapers, young lady," Mama Ruby said.

MiMi grinned as she gave Willa a sideways glance. "Yes, ma'am. I've been schooled."

"Anthony should be here instead of chasing some girl. This is family time." Mama Ruby gave Willa a pointed stare.

"He's almost eighteen and has his own social life. Besides, he gives y'all plenty of attention. Good Lord, mama. And I thought I'd have trouble cutting the apron strings." Willa rolled her eyes.

"At least we have most of the family here. I include you, Officer," Mama Ruby said. She beamed at him as though ready to call him her new son-in-law.

"Mama, don't start," Willa mumbled.

"I think it's wonderful that Jazz is happy," MiMi added. She laughed when Willa glared at her.

"Y'all need to stop meddling," Willa replied.

"Oh like you haven't?" MiMi retorted.

"Hey, listen," Jazz broke in.

"MiMi is right, Willa. Your nose ought to be sore stickin' it in Jazz's business." Mama Ruby winked at MiMi and turned to the stove again.

"Let's eat. Filling your mouths with food is a great

idea right about now," Willa said.

Willa, MiMi and Mama Ruby launched into a spirited debate over who was the worst busy body. Each one tried to out talk the other to present evidence. Despite the intensity of their discussion, there was more teasing than real conflict. Jazz tried to break in several times. Finally, after about ten seconds, Don spoke up loudly.

"Excuse me, but I didn't come for dinner. We need to talk." His deep voice rumbled like a threatening storm bouncing off the kitchen walls.

Mama Ruby stood, ladle poised over the open pot. She glanced at Willa. "Oh?"

Willa looked at Jazz. "Don't tell me you're tied up in another mess. Jazz, I swear..."

"Not me this time." Jazz looked at MiMi, one perfectly arched eyebrow raised.

"I need to talk to MiMi privately." Don wore a serious expression.

"He tried to get you at home, MiMi. You need to answer your damn texts. Anthony told us y'all were over here." Jazz crossed her arms.

"Me?" MiMi blinked at him and then looked to Jazz for some clue. When she shrugged, MiMi started to really worry.

"The kids might walk in, so maybe we should go somewhere else," Don said.

"I'll take them to the family room with Elton. He won't mind. Tell me what I missed when I get back," Mama Ruby said to Willa. Seconds later she led the two girls down the hall.

"The police department in Santo Domingo, a..." Don took out his phone to consult it.

"Detective Aguilar," MiMi said. Her chest felt as

though a huge rubber band tightened around it.

Don glanced up at her sharply. "No, Martinez."

"Never heard of him." MiMi sat down at the kitchen table.

"Her, Detective Ernesta Martinez. Her superior called our lieutenant, asked us to follow-up on one of their investigations. Seems Jazz left out a few details about her trip out of town," Don said in a dry tone without looking at Jazz.

Jazz leaned up against the tan marble at one end of the kitchen counter. "Like I told you, I visited a friend."

"Yeah, in prison. They have a murder and questions about money coming into the country to a bank called Banco something I can't pronounce." Don looked up from his phone at MiMi.

"Look, I have every right to follow-up on my fiancé's assets and..."

"This Roderick Jefferson guy is your fiancé?" Don broke in.

"Huh?" MiMi stared at him in confusion.

"Their victim has a connection to Jefferson. This guy also was hooked up to a local gang that's suspected of moving money in and through the country."

Jazz spoke up quickly before MiMi could reply. "You didn't mention anything about moving money, Don."

Don frowned at Jazz. "Look, don't play games. Tell me exactly why you ended up in the Dominican Republic with this guy. Seems the Feds are interested as well. My assistant chief wouldn't waste time unless there's more to it than a dead weed man."

Willa crossed her arms. "What Feds?"

"The US Marshals, the FBI and that's just a start. Jefferson has been a busy guy to generate this kind of attention." Don sighed. "You sure have a knack for picking complicated boyfriends."

"Roderick is from a fine old family. My father and brother have done business with his family on more than one occasion." MiMi lifted her chin as she defended him.

"You better hope he didn't involve them in his troubles," Don said. "I won't mention that to my boss just yet."

"Roddy made one small buy and he's a one man drug cartel?" MiMi worked herself into anintense outrage.

Willa's brow wrinkled as she seemed to consider what Don had said. "There must be more to this whole deal, pardon the pun."

"The Feds keep a lot to themselves, to protect their investigation." Don gave a short grunt to show what he thought of that explanation. "But Willa's on target, MiMi. I maybe need to talk to your dad."

MiMi's eyes widen in horror. "No, no, no. Daddy will absolutely have heart failure, not to mention blame me."

"You? He should be pissed at Roderick Jefferson," Willa said.

"Or himself for getting into business with him," Jazz added.

"Reputation is everything to Daddy. He'll say I got Roddy into trouble because of my unsavory associations." MiMi rubbed her forehead.

Jazz nudged Willa. "She means us, sis. Guess we can stop waiting for an invitation to Sunday dinner at the Landry house."

"The Black elite never blame their own, Don. They're so special." Willa gave a scornful laugh.

"Just stop it," MiMi snapped. "You're stereotyping them because they grew up different than you."

"I married into that world. Jack Crown, remember? I know what I'm talking about," Willa replied.

"His parents might have been difficult when it came to you," MiMi said.

"Try condescending on a good day, flat out insulting on a bad one," Willa lobbed back.

"Excuse me, let's get back to why Don came over here," Jazz said loudly.

Mama Ruby scurried in. "Okay, fill me in."

"There was a murder in the Dominican Republic, and the police over there think Roderick and MiMi are involved. Something about money laundering, too." Jazz rattled out the succinct summary with the wave of a hand.

"Money laundering, again?" Mama Ruby gaped at MiMi. "Child, no."

"I never..." MiMi sucked in air and then let it out noisily. "Look, all I did was go on vacation with my boyfriend and..."

"I thought he was your fiancé. That's what you said at first," Don broke in. His dark eyes focused on MiMi like the scope of a high powered rifle.

"Slip of the tongue. I'm hoping he puts a ring on it," MiMi said with a laugh.

"She's always trolling for a BMWM; you know, a Black Man With Money," Jazz added. She shared a high five with MiMi.

"You said something about his assets."

"Roderick said something about business opportunities in the DR or with some people there. I wasn't paying attention to be honest. Oh, he did visit a commercial plaza for sale. It included a few shops, and I have retail expertise."

"You sure that's the only business he was up to over there?" Don made notes on a small pad.

"I was with him just about every minute we were there, Don." MiMi matched his crossed arms pose.

"Except when he slipped off to buy drugs," Don said.

"You know what? I think the Feds are doing some racial profiling. White kids from those Ivy League schools go on spring break, tear up everything and do drugs. The FBI doesn't show up accusing them of drug smuggling and money laundering. I can't believe you bought into their bull." MiMi jabbed a finger in the air between them.

"Don is doing his job," Jazz put in. "But she does have a point about the profiling."

Don raised a dark eyebrow. "Pick a team and stay on it, Jazz."

"I'm not talking about *you*," Jazz said promptly. "On the other hand, look at the facts. A lot of people get locked up for stuff they didn't do."

"We follow the evidence. Speaking of profiling, the all 'cops are rotten apples' theme is getting very old." Don's eyes narrowed as he stared at Jazz.

"I didn't say..."

"No, she didn't, now let's not start attacking each other. Don is right. There's more going on than Roderick bought a little weed. Too many people are interested," Willa added fast when MiMi opened her mouth.

"Hmmm. He did lie, girl. You gotta wonder what else he hasn't told you." Jazz frowned and rubbed her chin as if in deep thought.

"I've known the Jeffersons since I was twelve. They're a fine family." MiMi sniffed.

"You sounded a lot like your mother just then," Willa murmured. When MiMi scowled at her, she held up both palms.

"I would say the same thing if someone accused you or Mama Ruby of being an international criminal," MiMi replied, putting ice in her tone.

"What about me?" Jazz's full lips lifted at one corner.

"No comment." MiMi ducked when Jazz took a playful swing at her.

"All I'm saying is..." Don raised his voice to get their attention back to the subject. "You might not want to book a wedding planner with this guy. He's got baggage."

"There's a little concept called innocent until *proven* guilty. As an officer of the law I'm sure you've heard of it." MiMi planted both fists on her hips.

"Everybody is guilty of something. We slap the cuffs on and make 'em take the walk of shame to booking." Don gave a cynical chuckle.

"Oh, now that's such an enlightened view of people." MiMi shook her head slowly.

"He's kidding," Jazz said. But she looked unsure as she glanced at Don.

"Okay, okay. Mr. Roderick Jefferson deserves his day in court. I suggest you have a chat with him about the FBI. Talk to your daddy while you're at it." Don looked around at them all. "Anything else you want to tell me?"

"No," MiMi, Jazz and Willa said at the same time.

Don gave them a pointed stare. "Uh-huh. Y'all do know I'm going to find out sooner and not later, right?"

"We don't know what you're talking about." MiMi hoped her tone had the right mixture of honesty and injured pride.

Don's cell phone vibrated. He glanced at the screen for a few seconds before he disappeared into the laundry room to make a call.

"Y'all need to practice not sounding guilty as sin." Mama Ruby shook her head as she went to the stove to check on the simmering gumbo.

"What do you really know about this dude, MiMi," Jazz hissed. She glanced in the direction Don had gone.

"I think the FBI is really trying to track down Jack's money and using what happened with Roderick as a cover," MiMi whispered. "They might have had us all under surveillance for the last year or longer."

"Oh come on," Willa blurted out.

"Not 'us', you two. I wasn't one of Jack's many women," Jazz put in.

"Two words, Felipe Perez," MiMi tossed back at her.

"Look, don't start with the wild theories. Sometimes it is what it is. I say we start by doing some research on Roderick and his family's business deals," Willa said softly.

"I'm telling you there is nothing to find. But if you want to waste resources when you should be running your own company, go ahead." MiMi huffed in frustration.

"Maybe you don't want to know about your father's business," Willa said carefully. She glanced at Mama Ruby.

"What's that supposed to mean?" MiMi was about to go on but Don returned.

"I have to go. I'll talk to y'all later. Stay out of trouble." Don kissed Jazz on her forehead.

"Ha! These three stay out of trouble?" Mama Ruby

laughed hard as she stirred.

"What's taking so long with the food?" Papa Elton boomed as he entered the kitchen. He grinned at Don. "Hey, Detective Addison."

Don shook hands with him. "Afternoon, Mr. Wilson. Sorry I can't stay. I'm on the clock."

"Keepin' the streets of Baton Rouge safe. Good man." Papa Elton nodded. Then his smile faded as he looked at Willa. "Wait a minute. I hope you're not here because these three have gotten into something else."

"I'll tell you later," Mama Ruby said quietly. She glanced at MiMi and then back to her husband.

"Bye everybody." Don gave a general wave and walked out.

Jazz followed him and came back a few seconds later. "Willa, get to digging on Roderick."

"MiMi's new rich boyfriend?" Papa Elton blinked at his wife, who nodded slowly. "I don't even want to know." He accepted a tray with his food and trudged back to the normalcy of television sports.

"Don is wrong. The FBI is wrong, and what y'all are thinking is *wrong*." MiMi shook a finger at everyone and the world.

"Fine. Then you don't care if I do some research. We'll face up to the results, no matter where the facts take us. Agreed?" Willa gazed at MiMi.

"Sure." Jazz looked at MiMi.

MiMi looked back at them. Anxiety took up residence in her chest. "Sure."

Chapter 7

The next week went quickly. Between taking care of Sage and work, MiMi had little time to worry about investigations. As the days passed, MiMi relaxed back into her routine. Willa had probably been right about one thing, she'd let her imagination go crazy. Still MiMi rehearsed bringing up the subject of his business deals to her father. She even wrote out a script of exactly how she'd lead into her questions. Staring into the mirror, MiMi practiced making her facial expression remain normal. Drexel James Landry, Jr. could sniff out a lie or half-truth like a psychic.

Yet every time she picked up the phone to call, MiMi thought of at least a half dozen other things to do. She could have stopped by her parents' home. Instead, her hands resisted turning the steering wheel in the direction of Oak Grove Estates, the neighborhood where they lived. So she gave up, convinced the timing was obviously not right.

The following Saturday after Don questioned her at Mama Ruby's house, MiMi got ready for a date with Roderick. Adrienne had jumped at the chance to babysit Sage. MiMi dropped the energetic toddler off at lunchtime. Her sister had assured her that getting Sage that early was no problem at all. With her day free, MiMi had time to get a manicure, pedicure and buy a new blouse to go over her skinny jeans. By six o'clock she was home and ready. They were going to the new cinema with six screens called Dinner and A Movie. Roderick reserved one of their tables where they could order a meal and watch a movie.

MiMi winked at her reflection in the full length mirror in her master bedroom. "Girl, you still got it. I'll have a one carat engagement ring by Christmas. No, two carats, because he owes me and can afford it."

When the doorbell rang she glanced in surprise at the digital clock on her nightstand. She winked again before going down the stairs humming an old school hip-hop tune from the nineties. On her way to the front door, the phone rang. She grabbed the cordless phone from a table in the foyer.

"Hello Mother. Yes, I'm going out with Roderick. I don't exactly need you to monitor my love life." MiMi frowned at the handset. Still talking, she pulled open the front door without looking outside. "I have to go because he's here."

A man the color of dark chocolate stared at her. He looked away to scan the surroundings. He was tall, lean and bald. A blonde woman only slightly shorter stood beside him. Both were dressed in what almost looked like duplicate charcoal gray suits.

"Ms. Landry? We're with the FBI and we'd like to talk to you," the woman said without smiling. "I'm Agent Morrison and this is Agent Young."

"What do you want with me? Not you, Mother. No, you can't talk to Roderick because... I'll call tomorrow or sometime." MiMi hit the "end" button cutting off her mother's insistent voice. She felt lightheaded as the two agents held up identification tags. She gazed at them through the clear glass storm door.

"May we come in?" Agent Morrison's expression made it into a command.

MiMi flinched when Agent Young turned his dark gaze back to her. She unlocked the door and stood back. "Yes, of course."

Both agents seemed to slide in silently as though they were used to moving without a sound. Agent Young turned his laser focus on MiMi's foyer. Agent Morrison gave MiMi a slight nod which indicated they expected to be invited farther inside.

"Hmm, let's go into the living room, and you can tell me what this is about." MiMi closed the door and started to put down the phone, but decided to keep it. She might need to call a lawyer. "It's not every day the FBI shows up on my doorstep. In fact, I'm not used to having any kind of law enforcement visit me. I can't imagine why you'd be here."

The two agents followed her without speaking. Once in the living room, they stood studying her with twin impassive expressions as she talked nervously. They seemed patient, as though used to their presence unnerving people to the point of useless rambling. Finally when MiMi willed herself to shut up, Agent Morrison nodded again and took out a small note pad.

"You were involved in a romantic relationship with Jackson Phillip Crown, is that accurate?" Agent Morrison consulted her notes as if to make sure she had the name correct.

MiMi took time to regain composure as she looked back at the female agent. She faltered a bit when Agent

Young's barely there left eyebrow shot up. She briefly wondered if he'd shaved those off at the same time he shaved his head. The man made her think of all the scary movies she'd seen about cold, ruthless government agents. Then she reminded herself they were in her home, and she still had constitutional rights.

"We were engaged, and he was practically divorced from his wife. I'm sure you have all the facts," MiMi replied crisply.

"Yes," Agent Morrison said with a chilly smile of judgment. "We're conducting a joint investigation with the U.S. Marshals and the Secret Service into possible money laundering."

"Secret Service," MiMi replied. Her legs felt numb as she sank onto a nearby chair. The agents sat down on the matching sofa at the same time.

"Yes, not uncommon that we pool investigative resources in cases such as this," Agent Morrison explained blandly.

"Cases like this?" MiMi blinked at them.

"You're familiar with Felipe Perez, a business associate of Mr. Crown's before he died." Agent Young spoke for the first time in a bass voice.

MiMi flinched again. He didn't ask a question because he already knew the answer. Still she felt growing anger at his attempt to intimidate her. She bristled at the good agent, scary agent routine.

"Look, you already must know that I have never been 'familiar' with Felipe Perez. Of course I know who he is. The facts about him and his gang came out during the investigation into Jack's murder. The police also proved that Jack had no direct connection to that gang."

"We've read the reports. There are indications that Mr. Crown and his brother knew who and what Felipe

Perez was," Agent Young replied, his tone heavy with indictment.

"By indications I take it you mean there is no hard evidence, and Jack isn't here to defend himself. Correct?" MiMi stared him down.

"His brother pretty much confirmed it though," Agent Young replied.

"Ryan Crown got himself into a lot of things Jack didn't approve of, Agent Young. Which brings me back to my original question; why are you at my home?"

"You're correct about one thing, Ms. Landry. We have no definitive evidence that Jackson Crown was involved in drug or gun smuggling," Agent Morrison said quietly.

MiMi stood. "Thank you for finally admitting what I already knew. He has three surviving children, as I'm sure you have in your files. Their father's memory shouldn't be tarnished, especially when you have no proof. Now I'm expecting company."

Agent Morrison tucked her note pad away and glanced at her partner as she stood. "Right."

"Mr. Roderick Jefferson," Agent Young said. He rose and towered over MiMi.

"Okay, you've established that you can dig up facts on the private lives of American citizens," MiMi replied.

"We're looking into his business as well. You seem to have a taste for men who like to move money out of the country, Ms. Landry." Agent Young spoke in a bland tone that managed to communicate sarcasm perfectly.

MiMi's eyes narrowed to slits. "Now you just wait a minute..."

"Let's stick to why we're here, the late Mr. Crown," Agent Morrison broke in with a brief sideways glance at her partner.

"Skip to the part about how any of this has to do with me please," MiMi shot back, still eyeing Agent Young. Her temper flared hotter when he affected a half smile at her.

"Our agency is trying to determine if Jackson Crown and Roderick Jefferson or his father were ever in business." Agent Morrison stopped as though waiting for a reaction.

MiMi crossed her arms and transferred her gaze to Morrison. "What you mean is you haven't found any connection and I can't give you one. In fact, I'm sure Roderick and Jack never formally met."

Agent Morrison nodded with a sympathetic expression. "Yes, you're right. As far as we can tell they didn't know each other."

"Then have a good evening. I support your efforts to catch *real* criminals." MiMi started for the door but Agent Morrison's voice stopped her.

"Then there's the matter of your assets."

MiMi faced the two agents, neither of whom had moved. "What do you mean?"

"As I said, Mr. Ryan Crown admitted knowing Felipe Perez was a drug dealer and selling stolen guns. The money earned was part of an illegal enterprise, as such they are subject to seizure."

"With all the resources at your fingertips I'm sure y'all will find it in no time. Now if you'll excuse me," MiMi replied.

"Not just money, but anything bought with that money, Ms. Landry. Like this house," Agent Morrison added.

"You can't be serious," MiMi hissed. "Jack ran a successful business for over eight years. I'd like to see you prove exactly where the money came from to buy my home."

"Our forensic accounting section is very good, Ms. Landry," Agent Young replied promptly. He glanced at his partner as if signaling her turn to be sympathetic.

Agent Morrison responded on cue. "I'm really sorry to drop this kind of news on your Ms. Landry. You've had a rough time in the last few weeks. We don't think you knew about the laundered money."

"At least not at the time Jack Crown got it. But you did visit a bank in the Dominican Republic." Agent Young stared at her intently.

"I don't have any idea what you're talking about. If you have any other questions, I'll have you get in touch with my lawyer." MiMi tried not to let her voice shake as much as her knees did at that moment. The calm manner of the two FBI agents unnerved her as much as the bomb they'd dropped.

"So you already hired a lawyer, huh?" Agent Young said.

"Unless you plan to put my furniture out tonight, please leave," MiMi snapped. Her boldness hid the fear that they would in fact start setting her belongings on the curb.

"The Marshals Service is working on it," Agent Young replied.

"What Agent Young means..." Agent Morrison glanced at her partner. After a silent message passed between them, the tall man turned to leave.

"I'll check in," he said over his shoulder. Seconds later the front door opened and bumped shut.

Agent Morrison let out a short breath. "I realize what a shock this must be, Ms. Landry."

"Don't bother with the 'I'm on your side' speech. I may have been born at night, but it wasn't last night.

Interview over," MiMi said.

"Things aren't looking good for you. First you get busted for drugs in a foreign country. Your new boyfriend has questionable business practices, and your ex-boyfriend--"

"Jack was my fiancé, Agent Morrison. Do I have to write it down on an index card so you'll remember?" MiMi didn't have to pretend. She was officially pissed off. "The judge in the Dominican Republic ruled that I didn't buy or sell drugs, but you already know that. You also have no proof Roderick, Jack or I committed a crime. So this little visit to rattle me and get a guilty confession wasted your time, and mine."

"I'm trying to help you." Agent Morrison wore a frown of regret.

"Good, find the truth and clear my name. Goodbye." MiMi squinted at her.

"We'll be in touch." Agent Morrison didn't wait to observe the effect of her words. She spun around to walk away.

MiMi beat her to the door and opened it. "Save our tax dollars and stop chasing the *wrong people.*"

She shut the door firmly once the woman was through it. MiMi clicked the locks hard. Then she backed away from the door, a hand over her mouth to keep from screaming. When the doorbell rang again she jumped. The agents had left only long enough to come back and take everything she owned. Looking around in desperation, MiMi tried to think of who she could call. Her parents would be mortified to take her in under such circumstances. The phone rang. Roderick's name displayed.

"Sorry I'm late, but come down and open the door. We can still make the seven fifteen showing if we hustle," Roderick said.

MiMi marched to the front door, phone still in her hand and pulled open the front door. She glared at him. "I suppose the delay was because you had a chat with my visitors. How many times do you plan to get me thrown in prison?"

"What the hell are you talking about?" Roderick realized he was talking into his cell phone. He frowned and ended the call.

MiMi grabbed him by the arm and pulled him inside. "Come in, *baby*, and explain a few minor details. The damn movie can wait."

****

Predictably, Monday came too soon. After a weekend of jumping at every sound in the house, the last place she wanted to be was at work. Tyler gazed at MiMi with undisguised disdain.

"You have to take off early. Again. After being gone for weeks."

"I'm leaving an hour early for an appointment," MiMi replied shortly. She kept tapping the keys of her laptop as she talked. "You can get me on my cell phone if anything urgent comes up. But I'm on top of my assignments."

"Kerry wants the team to meet on the summer in-store and window displays. Six of our stores have a deadline set by the mall managers."

"Right, they want stores to coordinate themes to give shoppers a consistent experience, I know. I don't leave for another two hours. I'm sending them graphics. Fred and his team did design suggestions. Harold is ready to help them order display supplies for the May

Day and Cinco De Mayo sales. Mr. Jenkins and Darcas gave the green light to the ideas we sent. Oh, and we're working the Fourth of July display drafts."

"Kerry has all these I assume?" Tyler tapped the stylus of his tablet computer against one cheek. "She doesn't like being blindsided."

MiMi stopped typing. She swiveled her chair and affected as much sincerity as possible in her expression. "I know how busy she's been with renovations of the store in Jacksonville, Florida. Plus she's got so many other priorities. These are details I took care of to relieve her."

"So the answer is no. Once again you went behind her back to the bosses," Tyler drawled. He made notes on the tablet, the stylus moving fast across the smooth surface.

"Unclench your sphincter muscles, Ty-Ty. Doing my job is not going behind Kerry's back. Mr. Jenkins always says we should pull in the same direction." MiMi smiled at him.

"Kerry is your boss, MiMi. You might want to stay on her good side," Tyler warned.

MiMi almost blurted out that the woman had no good side but swallowed the comeback. Even so, her voice held an edge. "I'm ahead of the curve on the whole display thing. My projects are on schedule. Those two facts should be doing wonders for her good side. Instead she's..."

Tyler gazed at her anticipation. "She's what?"

"She's worried for no good reason," MiMi replied mildly. Whew, that was close. She almost gave the little snitch ammunition to use against her.

"Yeah, I'll just bet that's what you meant to say," Tyler mumbled.

"What else?" MiMi blinked at him, a wide-eyed look of innocence on her face. Then she swiveled back to face her desk again. She hit a send button. "There, your concerns have just been addressed. I sent Kerry a link to the cloud with all the wonderful work the team has done. We've put in our best effort, all due to her leadership."

"Oh please." Tyler looked up at the ceiling and gave a snort.

"You're not saying her leadership is... lacking I hope." MiMi raised an eyebrow at him.

Tyler gasped. "You know that's not what I meant."

"Glad to hear it. By the way, did I mention Darcas asked for an update on the displays? I have her email from last week. So in the unlikely event *someone* says I went behind Kerry's back, well I have to respond to head of merchandising. Right?"

"Clever. Be careful you don't hurt yourself being smug," Tyler said crisply. He strode off.

MiMi's co-worker, Elle, came into her office seconds later. The tall strawberry blonde was an ex-model like Kerry. As usual, she was dressed in what fashion stylists called "casual elegance". Her spice orange tunic set off her coloring perfectly. Brown leggings tucked into distressed brown leather riding boots finished off the outfit. Many of MiMi's colleagues were former models, including the men. MiMi liked to joke that they all made her feel like a chubby munchkin. Elle looked over her shoulder in the direction Tyler had gone down the hall.

"Girl, what did you do to put that sour look on Tyler's face? I asked him a question and he got snippy." Elle's accent identified her as a "Yat" from New Orleans. She plopped her five foot eight inch frame in a chair in front of MiMi's desk.

"I just spoiled his plan to give Kerry dirt to use against me. Forget him. Thanks for helping me out. I'm sorry you had to add some of my work to your already crowded plate."

"Anything that that irritates Tyler gives me pleasure, baby," Elle quipped. Her expression turned serious. "Is there something you need to tell me? You've been looking mighty stressed today."

"I'm a single mother. Stress is my middle name," MiMi replied and gave a dramatic sigh.

"Uh-huh. Kerry has been asking around to see if you talked to anyone. I'll bet she has Tyler snooping to find out. What happens in Vegas don't always stay in Vegas, ya know?" Elle's expertly shaped eyebrows went up to the bangs of her pretty bob haircut.

"Yeah, except I wasn't in Vegas," MiMi quipped. Still, fear spiked in her chest.

"Vegas, Dominica, you know what I'm talkin' here," Elle replied.

"Dominican Republic, Elle. Dominica is a very different Caribbean Island several hundred miles away." MiMi flipped images saved on the Fashion Sense cloud used for staff collaboration.

Elle hitched her chair closer to the desk and lowered her voice. "Yeah, yeah, so I got a C in geography. Look, you don't have to tell me, okay? I got your back. Hell, you covered my ass more than a few times. I've got a plan."

"It's not that I don't trust you..." MiMi brushed a hand through her hair.

"I understand." Elle shrugged.

MiMi sighed. Then she got up and closed her office door. "Roderick bought weed and we both ended up in jail. Our parents got us lawyers, paid our fines and we got the hell outta there."

Elle stared at her, mouth open for a few seconds. "Wow."

"Yeah." MiMi slumped into her chair again. "Anyway, I don't think Kerry will find out. We didn't make the news down there."

"Humph, don't put anything past that devious hussy. Okay, so about my plan. We'll spread disinformation." Elle nodded to herself.

"What?"

"So Cal in IT and Nadia in HR are the worst gossips. I'll tell them some story about how you and the rich boyfriend had a falling out, he left you stranded and you were too humiliated to tell the truth."

MiMi laughed. "C'mon Elle."

"Yes, you were sick, but it was from the heartbreak which led to a deep depression. You didn't want to be the object of pity, so you kept the truth from everyone. You've been in therapy. But," Elle cut off another protest from MiMi. "There's a happy ending. You two crazy kids finally worked it out."

MiMi wiped her eyes with a tissue from the box on her desk. "No one is going to believe that mess."

"I'll tell them you broke down and told me what happened. The partial truth always makes a lie sound credible." Elle nodded.

"So you have a lot of experience telling lies. I hope you've used your powers for good." MiMi shook a forefinger at her.

Elle wore a smirk. "Mostly. Anyway, Kerry makes it obvious you're on her list."

"Yeah, but Darcas likes me. A lot. So does Mr. Jenkins, they kinda think I'm precious." MiMi patted her hair and sniffed.

"Bull crap," Elle said with a snort. "Their sales have gone up. You do a damn good job figuring out trends and what fashions customers want each season. But you are cute I have to admit."

MiMi started to smile back at her. Then remembered the grim faced agents on her doorstep. If she could get her cute power to work on the FBI, life would be awesome. "Yeah, but they'll drop kick my butt if those numbers start going in the wrong direction. So for the next few weeks, I'll come in early when possible, even work at home."

"You can't keep going at this pace, not without sacrificing time with your baby. Anyway, if the sales are good, but you bring bad publicity to the Fashion Sense brand..." Elle shrugged.

"Yeah, Kerry can't find out about... what happened." MiMi shivered. Not to mention an employee being investigated by the FBI and tied to a murder.

Elle leaned forward. "My story will keep them busy, re-direct her energy. She can't go after an emotionally fragile single mother. Not only will it make her look bad, but I'll remind her that it's illegal. Remember the Americans with Disabilities act?"

MiMi gazed at her friend. "I have a new appreciation for your devious mind, girl."

Chapter 8

That night MiMi put Sage to bed at eight o'clock. She'd convinced Roderick that they were going to have a romantic interlude. She set the scene with mood lighting and a silky wrap blouse over matching lounge pants. Roderick eagerly agreed to bring dinner. He showed up, bags in hand with a big smile.

"Am I on time, baby?" He came in and gave MiMi a peck on the forehead before heading to the kitchen. A delicious smell of garlic and onions trailed after him.

MiMi closed and locked the back door. "Right on time. Put the food on the counter. I'm going to heat it up."

"Yeah, by now it's room temperature. Baton Rouge traffic is a pain that never goes away." Roderick set the bags down. He faced her. "What's next, oh gorgeous one?"

"Let's have a little talk." MiMi forced a smile. She pointed to the long counter with three wooden stools. "Take a seat."

"Whoa, you sound too serious. This was going to be another special night like the last two we've had." Roderick walked to MiMi and put both arms around her waist. He tried to kiss her, but she turned her face away.

"Sit." MiMi pushed back from him.

Roderick sat down and leaned one elbow on the granite surface of the counter. Dressed in a long sleeved brown shirt and Army green slacks, he looked relaxed. "Okay then. But I thought we'd hashed out that whole incident in the DR."

"You left out a few details. Anything you need to tell me?" MiMi wrestled with the urge to blow up at him.

Roderick affected a thoughtful expression. After ten or fifteen seconds he shook his head. "Honestly, babe, I told you everything. I thought we had built up some trust. Come on now. Don't over think it and come up with more questions."

"Actually, I'm not talking about what happened on our trip. The FBI paid me a visit about Jack's death and his business deals." MiMi watched him. His short exhale signaled relief.

"Damn, Jack's issues won't die. Sorry, bad choice of words. Come here, girl. Let me make you forget, at least for a little while."

"You might need some comfort yourself. They mentioned you, too." MiMi crossed her arms.

He wore a puzzled frown. "Me? I never even met the guy, much less did business with him."

"The FBI is looking into your family's company. So I started wondering just what exactly haven't you told me."

"I don't understand. The FBI?" Roderick's smooth charmer facade slipped. He blinked rapidly as he pulled a hand over his face.

"So they haven't questioned you yet?" MiMi squinted at him.

"Wh-what exactly did they say? I mean their exact words." Roderick got up and started to pace. "Damn, I told dad and Uncle Harold not to..."

"So you know what they're talking about," MiMi said mildly.

"Look, it's not that bad. We helped with some exports to the Caribbean. One of the guys has a criminal record, but he's clean now; a totally legitimate businessman."

"Let me guess. This 'totally legit' businessman has his office in the Dominican Republic, specifically in Santo Domingo. I suppose you being so eager to go there was a crazy coincidence." MiMi walked up to Roderick. Luckily he jumped off the stool and started to pace, because MiMi was about to let go and slap him.

"The place is beautiful and... look at where we stayed. I mean it's a fabulous place to party." Roderick spoke to her as he paced. Yet clearly his mind wasn't on rum punches on the beach.

"So the fact that we just happened to end up arrested had nothing to do with your 'business.' The FBI mentioning your name is another crazy coincidence. Yeah, I totally get it." MiMi snorted to punctuate her lack of belief.

Roderick raked long fingers through his thick tight curls. Then he pulled his cell phone from the clip on the waistband of his pants. "I'm going to call dad so he can get our lawyer on the phone."

MiMi darted to him, deftly snatched the phone away and stepped out of his reach. "Hold it slick. We're going to talk first."

"But you don't understand..."

"You got me into even more trouble, so yeah I kinda understand for damn sure. Sit your ass down and explain," MiMi fired back.

"Don't pull the outraged act. You were tracking down funny money. Yeah, my lawyer told me. Sounds like you had an agenda. Hell, you suggested the DR." Roderick snapped his fingers and then pointed at her accusingly. "Yeah, you did."

She hissed at him. "Which doesn't change the fact that--"

"Our company has goals to go global. The FBI is being overzealous because one of our partners has a past." Roderick pulled a hand down his whole face as if trying to wake from a bad dream.

"Agent Morrison said they're investigating your business deals. She didn't mention anything about a business associate with a criminal record."

"Agent Morrison. What's her first name?" Roderick reached for his phone. "C'mon now, quit playing around. This is serious."

"You think I'm playing? They want to take my house. I have a child to raise, Roderick." MiMi glared at him. She swung back as though ready to throw the phone against the wall.

"No, no, wait. Calm down, baby. Let's just take this slow, talk things out. They want us at each other's throats. You know, divide and conquer." Roderick's words tumbled over each other as he reached toward her.

"Well it worked. Give me the truth and then get out of my house," MiMi replied.

Roderick's long-legged stride took him across the floor in a few steps. He grabbed the cordless phone before MiMi realized it. Long fingers tapped the keypad. "Dad, it's me. Yeah, yeah, but listen."

MiMi considered rushing him to pull the phone

away, but knew she couldn't win such a tussle. Instead she slapped his expensive phone down on the counter. She had to settle for shooting daggers at him. Roderick started out speaking normally. After a few moments, his voice dropped too low for her to hear. He glanced over at her when she took a few steps toward him.

Roderick met her halfway, the phone extended. "Here, Dad wants to talk to you."

MiMi blinked at the phone for a few seconds before she took it. She stared at Roderick as she put it to her ear. "Good evening, Mr. Jefferson."

Gentry Jefferson's commanding voice came through the phone. For the next five minutes he made the case that MiMi was overreacting. In fact, his explanation sounded plausible. At the end he pointed out that Jack Crown had unwittingly gotten involved with the wrong business partners.

"I'm sure a competitor is behind this FBI nonsense. Turner Industries is angry we've outbid and out classed them three times. Don't jump to conclusions without talking to your father," Mr. Jefferson's sonorous voice boomed through the handset like a lawyer ending his closing argument.

"Yes, sir. Thank you," was all she could think to say. She handed the phone to Roderick and sat down.

"Of course MiMi understands. Yes, when I leave here. Bye." Roderick placed the phone down on its base. He strolled over and sat on the stool next to MiMi. "I'll take some of the crawfish fettuccini now."

"You want to eat? You must be out of your mind."

"Dad and our lawyers will be on it before noon tomorrow. So yeah, my appetite is still good." Roderick shrugged, the picture of a privileged young man used to his father wielding power.

"You have a lot of confidence considering the *FBI* is dogging your footsteps," MiMi retorted.

Roderick laughed. "You'd be surprised at what Black business people have to face. We're under scrutiny more than our white counterparts. Not to say some don't break the law, or make missteps. We're not one of those companies though."

MiMi raised an eyebrow at him. "But you're calling in a team of lawyers."

"Which is a smart business move." Roderick pulled her to him. "What's more important is that you believe me. I know how it must look."

"No kidding." MiMi resisted his hug.

"First the DR, and now the FBI. I told Dad about the FBI saying they'll take your house, too. He says proving the money was earned from a criminal enterprise will be tough. The FBI will try to scare you into talking. Dad says they probably have little or nothing in the way of evidence."

"You didn't tell me your business was being investigated, Roddy." MiMi pointed a finger at the end of his nose.

"You didn't tell me about Jack's money stashed in the DR." Roderick gazed at her steadily. "Did I hold it against you?"

"Well... I don't know for sure it's there." MiMi searched for a hole in his logic and found none. She relaxed a bit in his arms.

Roderick continued to embrace her. He brushed his face against hers. "I'll be sure you get the best lawyer around."

"Wonderful, exactly what I need from a boyfriend. Flowers and the name of a good lawyer." MiMi frowned at him.

"I did tell you I'd take care of you in every way," Roderick whispered.

MiMi looked into his eyes. She couldn't deny that her past was far from squeaky clean. The fact that she had kind of used Roderick as an excuse to look for Jack's money... well, she didn't exactly have the moral high ground. Besides, he looked and smelled really good. Dinner waited for a couple of hours.

****

The next two days at work went smoothly enough. Tyler was too busy to bother MiMi, and she was too focused on doing her job to worry about him. She also didn't have time to dwell on Elle's scheme. And Elle played it cool. She stayed away from MiMi's office. Yet she gave MiMi a conspiratorial wink when they passed each other in a hallway. MiMi was bone tired by the time she quit at around six that evening. She picked up Sage from her sister's house and headed to Willa's house. They arranged it so that Sage could spend time with her big brother and sister. MiMi didn't have to cook at least one night a week, a huge bonus. When Willa wasn't being a tough business woman, she enjoyed playing homemaker. More and more Jazz showed up, too. Family nights became a tradition during the week as well as on Sundays.

Willa stood at the stove stirring a pot of her famous pasta sauce. She brought the large spoon to her mouth, tasted and frowned slightly. She took a bottle from the spice rack nearby and sprinkled something. "That ought to do it. Bring me the meatballs."

MiMi groaned as she pulled herself from the chair at the large kitchen table. "I knew you'd put me to work."

"Handing me the pan doesn't count as work," Willa retorted as she accepted it from MiMi. She put the large spoon in the sink and carefully put the meatballs in the sauce. "Don't panic. I think I can handle the pasta on my own."

"You don't know the days I'm having." MiMi was about to go on when Anthony strolled in.

"Hey, Aunt MiMi." The six foot tall teen kissed her on the cheek.

"Hello, big guy. How's school?" MiMi laughed. "I sound like the typical adult these days. Sorry about that."

"Yeah you do," he said with a grin. Then he grimaced. "School is a beast. At least the courses I don't like."

"Required core courses will come in handy more than you know," Willa lectured without turning from her cooking motions.

"Yes, ma'am."Anthony looked at the ceiling and mouthed the words as she spoke.

"As a future business owner good English and writing skills will be essential, and stop imitating me." Willa put the sauce on simmer, still without facing him.

"You're the best, ma." Anthony playfully tried to hug Willa.

She just as playfully brushed him off. "Go on, I'm trying to finish dinner. Get outta here before I forget you're taller than me and you get a spanking."

"You can't catch me," Anthony wisecracked. He did a little dance before dashing off.

"Don't be so sure," Willa yelled after him and laughed. Girlish squeals floated from the direction of the bedrooms. "Go check on those young'uns. I must have been crazy letting Mikayla's little friends come over on a school night."

MiMi went down the long hallway to the bedrooms. She peeked through the door to Mikayla's room. Sage sat in the playpen Willa had bought just for her visits. She happily divided her attention between playing with her toys and watching the big girls. MiMi returned to the kitchen moments later.

"All is well. They're just having fun." MiMi sank down onto the comfy chair again.

"Yeah well, they're supposed to be studying. They have to present their project tomorrow," Willa replied.

"Ten and eleven year olds have study groups? Are they teaching them, nuclear physics or something? I didn't do study groups until my junior year in high school."

Willa took out a tray of French bread slices covered in garlic butter. "I don't complain. The public schools are making big strides. And yeah, they're pretty close to studying nuclear physics."

MiMi's stomach rumbled at the delicious smells filling the air. When the kitchen doorbell chimed she stood. "Hurry up. I'm hungrier than I thought."

"I don't need the pressure," Willa quipped.

Jazz came in. She was dressed in a red tunic and black leggings. Long thick braids hung from beneath a knit Rasta hat. "Hey, when's the food ready?"

Willa faced them with one hand on her right hip. "You know, y'all are spoiled. One day you or you will be the hostess."

"Anytime you say," MiMi replied. "You can cook at my house just as well as here."

"Ha, ha." Willa went back to tossing the salad.

Soon everyone was around the table talking about

everything, yet nothing too important. Sage sat on a booster seat between her siblings. Mikayla and Sage shared a father, the late Jack Crown. Anthony had been Jack's stepson. Still Anthony treated Sage like his baby sister. A strange crew indeed. Jack would be amazed that his ex-wife and mistress had become friends. In an odd way, his murder three years before had brought them all together.

An hour and half later, the dishwasher hummed and the kids had gone back to their rooms. The adults sat around for serious talk not suitable for little ears. Jazz savored sour cream pound cake from Mama Ruby's oven. She licked the lemon glaze from a slice and sighed. Willa sipped a cup of coffee.

"I love family night." MiMi basked in the glow of acceptance. The sound of kids' voices added to her feeling of security.

"Your sister has been pretty supportive. She's keeping Sage a lot," Willa said.

"Yeah, I guess," MiMi said. Adrienne's behavior didn't inspire even a little spark. She couldn't put her finger on why though.

"This is all sweet and stuff, but let's get to the real reason for this pow-wow. What did the lawyer say?" As usual Jazz shied away from touchy-feely moments of sentimentality.

"Edselle Underwood is one of the best in Brad's practice, and that's saying something," Willa said to reassure MiMi. Brad Craft was Willa's former boss. He had a huge law practice with three offices, including one in Houston.

"He didn't bat an eye at the mention of the FBI when we met Monday. He's solid and calm, just what my jacked up nerves needed." MiMi sighed. "He says the US Marshals office has to follow a strict protocol. Judges don't make decisions about confiscation lightly."

"I told you," Willa said, slipping into her former paralegal tone. "They have to have solid evidence linking the money used to buy your house with a crime."

"Edselle says the FBI may know it's a long shot, but he didn't want to give me false hope. He's got the firm's investigator on it. I don't know. Those agents seemed real confident." MiMi felt the fear creeping back up her spine.

"Of course they show up with plenty swagga. It's a cop thing," Jazz said between chews.

"Has Don said anything?" MiMi got up to pour a cup of coffee. Maybe it would help her spike of nerves talking about bad possibilities.

Jazz shook her head. "The feds looked over their files on Jack's murder. They're deep into every detail connected to his business. Don didn't say, but we can be sure they're also looking at Felipe."

"Wait a minute. Let's get back to Roderick 'Smooth Talker' Jefferson. You believed him... again?" Willa shook her head slowly.

"Damn, he must put down some good, good stuff in the sheets," Jazz said quietly.

"I'm not that weak in the head or elsewhere," MiMi snapped.

"Let's review. You confront him about getting you arrested and sorta kinda trying to put the blame on you. Y'all end up bouncing the mattress. The FBI came to your house, mention he's under investigation. You confront him again. Y'all end up on the kitchen floor." Jazz let out a long hiss.

"We weren't on the floor. It was the sofa in the

den," MiMi added softly and cleared her throat.

"Oh, big difference," Jazz joked. "I guess that makes it less slutty."

"Don't make me go over your love rap sheet," MiMi shot back.

"You're catching up fast," Jazz said. They stuck out tongues at each other.

"Real grown up y'all," Willa broke in.

"Edselle said exactly what Mr. Jefferson told me the other night. The FBI is fishing because they need solid evidence," MiMi argued.

"Umm, so what? I could have come to the same conclusion," Willa countered.

"Jack had flaws, but he didn't do all the things he was accused of. I know Roderick can be selfish, a little shallow and a jerk." MiMi sighed.

"Oh please, get him to the altar quick before he's snatched up," Willa said, her cynicism punctuated with a snort.

"Hilarious. He feels really guilty about getting me involved. He's not faking it either. I can tell," MiMi added when Willa rolled her eyes.

"How many times did you believe Jack? What about the last boyfriend? What's his name; the creep who led you on for months." Willa sat back in her chair in a waiting pose.

Jazz finished the last chunk of cake, licked glaze from the fork and put it down. "Okay, now I gotta stick up for my girl. We both know being a jerk doesn't mean he's guilty of a crime."

"Thank you, Jazz." MiMi gave Willa the side-eye. "Some of us have forgotten that we've all been falsely accused."

"Fine, cling to him like a he's your last hope for a

rich husband. Oh wait, he is." Willa pretended to duck a punch.

"Keep the jokes coming. One of them will be funny eventually," MiMi grumbled. She emptied the cup of lukewarm coffee and poured more.

"Okay, okay. That was low," Willa said, yet still laughed. Then she grew serious. "The good news is Edselle is confident and has a plan."

"Yeah, but he doesn't know what the FBI knows," Jazz said.

"If they prosecute they have to share information with her lawyer."

MiMi came back and sat down again. "You give me hope then snatch it back."

"Edselle has experience with federal prosecutions. The time to worry is when he tells you to." Willa smiled.

"Thanks. I could use some good news. Hey, and even if Roderick isn't telling the truth, he's motivated to stand by me. We're in this mess together. Remember his dead weed man in Santo Domingo." MiMi looked at Willa and Jazz.

Jazz nodded slowly. "Yeah, let's not forget murder."

"Roderick needs me in case the DR National Police decides to arrest him. He better hope they don't have a strong extradition treaty with the U.S." MiMi cocked an eyebrow at her friends.

"I'll research it," Willa said promptly. She went to a notepad usually used for shopping list and began writing.

Jazz looked at MiMi. "Wait a minute. You were all trusting about the guy a minute ago."

"You taught me to always have a Plan B." MiMi wore a hard smile. "Call it a little insurance policy."

****

A week later MiMi and Roderick went out to dinner at Galatoire's, a perfect Saturday night date. Roderick seemed intent on courting her in style. MiMi wasn't one to refuse being treated royally. She had to admit Roderick knew his stuff. He'd sent flowers to her office twice. His romantic text messages brightened her days. All that, plus there had been no more visits from the FBI. MiMi could almost believe the storm would pass over her.

The waiter served them grilled redfish with garlic potatoes and tender spring vegetables. MiMi had to admit, Roderick had the whole charming dinner companion down to perfection. He kept her laughing with jokes about his father, and even a few about hers. His voice changes when he imitated were dead on.

"How do you keep a straight face when they're bumbling with computers and cell phones?" MiMi dabbed at the tears on her cheek from laughing hard.

"Your father is the worse. He won't admit he can't do much more than click send on an email. Mostly I just bite my tongue and pretend they're doing okay." Roderick shrugged with a cheeky grin. "It's not honest, but it's safer. Dad still signs my paychecks, and I'm still in the will."

"I doubt Daddy sends much email." MiMi puffed up and sat straight. "This is him. 'If I wanted to type, then...'"

"I would have gone to secretarial school," Roderick finished. They both dissolved into giggles. "

"But give them credit, they're both sharp when it comes to business decisions." MiMi finished the last of her fish. The delicate flavor was a delight.

"They might be old school when it comes to technology, but I listen when they give advice. They're the reason we both live so well, right?" Roderick winked at her.

"Since we were kids," MiMi agreed. "Of course it helped that our grandmothers and fathers left them nice estates. But they built on what they got."

"Exactly." Roderick became serious. "We both know people who pissed away assets on bad decisions, gambling, heavy drinking."

"Speaking of which, do you ever hear from Andre?" MiMi sipped water. "I heard he tried to get his life together. Y'all were tight in high school."

"Yeah, he took partying to the next level and it wasn't a good thing. I haven't heard from him in..." Roderick blew out air. "I want to say it's been a good ten years. He didn't make it to junior year at Hampton. I heard he was doing okay, but I don't know."

"Hmm, hope so." MiMi raised an eyebrow at him. "You were sweet on his sister for a minute."

"Whew, that's ancient history. She's married with three kids and living in San Jose, California," Roderick replied.

"Oh yeah? I notice you kept up with her marital status and whereabouts." MiMi grinned when he groaned. "You know I'm kidding."

"Seriously though, that stupid move on our trip is not usual me. I don't want to be like Andre. You know, the subject of a 'Such a shame how his life went off the rails' conversation over dinner."

"I understand," MiMi said. Then she started when Roderick took her hand and gazed at her intently.

Roderick stroked the back of MiMi's ring finger. The he produce a deep blue velvet box from a pocket and pushed it across the table. "Open it."

MiMi felt a shiver of excitement. She caressed the silky smooth surface as she enjoyed the anticipation. Finally she opened it and gasped. A two carat round diamond ring set in platinum nestled in the silver satin interior. Roderick kissed her on the lips. Then he removed the ring and slipped it on her right ring finger.

"I, I don't know what to say," MiMi murmured. The soft lighting combined with the exclusive ambiance maximized the romantic mood.

Roderick folded her hand in both his larger ones. "I want only the best for you and Sage. I'm going to work hard, make a lot of money for both our tech challenged fathers..."

"Please help the poor things," MiMi broke in with a soft laugh.

She held her breath when Roderick leaned even closer. The delicate scent of his cologne mixed with the warmth of his solid hands thrilled her. He brushed her lips with his, then gently nipped her bottom lip.

"I didn't start seeing you because of my parents, MiMi. I want to be with *you*. When I'm with you, it's real," Roderick said softly. Then he smiled teasingly. "Hey, I better stop before they put us out of here."

"No, don't. Let them stare." MiMi sighed. She swam happily in a haze of desire.

"So the answer is...?" Roderick kissed her again and pulled away.

"Yes, very much yes." MiMi wrapped both arms around his neck.

They kissed again, admired the way her new diamond caught the light and talked as if no one else existed in the world. Would they buy a new house or build? Live in town or move to a new development? Get married in Baton Rouge or on a beach in the Bahamas? So many delightful decisions. Finally they both wound down and simply gazed at each other.

"I'm going to the men's room. All that sweet tea is working on me. Be right back." Roderick gave her cheek a gentle pinch and left.

The waiter approached. "You need anything, ma'am?"

MiMi let out a slow breath. "No, I've got it all right here."

The young man gave her a knowing smile. A few older couples at nearby tables had been sneaking looks at MiMi and Roderick. MiMi beamed back at them as she waved her hand showing off her ring. The finest man in the room only had eyes for her. The world could stare all night if they wanted to. Worries about investigations and FBI questions shrank to nothing. She and Roderick, along with their powerful families, would face down anything. MiMi laughed to herself with delight. Then she heard the buzzing sound in her small purse. She unzipped the soft pink leather clutch.

"I hope everything is okay with Sage at Adrienne's," MiMi muttered as she pulled out the smart phone.

Then she wore a big grin. Roderick's cell number displayed along with his smiling face. She opened the text message and the attachment. MiMi sat frozen, watching the video that seemed to play in slow motion. Fifteen seconds later Roderick walked back to their table, turning heads and wearing his signature gorgeous smile. And hell broke loose.

Chapter 9

Sunday morning dawned, and MiMi dragged herself out of bed when Willa had shown up for support. Jazz stumbled in about an hour after Willa arrived, yawning and looking annoyed. Sage was still at Adrienne's house, so thankfully MiMi could give in to self-pity.

MiMi watched Willa move in and out of the kitchen. She straightened up the den. No doubt she'd been upstairs as well. Jazz treated the large mug of coffee she held like a long, lost lover. The oven bell pinged. Like a genie, Willa appeared and went straight for it.

"As usual, Willa is playing the role of mama," MiMi said with a sigh.

"Humph, as usual, Willa is the control junkie ready to order you around," Jazz retorted.

"You know I can hear you, right?" Willa called without turning from serving up helpings onto plates.

"Yeah, and you know I don't care. Right?" Jazz shot back. She picked up the first section of the Sunday paper. "Let's see if last night's Rumble in the Restaurant made the news."

MiMi shrank into her French terry robe until the collar hid part of her face. "That's not funny. Please tell me you don't see my face in there."

Jazz turned a few pages. "Hey, nice action shot."

MiMi moaned and jumped to her feet. "We have to go over to my parents' house."

"What in the world are you talking about?" Willa continued to put plates on a tray, along with two full coffee cups.

"I have to steal the Sunday paper before they get home from church. They go at seven and they read the paper when they get home like clockwork."

"Seven? In the morning? Not even God gets up that early on Sundays," Jazz joked. She raised the mug to her mouth with one hand while still reading the paper.

Willa deftly spun around, grabbed MiMi by the arm. She pushed MiMi back to the kitchen island and onto a barstool. "Shut up. You're gonna give her a seizure or something."

"Girl, I'm messin' with you. I was talking about this picture of a kid on his bicycle. Keep your panties on," Jazz said.

"Thank you, Jesus." MiMi slumped onto the counter top, her forehead on her folded arms. She was too relieved to be angry at Jazz's bad attempt at humor.

"Be grateful for sure, hitting Roderick over the head with a bottle of wine in a restaurant. Eat something, some protein. You'll feel better." Willa sat down. She ate a forkful of food.

MiMi sniffed the air and moved to the breakfast table and sat next to Jazz. "What is that?"

"Aunt Ametrine's famous breakfast casserole. You've got layers of eggs, two kinds of cheese, sausage and a hint of sour cream. It should be three kinds of cheese, but I only had two. I figured you needed us fast so I didn't stop at the store." Willa spoke around chews. She drank orange juice.

"She didn't need *me* at this hour. Y'all need to remember my club closes at two in the morning." Jazz yawned widely as if reminded she should be in bed.

"Yeah, right. You wanted to hear the details," Willa shot back and continued eating.

"Speaking of..." Jazz turned to MiMi. Her eyes lost the sleepy look. "Girl, you need to be thanking God and everybody else you didn't end up in jail, let alone on the news. You hit the man over the head with a wine bottle? He could be in a coma."

MiMi sat up. "I didn't hit him with a bottle! I threw my wine glass at him. It barely tapped him on the head."

Willa dabbed her mouth with a napkin. She spoke as if she hadn't heard MiMi's protest. "Y'all must not be familiar with the concept of keeping a low profile."

"And everybody says *I* get in trouble. Humph." Jazz sipped more coffee.

"Oh Lord, what if the FBI has been following me all this time? They already know about last night." MiMi covered her face with both hands again.

"Kill the drama, girl. I doubt the FBI thinks you're that important," Willa drawled.

"I wanna see the video. C'mon, let's have a show." Jazz wiggled her eyebrows.

"Here, she sent it to me. Got it on my tablet." Willa grabbed her large leather purse and pulled out a tablet computer. She hit the play button on her app.

"No, no, no." MiMi covered her ears and squeezed her eyes shut. Still she could hear the groans and shrieks.

"This girl is limber, and your man got skills. No wonder you stuck with him," Jazz said, and let out a low whistle.

At first sitting in the middle of the restaurant, MiMi didn't quite make out what she was seeing. Then she recognized the naked male's hip. Roderick's strawberry shaped birthmark was visible as the camera angle caught him gleefully pleasuring a woman. Someone definitely not MiMi. Roderick kept up a steady stream of dirty talk. The woman screamed back, urging him to go faster and then to slow down. One minute and twenty-two seconds of sex tape.

Willa tilted her head from side to side as she watched. "Wow."

MiMi grabbed the tablet and closed the app. "I should have thrown a bottle, no ten."

"Girl, I'm so, so sorry." Willa shook her head slowly. She gave MiMi a look of pity. "Glad I never got video of Jack cheating. Shoot, I'd have a whole library."

"Oh please, it's not like she was in love with frat boy. He's a meal ticket." Jazz got up and refilled her mug.

"Real sensitive," Willa scolded.

"Okay, watch this. Tell her, MiMi." Jazz started to sip coffee but froze. She gaped at MiMi. "Oh hell no. You actually fell for this jackass?"

MiMi swiped a tear from her cheek. "For the first time since Jack, I felt like a man cared for me. It wasn't the flowers or jewelry. He was so sweet with Sage. It was all the little things, like taking out the garbage and talking to the plumber who came to fix a pipe. And I thought, you know, for once maybe my parents were right."

"You could see y'all as a family," Willa said, her tone full of understanding.

"Yeah," MiMi whispered. "I feel like a prize dumb ass fool."

"This video could have been taken long before you guys started dating. Some heffa is just mad because he picked you," Willa offered. She glanced at Jazz for support.

"It's date stamped," Jazz said, pointing to the tablet.

"Oh, I missed that," Willa murmured.

"No wonder with all that action," Jazz blurted out. She shrugged when Willa hissed at her.

"Her name is Yvette. She's a lawyer he met at a Chamber of Commerce conference in New Orleans." MiMi sniffed into a paper napkin. "He told me about it, the conference I mean."

"You know her?" Willa said.

"No, she sent me texts to gloat. The conference was only a couple of weeks before we went to the DR."

"To top it off, she's wearing an ankle bracelet in the video, the same one he gave me." MiMi lifted her right leg. The eighteen karat gold sparkled in the sunlight coming through her breakfast area's bay window. Two bezel set diamonds on either side shined even brighter.

"And you still have it on? Humph." Jazz sat down.

MiMi let out an angry yelp and tried to yank the chain off. She only succeeded in scratching her ankle. "I'm going to get this crap off me."

"Hold on! I didn't say break it," Jazz protested. She put her mug down with a thump and grabbed MiMi by the arm.

Willa grabbed MiMi's other arm "No need to rip off

a leg over the guy."

"Okay, okay. But I'm taking it off." MiMi huffed a few times. Then she opened the lobster claw clasp, removed the bracelet and threw it across the room.

Jazz followed quickly to pick it up. "Don't be wasteful. You could probably sell this to one of those online auction sites and make some bucks."

"Jazz, you might want to be helpful here," Willa snapped.

"Hmm." Jazz was too busy examining the gold links to reply.

Willa rolled her eyes and turned her attention to MiMi again. "All I'm saying is talk to him and..."

"I did. Roderick started out apologizing. Then he got mad at *me*." MiMi snatched up a fresh table napkin and sniffed into it.

"Excuse me?" Willa blinked at her.

"Oh yes, he said I made a scene over nothing, and it's not like I'm a saint. He goes, 'We both know how this will end. We'll do what our parents want because it makes financial sense.' He told me to quit being a whiny little spoiled rich bitch. I'd get the best of everything. He'd get the instant family he needs. He even said I could have a lover every once in a while." MiMi grew sober as she recounted his reaction. Roderick's words fell over her like a bucket of ice water. The charmer had vanished, replaced by a calculating snake.

"At least he told you the real deal. How much is he worth again?" Jazz seemed reluctant to let go of the gold bracelet.

Willa reached out a hand, palm up. "Hand it over."

"Hey, if she's just going to throw it away... Fine." Jazz heaved a sigh as she dropped it in Willa's hand and sat down. "I could rock that with gold leggings, a black t-shirt and six inch gold and black pumps."

"I'm going to make you a cup of Blue Mountain coffee. I brought some just for you." Willa gave MiMi a brief shoulder rub. "You really out to eat though, MiMi. You're right about the casserole. It may be too rich on a delicate stomach."

"Uh-huh." MiMi stared out the window.

"I'll fix you two slices of toast and one scrambled egg, no butter." Willa spoke with her head in MiMi's stainless steel refrigerator.

"Yeah, right. You do that," Jazz replied loudly. Then she looked at MiMi as Willa got busy. "See what I mean? She likes to control everybody."

The doorbell of her front door rang just as MiMi started to reply. Instead she padded off with the napkin still clutched in one hand. When she parted the curtains and saw Adrienne holding Sage, MiMi hastily wiped her cheeks dry and raked fingers through her hair. She opened the door wearing a sunny smile; at least she hoped it was anyway.

"Good morning, sis! Hey mommy's little honey bunny." MiMi took Sage when the toddler grinned at her.

"Sis?" Adrienne wrinkled her nose. She studied MiMi with a critical eye as if noting every detail of her appearance. "Looks like you had an eventful night."

"No," MiMi said too sharply. Then she forced a light laugh when Adrienne's gaze sharpened to a laser point. "Nothing more exciting than dinner and a little conversation."

"I assume Roderick is still here." Adrienne looked around the house as if she expected him to walk out naked.

"Of course not. Was mommy's sweet girl good?"

MiMi kissed Sage's soft face and inhaled the welcome smell of baby lotion.

Adrienne closed and locked the front door before following MiMi to the kitchen. "I know Roderick's reputation, and I know you. I doubt you two spent last night discussing philosophy or current events. Besides, I see his SUV."

"That's Willa's SUV. She and Jazz dropped by to have breakfast with me." MiMi didn't look at her older sister.

"On a Sunday, after your date. That's strange."

"It's kind of a girlfriend tradition we have." MiMi walked fast ahead of her to cut off more questions. "Hey everybody, this is my sister Adrienne. That's Jazz and Willa is the cook."

Jazz gave Adrienne a quick head to toe scan. "Mornin'."

"So nice to meet you. Join us for breakfast." Willa put the plate of toast and eggs down into the oven

"We've eaten, but what exactly is this dish?" Adrienne looked at the stoneware dish on the counter top.

"This is an egg, sausage, cheese and sour cream casserole. Oh, and I have toast to go with it." Willa smiled at her. "Sunday morning comfort food."

"Ah." Adrienne eyed it for a few seconds longer before she put on a smile. She placed the bag holding Sage's things down on the floor. "I finally meet the famous Willa Crown and her sister. MiMi talks about you a lot."

"Not exactly famous." Willa's smile tightened.

"The news made it seem like you practically cracked the case on who killed poor Jack. Then you and MiMi became friends. Very progressive. I suppose sharing so much forged a bond." Adrienne nodded as she spoke, a sincere expression stamped on her almost too pretty face.

"Humph." Jazz studied her, head to one side.

"There's no reason why we can't be friends. MiMi and I want our children to have a relationship since they're siblings." Willa's voice dripped ice water.

"Of course," Adrienne said smoothly. She turned and kissed Sage's forehead. "I'm going to miss my little girl so much. Call if she starts fussing for me or Brayden. He's the perfect big brother."

"Sage has a big sister and a big brother to keep her company. She'll be just fine," Jazz said.

Adrienne spun to face Jazz for the first time. "I'm surrounded by celebrities. You're a dancer at a gentlemen's club."

"Yes, pole dancing in teeny weeny costumes." Jazz stood up and took a bow. "Damn good at it, too."

"Obviously since you now own it. Congratulations. I read how the city tried to shut it down. Well, I think we need more small businesses owned by women of color," Adrienne said with enthusiasm.

"Thanks. I don't have pole dancers by the way. It's a night club and restaurant," Jazz replied.

Adrienne smoothed back her long thick hair. "Even better."

Jazz's gaze narrowed. She marched over to MiMi and held out her arms. Sage leaned out. Jazz took her. "I'm going to get Lil' Bit upstairs so she can freshen up."

MiMi blinked at her. "What?"

Jazz spoke low. "Before I kick your sister's ass up in here."

"Right, you haven't seen Sage in a while," MiMi said loudly before Jazz finished speaking.

"Thank you." Jazz tossed a glare at Adrienne over her shoulder before she climbed the stairs.

Adrienne followed to the bottom of the staircase. "Bye sweetie. Aunt Adrienne will see you soon." She faced MiMi again. "Listen, you've got a lot going on. Why not let Sage come stay with me for a while?"

"Thanks for the offer, but as you can see I have plenty of support," MiMi said sharply.

Willa stepped closer to MiMi until they were shoulder to shoulder. She gave Adrienne a chilly smile. "MiMi has more babysitter's than Princess Kate in England."

"Sometimes family helping out is for the best, no offense," Adrienne added in her best honey sweet tone with matching smile.

"We're family," Willa said, smile still in place. Her equally sugared tone laced with battery acid came through loud and clear.

Anger flared briefly in Adrienne's eyes, but she recovered. "I'll be going. Next time Sage can stay until evening. That way you can recover from another one of your intense dates with Roderick."

"Bye," Willa said pointedly.

MiMi shot a warning glance at Willa. Then she steered Adrienne to the front door to avoid a bloodbath. "Thanks again, Adrienne."

Adrienne opened the door but spun around instead of leaving. "Next time wait until you get to the parking lot to make a scene, dear sister."

MiMi gasped. "How did you..."

"A friend of a friend saw the whole show. Don't worry. Shelia is discreet." Adrienne chuckled.

In other words everyone in their social circle would know by the time the sun set today. "Oh. No."

"Mother and daddy will be quite upset."

"Then tell Mother to take one of her pills to calm down. I so appreciate you keeping Sage, Adrienne. Have a good evening, and kiss Brayden for me."

"Goodbye," Adrienne said dryly. She strode to her BMW. Minutes later she drove off with a flip of the hand and a smirk as a going away present.

"Ding, dong the witch is gone?" Jazz gazed in the direction of the BMW. The taillights vanished when it turned the corner.

"Yes, and please don't threaten my sister." MiMi shooed her inside. She shut and locked the front door.

"Hey, I threaten my sister all the time. Admit it. You wanted me to take a swing at her." Jazz pointed a forefinger at MiMi.

"No, I didn't." MiMi went back to the kitchen. Willa played with Sage as she bumped around in her walker.

"Just a lick, right upside the head. C'mon, say the word and it's done." Jazz laughed.

MiMi giggled as she spun to face Jazz. "Girl, you're too crazy."

Willa leaned down and placed both palms over Sages tiny ears. "Adrienne is a bitch." Then she took her hands away.

"Willa!" MiMi put both hands on her hips.

"Sage didn't hear. Even if she did, baby girl doesn't know what it means. Do you sweetie?" Willa tickled Sage on the chin. A baby cute smile was her reward.

"She's been super helpful with Sage. So I give her points for being a good aunt." MiMi shrugged and sat at the table.

Jazz sat in the chair across from her. "That's no reason to let her wipe her four hundred dollar shoes on you. She pretty much thinks you don't take care of

Sage."

"Adrienne thinks she does everything better than everybody," MiMi said.

"Well you shouldn't be prim and proper. Cuss her out and be done with it. It'll bring y'all closer, like me and Willa." Jazz grabbed her mug of coffee. "Tell her, big sister."

"Oh yeah, a good profanity laced family fight works wonders as therapy," Willa drawled.

"Told ya," Jazz quipped.

MiMi shook her head. "My parents are going to find out. Someone Adrienne knows happened to be having dinner and saw us. My parents will be so mad. I try to stay on their good side since they've been so helpful. Daddy helped me with expenses a lot."

"Which means they get to control you," Willa shot back.

"Look, if I found Jack's money, I wouldn't have to ask them for anything. If you're so concerned about their controlling ways then help me find it." MiMi pressed on when Willa hissed. "Mikayla and Anthony should get their inheritance, too. Jack owes us all that much."

"Jack ended up... you know, over that money," Willa said with a glance at Sage. "And last but not least is Jazz's gangsta man. If he gets wind Jack ended up with his money, we're all toast."

"Hey, Felipe isn't my 'gangsta man'. I don't know why everybody keeps saying that," Jazz complained.

"But did you find checks deposited from that company? No," MiMi answered while Willa's mouth still hung open.

Jazz put the mug down. "Hey, she's making sense."

"I checked with Cedric. Jack had seven major

contracts. Well, Crown Protection had them anyway. Plus there were ten smaller ones. On paper the business was doing well, but the business accounts didn't add up. I think we've had it wrong this whole time. What if Jack was stealing from the company?" MiMi looked from Jazz to Willa.

"Okay, now you've stopped making sense. Jack didn't need to steal from himself." Jazz picked up her mug again. "I vote for the money being Felipe's drug cash, a healthy down payment. Felipe paid Jack to look the other way at what really went down at those warehouses Crown Protection was guarding at the Baton Rouge Port."

"Jack wasn't in on the arrangement with Felipe. Remember?" MiMi said, shooting a huge whole in their theory.

"The cops never found proof one way or the other. He could have taken the money as security, to escape," Willa said.

"Okay, I can see it." Jazz nodded in agreement.

"No, you're wrong and the FBI had it wrong. Jack didn't take drug money," MiMi said firmly.

"Again, Jack didn't have to steal money from Crown Protection. As sole owner he could take money anytime he chose as his salary. Except..." Willa's voice trailed off.

"If he didn't want to pay income taxes, payroll taxes, inventory taxes," MiMi ticked off each one on her fingers. "Jack had plans to not only expand but to change from a sole proprietorship to a corporation. A board of directors would have meant more scrutiny. I think he planned to stuff his personal account before that happened."

"Is she right?" Jazz looked at Willa.

"He talked about incorporating, but kept putting it off. He said it was hard giving up control," Willa said.

"Or maybe he stalled for time while he looted the accounts. Jack always said he'd take care of me and we'd be able to travel more." MiMi sighed as she thought of past good times.

Willa snorted. "Oh he traveled alright, just not with you. He bought lots of lingerie and jewelry while he was visiting The Caymans, too."

Jazz sucked in air. "Ouch."

"Even if he didn't take gang money, tax evasion and moving cash off shore is against the law. So the FBI would still be after it and *you*," Willa said and crossed her arms.

"Your smart lawyer buddy says it's tough to prove money is dirty," Jazz offered.

"But not impossible, and they probably have leads. Leave it alone," Willa countered.

MiMi opened her mouth three times, but closed it. No persuasive arguments came to mind at first. Then she sat straight and looked at Willa. "As one of his heirs, I'm requesting that the executor of Jack's estate investigate."

"The who?" Jazz blinked at MiMi.

"Me, that's who," Willa said. She threw her head back and groaned as if in agony.

"She has the duty to settle all debts and questions surrounding his succession, including any from heirs. As we all know, it's dragged on because of the questions about Crown Protection's assets," MiMi added.

"Check and mate," Jazz said and blinked at Willa, who whispered an expletive.

MiMi smiled. "When do we start looking for our money, ladies?"

Chapter 10

A week later, MiMi sat at the police station. She glared across a metal table at the two detectives. One, a tall redhead, frowned back. The short blonde wore a sympathetic expression. Detective Drake kept bobbing his head as if he agreed with every protest MiMi made. Harsh florescent lighting in the windowless room meant it could have been midnight or any time of day instead of nine in the morning.

"I don't appreciate being interrogated about a crime on foreign soil. I don't know anything about that man's murder. Ask Roderick. The victim was his weed man after all."

The blonde bobble head gazed at MiMi without a glance at his frowning partner. "We're following up as a courtesy to the Dominican Republic National Police, ma'am. You're not being detained or anything like that."

"They just need answers, and you were involved," blunt redhead added.

Thank goodness MiMi had a flexible work schedule. Kerry or her snitch of an assistant wouldn't think her absence on a Wednesday morning all that unusual. After forty minutes MiMi decided playing the outraged innocent citizen was a waste of precious energy. MiMi plastered on an apologetic smile.

"Detective Drake, Detective Forrester, I'm sorry for complaining. I understand you're doing your job. If I had remembered anything new or helpful. Believe me, I'd tell you. "

"Humph." Forrester, let the soft grunt deliver his message of skepticism.

MiMi continued to focus on Drake, the good cop. "I'm a hardworking single mother who chose the wrong vacation date."

"How long have you known Mr. Jefferson?" Detective Drake asked as if they hadn't asked her the same question in at least four different ways already.

"Our families have known each other for years, since we were in middle school at least. We dated briefly in high school, but it wasn't serious." MiMi tapped a finger on the purse in her lap.

"So the trip to the DR was planned or a last minute thing?" Detective Drake pressed on in a calm yet relentless way.

"We decided maybe a month before. Look, I'm sure Roderick can tell you where he first met this poor man. I wasn't even with Roddy, I mean Roderick, when he went to buy the marijuana. You must know all this from the Dominican court records."

"You've seen Mr. Jefferson several times since coming back, right?" Detective Forrester cut in sharply.

"Yes."

The interview room was about the size of her walk-in closet at home. The matching chair was slightly comfortable. She was between the two men. One to her left the other to her right. To get to the door, MiMi would have to slide sideways past Forrester. So she was hemmed in, or supposed to feel that way despite the 'you're free to go anytime' speech. Drake asked a few more questions which MiMi answered as her mind worked.

"Mr. Jefferson works for the family business, correct?" Drake said, looking at a note pad.

MiMi snapped out of auto pilot response mode. She noticed something significant. "If you're investigating Jefferson and Son, Inc. deals, then you're wasting even more time. I only know Roderick socially."

"Why do you think we're investigating his business?" Forrester leaned both elbows on the table.

"The FBI paid me a visit and implied they were looking into him. I'm sure they talked to you," MiMi shot back.

"Your father does business with the Jeffersons," Forrester said, a statement not a question.

"Then you should talk to him after you have a long talk with Roderick. Let me save y'all some time, okay? I've never worked for my father or conducted business with Roderick. So for the fifth time at least, *talk to Roderick*. Stop harassing me."

MiMi didn't think she needed to add the part about getting a lawyer. She slipped the strap of her purse over one shoulder and stood. Drake and Forrester stood at the same time, but only Drake spoke.

"Ms. Landry, Roderick Jefferson was found dead last night." Drake's smooth voice didn't match the rough news he'd just delivered.

Her legs went weak. MiMi dropped back to the vinyl cushioned metal chair. "But, but that can't be. He's healthy, works out twice a week at least."

"Do you know anyone else who had a grudge or a

problem with him?" Drake said. His cool gray eyes gazed at her with interest.

"No, I mean, of course not. I can't believe this." MiMi swallowed against the acid sensation in her throat. She took in three deep breaths and let them out. The detectives kept quiet, but she knew it wasn't out of concern. They wanted to observe her. "How did he die?"

"We're waiting on the coroner's report," Drake said.

"Where were you between Tuesday evening at around six until this morning," Forrester asked as Drake picked up his note pad.

MiMi fought to focus on her surroundings. She ignored the questions screaming inside her head. A dizzy spell threatened and she gripped the cold edge of the metal table. Both detectives sat again, as if they expected to spend a lot longer with her. *What would Jazz do?* MiMi had seen her face down cops, prosecutors and judges without breaking a sweat. Yes. MiMi needed to think her way through it, use the scant information the detectives had given her.

"You said 'who else had a grudge' which means two things. His death wasn't natural or an accident, and you think I had something against him. How did he die?" MiMi forced a composed tone that she damn sure didn't feel.

"You two fought a few days ago when you found out he was with another woman. You made quite a scene in a local restaurant. Took a swing at the guy," Forrester replied.

"Yes. Roderick hooked up with another woman. I told him he was dead to me." MiMi sucked in a sharp breath. "I only meant he no longer existed, that I'd pretend he was..." Forrester's almost joyful expression confirmed he was ready to bring out the handcuffs.

"You were angry. Emotions flare hot when it comes to a relationship gone wrong," Drake said in his reasonable 'I understand perfectly' way.

"The woman had the nerve to send me a video for God's sake. So I lost it, told him off. That's all." MiMi looked at him, but there was no real help from that corner. His next words proved it.

"So I'm assuming this video was, let's say explicit, that it showed them in an intimate situation," Drake continued, taking notes.

"Yes. Now I've answered you for over an hour. I cared about Roddy despite what happened. At least tell me how he died," MiMi said, her voice rising steadily.

"He was struck over the head twice, and shot. In the chest," Drake replied quietly.

"Yeah, through the heart," Forrester added. He stared at her. "So seems like it was personal."

"Roderick tried to convince me that she was a fling, that it didn't mean we couldn't become engaged. But I wouldn't have..." MiMi's fingers hurt from gripping the table. She let go, tried to center herself and channel some of Jazz's badass persona.

"Very much a shock I imagine," Drake put in.

"You must have been furious. I mean, the guy does that to you and then suggests you just get over it. His other woman throws their affair in your face, he goes 'No biggie'. All this after he got you arrested, and you forgave him. I can see why you lost it, like you said." Forrester stared at her.

His gaze wasn't hostile nor was his tone confrontational anymore. No, he seemed like more like the unemotional executioner leading her to doomsday.

Except she wasn't going. Not today. Not ever.

MiMi narrowed her gaze at him to help send her message. "I'm not going to say anything more until I speak to my attorney."

****

Five hours later MiMi allowed herself to freak out. She paced around Willa's office at Crown Protection ranting about police brutality, racial profiling and injustice. Willa and Cedric, Willa's second in command, let her go until she ran down. When MiMi collapsed onto one of the leather chairs, Cedric placed a large steady hand on her shoulder. Coffee, a glass carafe of fruit juice and a tray of sandwiches were set up on the table in a corner of Willa's spacious office. Willa filled a glass and brought it to her. MiMi promptly burst into tears at the caring gesture. A box of tissues appeared in front of her. MiMi yanked out two fistfuls and pressed them to her face.

"Daddy won't pay my bail or for a lawyer this time. They say I killed one of his business partners. Which means Daddy won't make piles of money with the Jeffersons. He'll never forgive me." MiMi went back to bawling into the tissue.

"What the...?" Cedric perched on the edge of Willa's desk.

"Money means a lot to the Landry clan. She thinks her parents don't care about her." Willa gave him the abbreviated version of MiMi's issues in a crisp tone, like a therapist. She pulled a chair next to MiMi, sat down and rubbed her back. "Honey, you need to calm down. I don't think your father is that cold blooded."

MiMi wiped her face with the wad of tissue. She frowned at the black mascara and foundation that came off. "You don't know him like I do."

"I know a little something about parents who eat their young."

"Hey, we need MiMi to pull it together," Cedric put in.

"I'd love to say my parents only seem unfeeling on the outside, and underneath they're warm and cuddly, loving parents. I'd be lying. Mother rarely visits Sage."

"You should be grateful then," Willa said flatly. "Don't give me that look, Cedric. Better to have an absent cold grandmother than to have her messing up the next generation."

"Amen. I don't complain. Not at all." MiMi shivered.

Cedric heaved a sigh. "Okay, no help from the family."

"Why do you think I called Willa instead of them? Thank you for tracking down my lawyer." MiMi sniffed a few times.

She rose, found her purse where she'd dropped it on another chair and took out her small make bag. As she repaired her look, MiMi cleared her head. Looking her best had always steadied her nerves.

"Smart of you to assume he'd be in court or tied up. Lawyers don't sit in their offices all day like most people think," Willa said. "Drink your juice. Kay swears it will smooth out the rough edges. She convinced me to get one of those fancy blenders for the office."

"Four hundred bucks to mash up stuff," Cedric said dryly, ever the keeper of the company cash flow.

MiMi managed a weak smile as she put her make-up away and sat down. She sipped from the glass.

"Hmm, that's not bad."

"I wouldn't drink that green concoction," Cedric joked.

"No, it's really good. What's in it?" MiMi drank more.

"Fresh pineapple and an apple to sweeten it, also for fiber. Cucumber, lemon and celery. Since you didn't heave, I'll try." Willa poured another glass.

"You haven't tasted it? Thanks a lot," MiMi spluttered. Still she drained her glass. "Whew. Okay, I think I can make sense now."

"Maybe we need to bottle the stuff and sell it. Cause a whole lot of people are acting crazy these days," Cedric said with a smile.

"Yeah." MiMi tried to smile, but couldn't quite muster the effort. She lifted her chin, let out a slow breath and gazed at Willa. "We better figure this out."

"Hell yes. Did Roderick get shot, beaten or stabbed," Willa was about to go on when Cedric cleared his throat. "What?"

"Give her more than a minute to get steady," Cedric said dryly.

MiMi fought off the shakes that started when Willa listed the grim reaper possibilities. "He died from a gunshot to the chest."

"Damn. I'm surprised they came straight for you though." Willa blinked as she tried to sort through cop logic.

"Most murders are committed by people known to the victim. If evidence pointed to a robbery they'd have said so." Cedric's good humor had vanished, replaced by a serious expression. "They didn't give you more facts for a good reason."

"Yeah, they wanted to see if you'd slip and say

something only the murderer would know. Then they'd pounce," Willa put in.

"Oh God, you think I blurted out something they could use against me?" MiMi squeezed her eyes shut to blot out such a reality. "I'm on my way to prison. Again."

"They may be eliminating you as a suspect. Obviously you didn't know how he died, so they went ahead and told you. Plus it was probably about to be in the news." Cedric started to go on, but stopped when his smart phone buzzed. He stood, unclipped it from his belt, and gazed at the screen. He waved to them as he left the office.

"Has Jazz called? Maybe Don can tell us something." MiMi couldn't sit or stand still. She moved to the window. Willa's office looked down on an interior courtyard. People sat at tables eating lunch. Afternoon sunlight gave the scene a cheerful look.

"We can't put him in a difficult position by asking him questions."

"That an exact quote?" MiMi didn't turn around.

"Yep, Jazz is starting to sound downright conventional. She's protective of him." Willa smiled as she shook her head.

"She loves him," MiMi replied.

"Jazz is too busy pretending they're friends who have good sex. That makes her feel safe." Willa waved a hand. "Anyway, back to your pressing problem."

"Roderick was no good, but he didn't deserve to die. Hell, if people who were scum got the death penalty the streets would be littered with bodies. Besides, he was genuinely sweet to Sage."

"Hmmm." Willa raised her eyebrows, sipped coffee but said no more.

"Okay, maybe he was setting us up to be his trophy family. We'd make a nice respectability cover for him, especially if he expected to be in legal trouble." MiMi chewed on her thumb for a few seconds, a habit her mother had nagged her about since childhood.

Willa gave a short chuckle. "His *stunning* wife, huh? How modest of you. What about his wife with a rich daddy who could give his business bottom line a much needed bump?"

"That too," MiMi agreed. She grimaced as if Roderick stood in front of her. "What a low down sleazy waste of space."

"At least one other person thought so," Willa clipped.

MiMi shivered. "No, someone hated Roderick enough to kill him. If only we knew more."

Cedric came back and shut the office door as if on cue. "That was Edselle. He's found out more. Roderick suffered blunt force trauma and was shot in the leg. The bullet hit a major artery. He bled to death."

MiMi's legs went weak. She stumbled to a nearby chair and dropped onto it. "Oh God, that's awful. They wanted him to suffer. Wait a minute, Forrester said he was shot in the chest."

"He probably wanted to surprise you into saying something like, 'I hit his leg'. You'd be surprised how many suspects give themselves away so easily." Cedric checked his texts messages as he talked.

"No wonder the police are questioning people close to him. Sounds personal to me." Willa looked at Cedric.

"It could have been a robbery. His home and his office had stuff thrown around, like someone searched them. But... I don't know." Cedric sat on the edge of

Willa's desk.

Willa sat straight. "Wait, that's good news. The police will cover all the bases. He could have interrupted a burglary and been attacked."

Cedric scratched his jaw and turned over her premise for a few seconds. "Yeah, I guess."

"You don't believe it though." Willa lifted her mug. When Cedric nodded, she got up and poured coffee into an empty mug for him.

He took it from her. "Thanks, babe. He either interrupted a thief at his house or his office, not both. Burglars typically don't go to a victim's house, figure out where he works and go there, too. Doesn't make sense."

"Maybe they forced him to his house or office when they couldn't enough money. Anyway, it weakens any theory that makes MiMi the likeliest suspect," Willa said.

Cedric frowned. "They could have taken to the nearest ATM and forced him to withdraw cash. And..."

Willa gazed at him. "What else?"

"In criminal cases the authorities can't hold back information from a defense attorney," Cedric replied.

"She hasn't been charged. They could have told him because the details are about to become public anyway, probably in the news." Willa pointed her mug at him.

"Good point. Ed didn't say she was going to be arrested." Cedric took out his cell phone and dialed. He spoke for a few minutes. "You're right. Ed says he saw a breaking news bulletin on his tablet about Roderick's murder. He called the police and got more information. The detective, Drake, told him they were following more leads."

"Which is the same as saying they don't have enough to charge MiMi or anyone else," Willa added.

"Good catch." Cedric smiled at her.

MiMi listened to them bat ideas back and forth for a few minutes. She massaged her forehead in an effort to fight off a migraine. Yet the first stab of pain started behind her left eye. Willa's assistant slipped in to press an object into her hand. MiMi looked at the foil with two white tablets encased in plastic. Kay handed MiMi a large paper cup filled with water. She waited as MiMi tore open the package, took the pills and gulped down half the water.

"Thanks," MiMi said softly and accepted a hug from Kay, who then left just as unobtrusively.

Willa and Cedric spoke quietly. With her eyes closed, MiMi rested her head on the back of her chair. Tension eased from her neck and shoulders. The pills kept the thud from turning into a full-fledged sledge hammer of agony. After a few moments her thinking cleared. MiMi opened her eyes. Aware that the headache could still hit hard, MiMi moved slowly to sit up. She wanted to be strong, to help them examine alternatives. After all, this was her mess, not theirs. But she couldn't.

"I just want to go home, take care of my little girl and crawl under my comforter," MiMi said, her voice shaky.

Willa gave Cedric a look full of meaning. He nodded and crossed to MiMi. Without saying a word, he gave MiMi a solid warm embrace and then walked out. He didn't have to make a speech. Cedric would juggle his work at Crown Protection with finding facts to help her. Just as Kay hadn't needed to speak as she looked after MiMi.

"Kissing my kids has always been my best medicine. I'll drive you home. Kay can follow and bring me back to the office," Willa said gently.

She helped MiMi to her feet, dried tears from her cheeks and handed MiMi her purse as she talked. Overwhelmed, MiMi could only follow directions. She let Willa and Kay take control for the next forty-five minutes. They collected Sage from daycare. Three hours later, MiMi felt much better. Going through her typical mommy routine helped. Sage cooed in a warm soapy bath as she played with her toys. MiMi fed her mashed potatoes and green peas. By the time the sun slipped down, MiMi could almost believe the awful day had been all her imagination. Almost. By eight o'clock she'd put Sage in bed. MiMi smiled as Sage's eyes fluttered. She kicked her chubby legs in an attempt to stay awake, but it didn't work. MiMi jumped at the sound of the doorbell. Thankfully Sage seemed too tired to be disturbed by the chime that echoed through the house. MiMi made sure the baby monitor was set. She left the bedroom door halfway open. Then she went down stairs.

"I don't care if a truck load of burly FBI agents, cops or both is at this door. If they disturb my baby, I'm going off, on somebody," MiMi muttered.

She peered through the window next to the front door. What she saw surprised her. A slender elegantly dressed woman the color of nutmeg stood in the light. Long black hair draped her shoulders. The woman's form fitting black dress and bright teal blue pumps caused a flash of admiration in MiMi. Long contemporary silver earrings swung as the stranger scanned her surroundings. A dark Mercedes sedan sat in MiMi's driveway. When a tall man with broad shoulders and a bald head stepped out of the driver's side, the woman waved him away. Then she faced the door again.

"Hello, Ms. Landry. May I speak with you one moment, please?" she said. Her soft Dominican accent made her request sound quite pleasant.

MiMi didn't move. The presence of the man made her invitation a lot less inviting. "It's late and I'm dressed for bed."

"Tsk, tsk, Ms. Landry. This isn't the southern hospitality I'm told is so famous," the woman replied. "Your fancy neighbors might find out about Jack stealing my money and why this property belongs to me."

"What the..." MiMi slammed open the locks and jerked the door open.

A tan SUV pulled up just suddenly. Three guys piled out of the passenger front and back doors. A fourth man bounded around from the other side. He pointed at the woman's male companion who was coming from the BMW.

"Hey, man. You don't wanna do that. Just be cool right where you at," the fourth guy shouted.

His three companions positioned themselves in a line blocking a path up MiMi's sidewalk to her front door. Then a black SUV screeched around the corner. Seconds later it parked behind the Mercedes so that the car couldn't back out. The bald headed companion slapped a palm on the car's roof in frustration. Jazz appeared from the SUV passenger door. Don Addison, emerged from the driver's side seconds later.

"Hey, didn't your mama teach you not to open the door to strangers?" Jazz yelled at MiMi.

Chapter 11

Ten minutes later they all sat in MiMi's living room. The elegant woman wore an impassive expression as she studied Jazz first. She seemed to reach some kind of conclusion as she gave a short hiss. Then she looked at Don. Her milk chocolate gaze lingered on his tall, muscular frame. Her deep wine colored lips parted to reveal white teeth.

"Your police officers are a lot sexier here. Or is that just the way you grow them in the southern states?" the woman purred.

"He's kinda unique," Jazz replied. She draped an arm around Don's shoulder for a second and then took it away.

The woman raised a dark eyebrow. "Lucky girl."

"Luck ain't got nothin' to do with it." Jazz flashed a cocky grin at the woman.

"Hey, cut it out," Don mumbled, a quick side-eye at Jazz.

The woman laughed. "Enjoy being a sex object, my darling. Women have to put up with it all the time."

MiMi had time to dress in a red tunic sweater over

jeans while Jazz and Don babysat her visitor. She cut in before the woman could go on flirting. "Excuse me if I ask a rude question, but who the hell are you?"

The woman started to stand, but changed her mind when Jazz took a step toward her. She sighed as she settled in the chair again. "You people are so dramatic. I'm Nairoby Villa. I don't think you want an officer of the law to hear the rest of what I have to say."

"You're not in a position to set the damn rules," Jazz shot back.

Don tapped Jazz on the shoulder. "Lemme have a minute."

Jazz followed him to a corner, they whispered back and forth. Don finally did most of the talking as Jazz nodded. They both shot side glances at the newcomer from time to time.

"Her handsome policeman is very smart. He's probably explaining to your hot-headed friend that any illegal activity I disclose would place him in an awkward position.

"What are you talking about?" MiMi squinted at the woman.

"You'll see soon."

Nairoby gave a short nod in the direction of Jazz and Don. Don went out the front door without looking back. Jazz joined them again. She sat down on the edge of MiMi's sofa, but didn't relax.

"You were about to say." Jazz gazed at her.

"I could use such a fine *asset* in my business." Nairoby glanced at the door. "What's his name again?"

"Mr. Don't Even Try It," Jazz replied mildly. She crossed her shapely legs. "You didn't come thousands of miles to get your ass handed to you over a man. Explain why you disturbed my girl."

Nairoby laughed. "I like you. I'm sure we could talk business. Now this one..." She glanced at MiMi.

MiMi strode to the woman and stood in front of her. "The police officer that might have kept me from beating you senseless is gone. I've been through enough crap that my patience is thin. So you need to start talking."

"Fine," Nairoby said with a sour expression of distaste. "I can't believe Jackson would bother with you. But that's neither here nor there now. Jackson and I had a business arrangement. He helped me export merchandise, trained my security staff and we shared in the profits."

"What kind of merchandise?" MiMi frowned at her.

"Mainly textiles. Later I expanded into garments for expensive specialty boutiques. Then I developed a line of cheaper clothing." Nairoby gave a short laugh. "I have you to thank for that. Jackson gave me advice based on your experience. You may have noticed he took an interest in your work."

"What?" MiMi yelped. She jammed both fists on her hips.

"You thought his pillow talk about the clothing business meant he was fascinated with you? He did it for me." Nairoby ignored the odds against her and stood.

"That no-good lying son-of-a..." MiMi huffed and cut off the rest. He was Sage's father after all. Even so, if Jack hadn't already died, MiMi would have happily taken a bat to him.

Jazz rose quickly. She went to MiMi and pulled her a few feet away from Nairoby. "Focus."

"He cheated on me with this piece of foreign

trash," MiMi spluttered.

"We need information, not a cat fight over a dead guy. Let it go," Jazz whispered. She glanced over MiMi's shoulder at Nairoby, who had sat down again and looked satisfied with herself. "She's pushing your buttons and enjoying it. She must need something bad to come all this way."

MiMi huffed and puffed a few times, then gained control. "Okay."

"I'll do the talking, in case you're tempted to take a swing at her," Jazz replied after a few seconds.

"I'm good." MiMi tried not to think of Jack wrapped up in a naked embrace with the leggy woman, and failed.

"Uh-huh." Jazz gave a snort of skepticism, then went to sit across from Nairoby again. The young man who'd come inside with Jazz seemed to be enjoying the show.

"Good you talked some sense into her. She's decorative and not much use otherwise," Nairoby said to Jazz.

Jazz glanced at her male companion. He moved closer to the woman. "Stop wasting time and get to the damn point."

The smile faded from Nairoby's face. "Jackson made a lot of money because of me, but he had expensive habits. I never cared about her," she jerked a head. "But I discovered he raided a joint account we had. He bought this house, a Jaguar and a car for her. Why? Because she was stupid enough to get pregnant."

Jazz studied Nairoby for a few moments. Then she smiled. "Jack had his faults, but he'd do anything for his kids. And his baby's mama."

"He stole from me for to support that breed cow of

a bitch! What he bought belongs to me. This house, those fancy cars are mine." Nairoby tapped her chest with a teal lacquered fingernail.

"Ha, how you gone get 'em?" Jazz retorted.

"Not all of the deals Jack and I did were exactly legal. The FBI would like to know about your property, huh? Yes, I know a bit about American laws. I could put his entire estate in jeopardy without causing much trouble for me or my business partners. Maybe he put some of that dirty money into Crown Protection. Felipe Perez would be disturbed to learn that your friends are living off his money while he sits in prison. Things could get nasty for you in a variety of ways." Nairoby pursed her lips.

MiMi gasped. In one big swoop this woman neatly threatened her, Willa and Jazz. Her mind spun in crazy circles trying to sort through the twists. "Oh. My. God."

"You, watch her," Jazz said to the young man as she stood.

"Sure," he rumbled. He didn't move, but remained close to Nairoby with his hands clasped in front of him. "Relax, baby. Look like we gone be here a while longer. Don't worry. My guys are keepin' your dude company outside."

Nairoby surprised him by merely shrugging. She sank down to the chair. "I'm not worried. Your police officer friend won't be a party to us getting hurt."

"Like he cares." When Nairoby blinked rapidly at him, the man smiled widely as his gold tooth gleamed.

Jazz heaved a sigh and went to MiMi. "Get your shit together. Show panic and she'll know she's holding all the damn cards."

"Are you kidding?" MiMi shouted, then took a deep breath and lowered her voice. "She already knows that, Jazz."

"Maybe." Jazz glanced back at Nairoby with a thoughtful frown. "Why didn't she go to the judge over Jack's estate and demand her property."

"She still might, the evil witch," MiMi spat. Then she breathed in and out. "No, she didn't present a claim to the courts. If she's telling the truth, then she would be a creditor of the estate. So that means she has a problem."

"Now you're thinking clearly." Jazz gave a nod.

They both turned to stare at Nairoby. The longer they stood across the room without speaking, the more uneasy Nairoby seemed to become. She tried to hide it, but MiMi could smell the sweat of anxiety.

"She mentioned business partners, right?" MiMi said quietly.

"Yeah, so?" Jazz gave her a puzzled look.

"I have an idea." MiMi marched back across the room as Jazz started to speak. "Why don't you cause us all this trouble you're talking about? Go on. Tell the world Jack stole your money."

"I'm not an unkind person. I know what it's like to be poor, and Jackson's little girl would suffer. A reasonable settlement will quietly resolve the matter," Nairoby said.

"Bull. You don't strike me as reasonable at all. I want to negotiate with the full team." MiMi sat across from Nairoby.

"Don't be ridiculous," Nairoby blurted out. "What--"

"You mentioned other business partners. Maybe they will be less willing to go public, air their problems in a court. The police could start to get a little too interested. Let's have a nice chat in the morning." MiMi looked at Jazz.

"We can use Willa's conference line," Jazz chimed in with a grin.

"Great idea since this involves Crown Protection, not to mention her children. There's no need for threats. We're reasonable women just like you, Ms. Villa." MiMi felt much better as she watched the woman's face. The warm brown color took on a grayish look.

"Hmm, let's think it through first." Jazz got up and pulled MiMi aside. She turned her back to Nairoby, but only lowered her voice a little. She gave MiMi a play-along-with-me wink. "Girl, don't negotiate with these Dominican thugs. It's too dangerous."

"She says they're business people," MiMi replied in a stage whisper.

"Yeah, and I'm Michelle Obama," Jazz retorted with a short laugh. "You know damn well what's up. Look, give her to the FBI. They wanna follow the money. Maybe they'll give you a deal, forget about taking your house."

"Makes a lot of sense. I get her and the FBI off my back in one move." MiMi nodded slowly.

"Excuse me, but I have excellent hearing," Nairoby called out. "You don't want to involve those FBI scum in our affairs. You'll lose a lot more than a house."

Jazz's companion standing guard reached down and snatched something from her ear. He held up a small blue tooth hands free headset. "This ain't for her cell phone. You can use it to listen in on people. We got a couple of 'em from overseas. Latest tech shit."

MiMi leaned close to Jazz. "Who is the 'we' he's talking about?"

"Freelance security. I'll give you details later," Jazz

whispered, and then she spun around.

"Here's the thing, Nairoby. MiMi has less to lose because she really wasn't involved in the game. Aside from being dumb enough to fall for Jack Crown..."

"Hey!" MiMi protested.

"Jazz continued as if MiMi hadn't spoken. "Sure, the FBI will make her life difficult for a minute. But eventually they'll clear her."

"*You* on the other hand won't be so lucky," MiMi picked up. "I suspect your partners didn't know you had a side hustle going with Jack. Maybe you want cash fast to fix *your* problem."

Fear, anger and calculation took turns chasing across Nairoby's pretty face. Calculation won. She gave MiMi a sly smile. "I must apologize, MiMi. You're not the empty-headed decorative piece of ass Jack described. I've totally underestimated you."

"I'm flattered," MiMi shot back. "Convince me not to sick the FBI on you."

Nairoby nodded. "You're only partially correct in your assessment of my situation. My associates found out about the money. I had to tell them because they were about to audit the books."

"Crooks who audit?" MiMi glanced at Jazz.

"They keep track of their transactions like any business," Jazz replied.

MiMi blinked at her friend. Jazz knew way too much about organized criminal enterprises for her own good. She'd talk to her about that later. "I see."

"They're not happy with me, but that doesn't mean they don't want their money. They'll contact you, dear, once they... chastise me." Nairoby wore a tight smile.

"What?" MiMi turned to Jazz for translation, but the man spoke first.

"They'll deal with her and still come for you. Gettin' her picked up by the police won't get you off the hook," the man said. He shrugged when MiMi and Jazz both stared at him in surprise.

"They know where to find you," Nairoby said more bluntly. "So we're in this thing together."

"She's right," MiMi said.

Nairoby stood with a cautious glance over her shoulder at the rough young man. "I suggest you find a way to raise cash. Paying me is the only way to satisfy my associates. Now I'll be going. I hope my driver is in good health."

"Humph, they didn't trust her to come alone," Jazz said quietly to MiMi. Then she nodded to the young man. "He's fine. I just wanted to make sure we could talk without interruption. Now that I know he works for your buddies, even better we kept him outside."

Nairoby nodded. "Ramon works for me."

"Tell your pals you stuck to the script," Jazz said promptly. "Keep letting them think MiMi is a, how did you put it?"

"An empty-headed decorative piece of ass," Nairoby said with a relish at each word.

"Yeah, that," Jazz said. "We'll figure something out to satisfy them."

"Only money will satisfy them," Nairoby replied sharply. "Nothing less than the six hundred thousand dollars Jack owes me."

MiMi swallowed hard. She glanced from Jazz to the young thug. He responded with a low whistle. "Six... Did she just say six hundred thousand?"

"Damn," Jazz said, drawing out the word until it had four syllables.

"I'm in so much trouble." MiMi gazed at the stylish

messenger of doom.

****

Life had to go on. MiMi had a baby to take care and a job to keep. She worked at home the next day. To her surprise Kerry didn't object. But eventually she had to go into the office. So off she went despite a throbbing headache. Elle asked her several times if she was okay. Tyler kept eyeing MiMi each time he passed her office. The fourth time he walked by MiMi stood at her desk.

"Yes, Tyler. I'm still in the office. You can take a break from stalking me," she called out.

Tyler came back to stand in her open door. "You're not that important."

"Funny, Darcas thinks so. Just got an email praising my last marketing idea. Wanna see?" MiMi pointed to her lap top.

"Humph." Tyler gave her a sour expression and strode in the direction of his office.

MiMi resisted the strong urge to throw her heavy paperweight at his back. She'd earned and a bonus for exceptional performance. Not even for the satisfaction of seeing Tyler drop like a stone. Instead she settled for muttering insults about him. Elle's voice interrupted her revenge fantasies.

"I'm pretty sure assault is against the law." Elle folded her lanky frame into a chair. As usual she looked comfortable and elegant at the same time. "What's the little chump done now?"

"Spying on me as usual," MiMi plopped down in her chair and massaged the back of her neck.

"Yeah, me and half the office noticed." Elle's expression turned serious. "Something is going on. I don't know if we're going to have a layoff or the company is being bought out or what."

"Could be both. They go hand in hand you know," MiMi said. She rested her head against the back of her chair and closed her eyes.

"Gee thanks, Miss Sunshine. Now I'll look as haunted as you. So you want to tell me what's up?" Elle crossed her arms. "I'm not buying you lunch until you tell me."

"I'm not hungry," MiMi retorted, eyes still closed.

"Crap, but I am. Now I have to come up with another way to twist your arm." Elle pretended to pout.

"I've got one. Threaten to force me on a work retreat alone with Kerry and Tyler."

Elle gave a grunt. "Nah, I'm not that cruel. C'mon, just tell me."

"I'm stressed about life. My sister and parents are acting... like they do. I have bills to pay. The usual." MiMi sat up straight. She wasn't about to pull Elle into the world of FBI investigations, Dominican underworld figures and murder.

"I know what it is," Elle said, her tone serious. "Roderick's death must be hitting you hard. When is the funeral?"

"Saturday, but I'm not going. I'll just send flowers and a card to his parents." MiMi didn't want to see the handsome man she knew lying in a coffin.

"Let me know if there's anything I can do. Grieving can sneak up on you, even though he was a lying, narcissistic over-sexed cheater. Forgive me for speaking ill of the dead," Elle whispered with a look toward the ceiling.

"Girl, the Lord knows you aren't sorry."

"Yeah, you're right. Forgive me for not being sorry,

Lord," Elle joked. "Sure you're okay?"

"If you ask me that one more time..." MiMi squinted at her.

"Last time, promise. So like I told you, something is up. Yesterday two grim looking guys in suits showed up. They were in Kerry's office for almost two hours. I can't find out who they are though..." Elle gave a grunt of irritation.

"I thought you had Chuck and Drew so whipped they'd do anything for you," MiMi replied, referring to the building security guards.

Elle frowned. "They wouldn't talk."

"So ask Lana," MiMi said, referring to the receptionist on their floor.

"She called in sick yesterday. Tyler got the call from downstairs. You know he won't tell me."

"Then for once you'll have to settle for finding out the facts along with the rest of us," MiMi said. She tapped out a reply to one of the reps at a clothing manufacturer.

"Devon, from the warehouse, happened to be here for a meeting. He swears they were cops. Why would the police be here? Nah, I think his past scrapes with the law has him paranoid." Elle picked up a mint from a bowl on the edge of MiMi's desk. "Let's get barbecue. I'm starving."

"What was that?" MiMi lost interest in the still long list of unread emails, some flagged as important.

"There's a new deli on Fourth Street. Trina in marketing says the food is awesome," Elle said around the candy in her mouth.

"No cops, you said the two guys that came were cops," MiMi pressed.

"I said Devon thinks they were cops. You know he's

twitchy about the police since he got busted twice for speeding." Elle gave a chuckle.

"Was one guy tall with red hair, the other one short and compact?"

"Yeah, he was kinda cute for a short guy. The tall one works out, I can tell. Tried to see if they were wearing wedding rings and..." Elle blinked back from her wandering train thought when Kerry stomped in.

"MiMi, we need to meet right now." Kerry left without waiting to see if MiMi would follow.

"What the hell?" Elle whispered.

MiMi shrugged and forced a smile. "Probably has another bee up her butt about one of my projects. She's got nothing better to do than to pick on us lowly worker bees."

Elle wore a worried frown. "Watch your back. I got a bad feeling."

"You and your bad feelings."

MiMi tried to laugh, but it came out like a hoarse cough because of the tension grabbing her by the throat. Elle shoved a mint into MiMi's pocket. With a sigh of resignation that Elle's intuition was on target, MiMi went to Kerry's office. Once there her heart beat even harder when she saw a tall man in a dark gray suit. Tyler stood to one side of Kerry's desk. His thin lips twitched briefly into a smirk before it disappeared again.

"This is Glenn Stuart from our corporate office, VP of the Logistics and Operations division. He's representing corporate executive management," Kerry said, aiming the words like darts at MiMi. Her expression radiated hostility and satisfaction at the same time. "He also happens to be a lawyer."

"Nice to meet you. Please, have a seat. Why don't

we have coffee?"

"Here's a carafe on the table with cups, sugar and cream." Tyler waved at hand at the round meeting table set in a corner of Kerry's spacious office.

"Thanks,Tyler. That will be all," Glenn said. He inclined his head slightly to signal dismissal.

"I, uh..." Tyler looked to Kerry for a sign.

"Follow-up on those calls we talked about. Also set up the conference room for the ad layout meeting at three today." Kerry cleared her throat.

"Right. Of course." Tyler grimaced as if walking out of the office hurt.

MiMi would have enjoyed his obvious disappointment at being shown the door any other time. But his departure was a more ominous signal. Taking a page from Jazz's bold playbook, MiMi decided to make the first move.

"So, Mr. Stuart, what brings you all the way from corporate in Dallas?" MiMi looked at him without paying attention to Kerry.

Rather than answer, he went to the table and poured coffee into a cup. "Call me Glenn. What would youlike added?"

"Cream, two packets of sweetener. The pink stuff," MiMi said with a smile. She relished the soft hiss of annoyance from Kerry.

Apparently Stuart noticed as well. "Most meetings go better with coffee, don't you agree?"

Kerry's face tinged pink as she gave a brittle smile. "Yes, of course. None for me thanks. I've been running on the stuff all morning. One more cup and I'll be a jittery mess."

"We wouldn't want that for sure," Glenn said mildly.

MiMi glanced from him to Kerry. His tone carried a hint of warning, maybe even reprimand. Kerry's nostrils flared and she cleared her throat. The reaction seemed to confirm Kerry had made some kind of misstep. Kerry glared at MiMi as if she were to blame.

"We have a serious issue to discuss with you."

"About my work?" MiMi raised an eyebrow at her boss.

"Not directly, I had the unpleasant experience of being visited by the police. Someone you know was murdered, and you're involved," Kerry snapped.

"What Kerry means is, we need to know if Fashion Sense or Zen Corporation has any exposure to negative publicity," Glen put in. He came over, handed MiMi a cup.

"I'm not a suspect." MiMi answered Glenn, but she scowled at Kerry. She put the cup on Kerry's desk. "So there is no danger to the company image."

"You left out a few minor details about your trip to the Dominican Republic, like being jailed on drug charges. This company could be dragged through the mud with you if the media gets wind of it. That's why you're going to be placed on an indefinite leave of absence, with pay for the first two weeks." Kerry glanced at Glenn.

"Let me repeat, I'm not a suspect, and nothing has been in the news. I was found not guilty of the charges in the Dominican Republic. My work has been outstanding. I also haven't violated any company policy, and I have a contract," MiMI shot back with heat.

"We can't let employees with complicated personal lives damage Fashion Sense." Kerry stood and crossed her arms.

"Really? Then we'll have to shut the place down,

because that describes about sixty percent of the office. Including you." MiMi pointed at her.

"Don't change the subject," Kerry shouted and slapped a hand on her desk.

Stuart put his cup down with a thump. "Enough. Outbursts and trading accusations are extremely unhelpful."

Kerry stood fuming. She seemed ready to burst from the effort of not speaking. After about ten seconds she sat down again. Stuart gave her a clear look that said, "Pull yourself together." Then he faced MiMi.

"We have no intention of terminating you," Glenn said. The word "yet" hung in the air unspoken. "You'll be paid for a month. By then I'm sure you can can resolve any issues."

"But we..." Kerry squeaked but clamped her lips together at a sharp glance from Stuart.

His affable expression had vanished. He'd turned into a bottom line executive. He let his gaze rest on MiMi for a few seconds. "You're correct. You haven't violated company policy or committed any kind of criminal offense against Zen or its subsidiaries. You do have a contract, which includes a clause about causing damage to Zen in any way. Legally that can be considered pretty broadly."

"My attorney might see it differently." MiMi tried to sound tough, but her stomach twisted.

Glenn let out a sigh. "Look, MiMi. You love your job, am I right? You've worked hard to make Fashion Sense a retail powerhouse."

"I love working with the rest of the team." MiMi gave Kerry a side-eye.

"And believe me the executive office appreciates your dedication, and your *results*. Time will help you and us. Protecting the company is in everyone's best interest. Agreed?" Glenn took a step closer to where MiMi stood. He blocked her view of Kerry. "In the end we both have the same goals."

"Yes, of course," MiMi murmured.

Thirty minutes later she drove out of the parking garage, a box of items from her desk on the seat next to her. The one concession she'd wrung from Glenn was working a few hours from home to wrap up three major projects. MiMi concentrated on getting through the next few days without sobbing in front of Sage.

Chapter 12

Adrienne called MiMi that night. Emotionally drained, MiMi found herself crying into the phone within seconds. MiMi agreed to have lunch at Adrienne's house once she finally gained control. So the next day MiMi was seated in what Adrienne called her garden room. Rattan furniture upholstered in fabrics with vines and small flowers filled most of the space. Two hanging baskets held vibrant green trailing plants. A round cast iron table with four chairs sat in one corner. The room stretched the length of the house, large enough to host a party of up to twenty people. Waist high windows gave a view of Adrienne's professionally designed garden. Adrienne hosted teas and brunches frequently in the garden room. Though she couldn't be bothered with housework, Adrienne loved puttering among her prized pink, white and red roses. Her lawn service did the dirty work like fertilizing, planting and heavy duty weeding.

Adrienne handed her a glass of sweet tea in a lovely tall glass with a straw once MiMi settled into a chair. "Thanks for making time in your schedule. Isn't this the day you have lunch with your business women's group?"

Adrienne waved a hand. "I can miss one. They've become kind of boring to be honest. I'll run for president next year. When I take over we'll have a more dynamic strategic plan."

"You'll be president next year, huh?" MiMi smiled. Competitive, Adrienne expected to get anything she went after. She usually did, too.

"I know what you're thinking. Yes, there's a small detail called an election. But trust me, the members are ready for a change."

"You've started campaigning already." MiMi breathed in the lovely scent of flowers in a crystal vase on the table nearby.

"Informally since it's still early." Adrienne sighed as she relaxed on the small stuffed loveseat. She gazed through the sparkling clean glass.

"Okay. Good luck."

MiMi pursed her lips to keep from saying more. She knew Adrienne too well. Her informal campaign most likely had been in motion for months. First she'd plant seeds of doubt about the current president's leadership. Then a few carefully dropped hints would take root questioning their competency. Luck would have little to do with Adrienne's victory.

"So, you could have brought Sage. She loves running around this big old house," Adrienne said.

"I want her to get back into her routine at daycare. Besides, Sage loves Caring Hands. She's developing social skills with her little group of friends," MiMi replied. She put down her glass. "At least she's doing good."

"You've had a pretty tough few months. First that mess in the Dominican Republic and then Roddy's death. One minute you guys were just old class mates. The next minute you were close to marching down the aisle."

"He was the worse guy I've ever met." MiMi suddenly felt a rush of emotion at the memory of the good times she'd shared with Roderick. She blinked as tears formed.

"Roddy had faults. The important thing is he wanted to marry *you*. What matters is who holds the keys to treasury. As long as he pays, Chris can play. I don't have to sit at home all alone either," Adrienne said with a chuckle.

MiMi glanced at her in surprise. "I don't get what you mean."

Adrienne crossed her toned brown legs. Dressed in casually white French terry shorts and a pink t-shirt, she looked every inch the prosperous work-at-home wife and mother. Pink thong sandals completed the outfit.

"Yes you do. Roderick would have given you a mighty fine life and we both know it." She raised her glass as if to punctuate her point with a toast. Then she sipped more tea.

"He was more than a big bank account, Adrienne. I *cared* for him," MiMi protested even guilt pricked at her.

"Of course you did. We all saw the way you two looked at each other." Adrienne sat forward and placed a hand on MiMi's knee. "You can talk to me. I know I can be a bit strong-willed and blunt. But family comes first."

"Thanks." MiMi felt odd at Adrienne's uncharacteristic shift into a warm family moment.

"Seriously, MiMi. I get the feeling a lot more is going on. It's not like you to go all to pieces like you did on the phone last night. Mother and daddy don't show affection exactly."

"That's a mild way of putting it," MiMi retorted.

"Which makes it even more important that we kids stick together. They push Drex way too hard. They don't support you as much as they should. And at times I feel smothered, like I can't breathe." Adrienne pulled back from MiMi and rubbed her forehead.

"Really?" MiMi stared at her amazed.

"Yes, I know you think I'm the favorite. Well let me tell you, there's a big downside to that. Mother hovers around me trying to take over my son. Daddy keeps trying to push Chris to work for him. Thank God we had sense enough not to get sucked into the family business. They'd be controlling every inch of our lives." Adrienne bit her lower lip for a few seconds. "I feel so alone sometimes."

"Wow, Adrienne. I never realized." MiMi felt more guilt about some of the bad things she'd said about her.

"It's my fault we're not closer, but I want that to change." Adrienne gazed at MiMi and reached out to her.

"Thank you again for taking care of Sage. The way you took care of her was... so sweet." MiMi felt tears form as she grasped Adrienne's soft, expertly manicured hand.

"I'm so sorry for all the stupid fights we've had. Half the time over nothing when you think about it" Adrienne swallowed hard and squeezed MiMi's hand.

"Yeah, you're right. Family should always come first." MiMi swiped at a tear that had escaped down her cheek.

"The children brought us together, made us realize we should always be there for each other." Adrienne sniffed as she smiled at MiMi.

MiMi soon found herself pouring out everything to Adrienne. She told Adrienne about the events leading up to her arrest in the Dominican Republic. MiMi described her Najayo Prison stay, and the shock of a visit from the FBI. Then she told the story of Jack, his betrayal and how his other "other" woman landed on her doorstep days ago.

"Oh girl. What a seriously messed pile of crap," Adrienne breathed, eyes wide with shock.

"Yeah." MiMi sniffed and dabbed her eyes with the fancy paper napkin Adrienne handed her. "Not to mention the police questioned me about Roddy's murder."

Adrienne pressed a hand to her chest. "Are you kidding me? Daddy must have exploded when you told him. I'll bet he had a hot conference call with police chief. Those detectives are probably still trying to screw their asses back on."

"Don't mention anything I told you to Mother or Daddy, Adrienne. You know how they are. Please."

"But Daddy knows everyone important in south Louisiana. And he could get one of the best lawyers in the country to make them back off fast," Adrienne said.

"Like you said, their help comes with a big price tag. They'd want to control my life and tell me how to raise Sage. No, promise you won't tell them anything we talked about." MiMi shivered as she looked at her sister. Maybe she'd been foolish to let her guard down.

Adrienne gazed back at her for a few seconds. "If you say so. At least let me do something. I know people."

"Willa helped me hire a really good attorney. She and Jazz have been great." MiMi saw the flash of disapproval and even distaste on her sister's face. "You should get to know them, Adrienne. They're wonderful friends, really."

After a few seconds Adrienne smiled. "Of course they are. Now how about we have a slice of lemon ice box pie and coffee?"

MiMi let out a soft laugh. "If you took the trouble to make it, I can't refuse."

"Oh, no. It's from that nouveau soul food place downtown. I'll only go homemaker just so far, even to lift little sister's spirits." Adrienne let out her signature musical laugh.

Her sister continued to be witty and attentive. MiMi's troubles hadn't gone away, but she felt close to her sister for the first time in years.

****

MiMi met with her attorney on a sunny Friday morning. Yet instead of a happy TGIF mood, everyone looked grim. Willa and Cedric used their investigative resources to get facts on Nairoby Villa and Roderick, so they met in the conference room at Crown Protection. The lawyer wore an apologetic frown. He clearly didn't like being the bearer of bad news.

"So this woman, what's her name..." Willa glanced at MiMi.

"Nairoby Villa."

"Yeah, she's not part of a Dominican gang after all. So maybe Jack didn't launder dirty money." Willa lifted both hands palms up. "What am I missing? That's a silver lining to one big old cloud."

"Nah, too early to tell. What we found out could just touch the surface," Cedric said. He glanced at

Edselle.

"Her partners left a message. I called their international toll free number. One thing is obvious, Ms. Villa isn't a senior partner, if she's a partner at all. They talk more like she's an employee. She may have exaggerated her importance to intimidate you. Whatever she is, I got the feeling they're not pleased with her." Edselle opened the button of his expensive suit jacket.

"Hmm, so MiMi's bluff turned out to be on target," Willa said.

"I smelled the anxiety beneath her slick talk," MiMi replied in a cool tone.

"Now you're a player?" Willa pursed her lips.

"Humph. Recognize." MiMi waved a hand.

Cedric covered a laugh by pretending to cough. He stopped when MiMi squinted at him. "Sorry. So Edselle, what are MiMI's legal options."

"Okay, let's examine the pros first. Mr. Reyes, their spokesperson, says they're a legitimate business consortium. They have a large clothing manufacturing plant in the DR, export jewelry, and craft items made in the DR and Haiti. They also have other businesses, but they didn't go into detail," Edselle said.

Willa nodded. "Okay, then it's quite possible that Ms. Villa was telling the truth. She and Jack could have had a deal to sell clothing in the states."

"Humph." MiMi crossed her arms.

"Yes, and he was romancing the woman. Get over it. I did when I was married to him," Willa wisecracked. She turned her attention back to the lawyer. "So you can make a case to the FBI that any money Jack made with them was perfectly legal. Which stops their whole seizure of assets process."

"Or at least weakens their case enough to make U.S. Attorney's office drop it." Edselle nodded.

"Which means the FBI backs off and MiMi keeps the house," Cedric added.

"And we can finally wrap up Jack's succession, praise the heavens." Willa clapped her hands together.

"Hold on, let's look at the cons. This consortium can present evidence that Ms. Villa didn't have the authority to enter into business agreements." Edselle glanced at each of them in turn.

"Which means any money she loaned Jack was without their approval," MiMi said and heaved a sigh.

"And they could make a claim to profits and demand a settlement. They've hired a local attorney to explore their options. I should hear from him any day now." Edselle sat back as if allowing them to digest his summary.

"One alternative is to settle with them to avoid drawn out legal wrangling," MiMi said. "I'll have to sell the house and empty my pitiful savings account."

"Sixty thousand dollars isn't that 'pitiful'. The house is worth maybe two hundred fifty thousand." Willa looked thoughtful.

"I could be out of a job soon. Then I'll need money to live on."

"Her house is worth more. Real estate values have gone up in that part of town. MiMi's neighborhood is smack in the middle of gentrification in Mid City," Cedric said.

"So maybe she can negotiate with them and keep her savings. Even better," Willa replied.

"Wait a minute. Before we break out the champagne, remember Sage will lose the only home she's ever known. And I happen to love my house."

MiMi's voice broke. Then she breathed in and out to steady herself. "Do we know for sure this consortium's businesses are all legal?"

Edselle rubbed his top lip and frowned before speaking. "Hard to say, but I would guess there's probably something shady. Without contacts in the DR we'd have one hell of a time tracking it down. Still they're most likely bluffing. They probably hope you're more scared of the authorities than they are. They're out of the US and harder to reach. But not impossible."

"We could hire a private detective." MiMi looked at Cedric and then Willa. "Track down exactly who they are for leverage."

"And prove they're crooks, which means the FBI swoops in again because we've done their jobs for them," Willa reminded her.

"What if I offered to cooperate? I might be able to make a deal with them. I got the feeling they used taking my house as pressure to make me talk." MiMi sat straight, liking her own logic the more she talked.

"I wouldn't advise, not yet. The feds have a high hurdle to jump. First they have to follow the money trail, and that's tough to do. Then they have to prove the source of the money was illegal." Edselle's grave expression brightened as he laid out his own train of thought.

"They could get desperate enough to come after you if they feel threatened," Cedric said.

"Besides, you don't have a whole lot to offer them. You don't know anything about these folks," Willa said to MiMi.

"I could find out more. I'll probably be positioned to pluck out some useful information once we decide to negotiate." MiMi nodded.

Willa turned to Cedric "Is she talking about some kind of undercover sting? I must not have heard that right."

"MiMi, playing a game when none of us knows the rules is way too dangerous," Cedric said.

"I don't mean flying to the DR and pretending to be their new best friend. Give me some credit. I meant open a dialog maybe with Nairoby. She seems to actually like Jazz, and..."

"No," Willa cut in and waved a forefinger at the end of MiMi's nose. "You and Jazz will stir up twice the trouble getting into some kind of crazy scheme."

"Well I have to do *something*. I feel like I'm being watched all the time. I can't just sit at home with the axe of doom swinging over my head. I'm not sure I can keep my house or my job." MiMi's voice trembled. She stood up and paced.

"Calm down, we're going to figure a way out. Right?" Willa glanced at the two men for support.

"Have you seen a car parked on your street that doesn't belong to a neighbor, or seen the odd jogger lately? I mean somebody you don't know," Cedric said.

"Or outside the building where you work?" Edselle added.

"Or a car following yours when you go out?" Cedric frowned and rubbed his jaw.

"Hey, you guys are supposed to be *helping* me reassure MiMi," Willa protested.

"The FBI, the Baton Rouge PD, and now these Dominicans," Edselle replied. His expression had gone back to somber. "Look at the facts. MiMi was arrested, there are two murders and the FBI are in the mix. I'd be surprised if she's *not* being followed."

"How long have you had that feeling?" Cedric

asked.

"For at least a week. My street is quiet with barely any traffic most days. But in the past week or so more cars drive by my house. My neighbor Brenda even mentioned it to me. Then I got a series of phone calls. Some were wrong numbers. I'd swear it was the same person trying to sound different. Or it could be a woman with a throaty voice."

Willa sighed. "I think it's nerves. Most surveillance is electronic. Baton Rouge has street cameras even."

"Well, I feel a whole lot better now. Thanks," MiMi retorted. She rubbed the tight muscles in her neck. The memory of Roderick massaging her slowly until her whole body relaxed popped into her head. "Poor Roderick. Being a jerk isn't grounds for the death penalty."

"At least one person obviously disagrees with you," Willa replied. "There was anger behind his murder."

"Money can cause that kind of anger, particularly large sums," Edselle said.

"Greed and sex, are the most common motivations for murder. Two sets of cops think I may have both." MiMi tried not to start bawling again.

"There is a bright side," Willa said gently and sat next to MiMi. "Edselle is of the expert opinion that you're in a good negotiating position with the Dominicans."

"Well, we've got a lot more going for us than it looks like on the surface. We could push back against their claim." Edselle looked at MiMi, a question in his dark eyes.

"My gut says they don't want a quick and quiet solution despite all the big talk, but it's your decision," Cedric said.

MiMi had an image of packing Sage's toys for a move from their house. Anger replaced the pity party she had slipped into moments before. "Do it."

"Think carefully. Are you sure?" Edselle said, becoming the cautious attorney. "There's a chance they'll press forward with their claim. Cedric is right about them being an unknown quantity."

"Nairoby Villa doesn't impress me as someone who plays by rules. I'm willing to bet her business associates don't think our laws are a big deal either. Let's push back. Hard." MiMi grimaced as though she could see her adversaries.

Edselle's milk chocolate face eased into a smile. "I agree, but I wanted you to consider all of the possibilities. As for the FBI, they've played all the cards they have for now. It could take months, longer, for them to bring a case to confiscate your home. By then we'll be ready for them."

"That just leaves the investigation into Roderick's murder," Willa said. She lifted both hands when they looked at her. "Hey, somebody needed to say what we were all thinking."

"Yeah, we have to find Roderick's killer. Who's with me?" MiMi stood up and put both hands on her hips. Dead silence followed instead of a chorus of assent.

Willa stood and faced her. "Hell. No."

"We need to make the police look at all of the evidence. They're stuck on me." MiMi slapped her chest. She looked at Cedric for support, but found disappointment instead.

Cedric crossed his arms. "Crown Protection resources will stick to on-site security and civil matters. No amateur homicide investigations."

"We'll give Edselle any background information we

can dig using electronic searches. But no private eye stuff. We're talking two murders and maybe a dangerous gang." Willa said with force.

MiMi blinked as if the last three words had slapped her on the forehead. "Yeah, you're right."

"Now you're talking sense," Willa replied. The tension drained from her expression.

"We could track down who else had a motive," MiMi replied quickly. "I mean, dang, we've got a lot of suspects."

"She's right," Edselle cut in just as Willa scowled and opened her mouth. "I'm not saying I expect them arrest and charge MiMi, but it could happen. Her defense attorney will need alternate theories of the crime. More suspects equal reasonable doubt."

"Hey, what do you mean my defense attorney? You're my lawyer." MiMi blinked at him.

"I'm busy on two fronts with the FBI and the Dominican business consortium. Besides, you'll need an attorney with extensive criminal trial experience. I specialize in civil litigation and white collar crime."

"Murder defense is a different game," Willa added.

"But don't worry. I know at least five top criminal defense lawyers." Edselle smiled at her.

"Oh good," MiMi said with much less enthusiasm.

Chapter 13

The next morning MiMi dropped Sage off at daycare. She gave the cheerful toddler an equally bright goodbye. MiMi drove away at least satisfied that so far Sage hadn't been affected. She'd managed to keep to Sage's routine. Her paychecks continued thanks to the high stock she still had with Darcas. She didn't have to dip into savings for the moment. But who knew how long Darca could keep Kerry on a leash?

When MiMi pulled up to a red light, she glanced into the rear view mirror at herself. "Okay. Here's the plan, girl. Keep doing a damn good job and let the dollars speak for you."

With her determination to hang tough firmly back in place, MiMi set out for her next stop. She pulled into the busy parking lot of Costco. The huge plain building reminded her of exactly what it was, a warehouse. Inside was a lot more welcoming though. A sleek white Acura sedan drove behind her SUV. At first MiMi didn't find it odd. Other cars circled as shoppers looked for empty spaces or waited for cars to pull out. MiMi grabbed her leather hobo bag. Then she noticed the car didn't move. She waved toward the store.

"I just got here," MiMi called to the driver. When there was no response, she shrugged and started to leave.

"Yeah, I know," a voice called back. "You stopped at the drive through window of the Smoothie Palace, dropped off your kid and headed here."

MiMi squinted at the stranger through her sunglasses, her heart thumping. Here was proof she wasn't being paranoid. "Who are you?"

The woman's thick natural hair was swept back into a neat bundle of curls. Her full mouth curved up. Dark wine lipstick set against her nut brown skin accentuated the sensual look. She was dressed in navy blue pins stripped suit. The heels of her dark red pumps clicked on the pavement as she took a few steps closer.

"Who do you think, sweetie?"

MiMi started to give a tart reply about wasting her time, but stopped. She and the woman removed their sunglasses in sync. They gazed at each other in silence. It took a few seconds, but then MiMi hissed. "You."

"So you didn't recognize me. Yvette Theirry. Nice to finally meet you." Yvette's smile lacked any trace if friendliness.

"It took a minute. Now if you'd been naked, bent over and grunting like a pig in heat... well, that would have helped a lot." MiMi put her sunglasses back on.

Yvette's smiled slipped a notch. "Hope you enjoyed the visual of me giving your fiancé what you couldn't."

"You mean an STD?" MiMi shot back.

"Listen, you little pie-faced bitch. You might have been the society princess he was going to wed. But I'm the freak he just loved to bed. Every chance he got. He'd leave you and call me. You didn't have what it took," Yvette spat.

"What I had was a marriage proposal. Roderick wasn't going to take you home to meet his folks. His parents are allergic to trash."

"I could pound your silly ass into this pavement right here, right now," Yvette growled.

MiMi dropped her purse on the ground and spread her arms out. "I just wish you would, heffa."

The woman huffed like an enraged lioness for a few seconds, but she didn't make a move. Finally she took a step back. "I have bets placed on how long it takes the police to arrest you for Rod's murder. Jealous society princess goes after him when she finds out he was in love with another woman. Thank goodness for anonymous tips." She smiled at MiMi's reaction.

"You evil rotten..." MiMi stammered as she searched for a foul enough insult to hurl.

Yvette cackled. "Good luck with the investigation, honey. I'll help all I can. Help the DA get evidence to convict *you* that is."

"You're insane!" MiMi shouted. "But for the record, Roderick wasn't in love with you. He begged me to forgive him. He said, and this is a direct quote, 'She was a big mistake and it didn't mean anything to me'."

"You're a liar," Yvette hurled at her.

"Face it, sweetie. You were barely a bump in the road on his way to *me*." MiMi gave a sharp, nasty laugh.

"I'll be watching when the police put the cuffs on you," Yvette screeched.

"By the way thanks for helping me. I know your name. Roderick told me you're an attorney, too. Did work for the Chamber of Commerce. Quite the career, he said. I can tell the police all about you." MiMi placed a finger under her chin and struck a pose. "Hmm, let's see. Enraged side piece learns her lover plans to dump her and marry another woman. I believe you lawyers call that *reasonable doubt.*"

"Bitch, bitch, bitch!" Yvette pounded the hood of her BMW. She spun around and stomped to the passenger door. Only then did she notice a group of onlookers. "What the fuck are you assholes looking at? Mind your own damn business."

"Have a good one," MiMi shouted over the roar of the Acura's engine.

Yvette drove off much too fast and barely missed another car. She laid on the horn and gave the other drive the finger. Seconds later she peeled off. The horn sounded three more times before MiMi guessed she exited the car lot. Only then did MiMi give in to fear. She leaned against the SUV as her legs went weak.

"Are you okay, ma'am?" A lanky redheaded teenager said. An older woman peered over his shoulder. "Mom called security in the store."

His mother mustered enough courage to step around her son. "They should be here any minute. I got her license plate just in case. You should get a protective order, sugar. Over a man, right?" The woman had dark auburn hair and freckles.

"Mom, seriously?" Her son wore an embarrassed frown.

"My second ex-husband put me through it. His mistress called me at work. Take my advice and get rid of the bum." The woman gave a sharp nod.

"Already taken care of," MiMi muttered. She squinted in the direction Yvette had gone.

****

Three and half hours later Jazz showed up at

MiMi's house for lunch. Their get together was decidedly more urban casual in fact than lunch with Adrienne. They sat on MiMi's patio. The April heat promised the typical south Louisiana summer to come. A breeze stirred making the late spring day pleasant. Still they also sat outside so Jazz could smoke her usual cigarillos.

"You need to give up those things." MiMi stared at her uneaten chicken salad sandwich from Jason's Deli. She loved their gourmet version of the dish, but her appetite was off.

"You could use one after facing Satan's second cousin this morning," Jazz retorted. She shook her head as she tapped the end of the cigarillo on the ash tray. "Damn, the crazy is *real*. She's actually going after you. I mean shit; the man is stone cold dead."

"Please, be a little more sensitive. He was my fiancé after all," MiMi murmured. She chewed on her fingernail. "Thanks for adding me to your Costco membership card. I'll need to stock up on staples when I lose my job."

"Stop thinking the worse is about to happen." Jazz waved a hand.

MiMi laughed so hard she bent double for a few seconds. Seconds later she gasped for air until she could talk. "The FBI, the local cops, a Dominican cartel and a crazy woman. I'm already up to my neck in the worse that could happen."

Jazz gaped at her for several seconds before she burst out laughing. "You're right. Anything else got to be a big improvement. You just stole my damn record for being in deep shit." She howled.

"Stop it," MiMi rasped between giggles. "I'm going to pee in my pants."

"Wait, wait. I got something worse. Your mama and daddy move in with you." Jazz pointed at MiMi and snapped her fingers.

MiMi let out a squeak of horror. Wiped her eyes and took a gulp of her lemonade. "If I lose everything, I could have to move in with them."

Jazz put out her cigarillo. "Nope, you don't. My business is going good. I bought a small complex of condos as an investment. Got a good deal on it before gentrification sent prices way up. The renovation is about finished."

"You're kidding."

"If you don't mind living in a house bought with the profits from almost naked pole dancers, it's all yours." Jazz's pretty cinnamon brown eyes sparkled.

MiMi sat still and quiet for a few minutes, tears sliding down her face. Then she was sobbing into both hands. Jazz put one arm around her shoulder and kept handing her paper napkins. MiMi tried to gain control, but it was no use. So she rode the wave of her crying jag. After a minute or so, she hiccupped to a halt. Blinking hard, she blew into the wad of soggy napkins.

"Here, dump that mess in here." Jazz stood next to her holding the kitchen trash can.

"Thanks." MiMi tossed them in, then went into the half bath on the first floor. She returned to the patio after freshening up.

"Feel better?" Jazz lit another cigarillo.

"Yes."

"Good for you. Now my damn nerves are shot. Dealing with hysterical folks ain't in my vocabulary." Jazz puffed and aimed a stream of smoke over her head.

"Yeah, yeah, you're trying to play so cool. But you put it on the line for people you care about. Willa is the same; Mama Ruby, Mr. Elton, your brothers. Even Cedric and Kay are so good to me." MiMi's lip trembled.

Hey, don't start again. Sheesh."

MiMi sniffed. "What you offered means a lot to me. I tried to hang tough for the past few weeks. It seems like the entire universe is out to get me in one way or another."

"I know that feeling." Jazz sat forward. "Look, just how crazy is this whatever-her-name-is bitch?"

"Yvette Theirry, and I'll bet crazy is her middle name. She had this wild look in her eyes. I think she was obsessed with Roderick, almost like she *owned* him." MiMi shook her head as she remembered their encounter.

"Hmm, crazy enough to kill him sounds like. We need to keep eyes on her. A psycho like that could do something nuts like set your house on fire, with you in it." Jazz stabbed out her cigarillo. She took out her cell phone and texted.

"Yeah, well I lost my temper and made things worse." MiMi let her head fall back.

"How?" Jazz continued to text.

"I called her a side piece, Roddy's freak for a temporary thrill. But his real life would be with me." MiMi heaved a deep sigh and reached for the glass of lemonade.

"Truth?"

"Yes, as a matter of fact. Roderick would have married me. A lot of society wives look the other way to keep their fancy lifestyles."

"I'm shocked," Jazz drawled, still texting persons unknown for the moment.

MiMi sat forward. "I couldn't play by those rules. You know my sister basically told me that's how her marriage is? The perfect upper-class family in the big house is just a front. Chris has a lover. She all but admitted she has one, too."

"Gasp. You've shaken my faith in humanity."

"I'm serious, Jazz. I always thought Adrienne would gut Chris if she found out he had a mistress. But she shrugged it off." MiMi relaxed back in her chair and sipped more lemonade.

"Fascinating," Jazz mumbled without looking up from her phone.

"Guess they've grown jaded, love turned to bitterness. Like Mother and Daddy." MiMi gasped, eyes wide. "You don't think my parents have lovers? No, I don't even want to think about it."

"Then don't, but they probably have gotten their freak on at some point," Jazz tossed back casually still reading the screen.

"Oh geez, thanks for putting that picture in my brain," MiMi blurted out.

"Okay, look, Willa and Cedric are going to get information on Yvette the Weird. If she makes a move to head this way, my guys will deal with her." Jazz tapped a message and then put the cell phone on the table.

"You're going to have them shoot her or something!" MiMi grabbed Jazz's arm.

Jazz shook free and picked up her glass of cola. "Stop being a soap opera drama queen. You think I go around ordering hits on people? Don't answer."

"Well, you have been known to hang out with gangsters. Guys with gold chains, no jobs and lots of cash," MiMi said.

She rolled her eyes at MiMi. "Marlon, D-Day and Zedonté work security for me at the club and my rental property."

"D-Day?"

"He knows how to launch an all-out attack when needed, but he's reformed. Mostly." Jazz shrugged. "The point is they're not gang members."

"You mean they're not gang members *now*," MiMi added.

"Exactly the kind of security I need. Reverend Fisher ran them through the program at his church. They're good guys. All they want is to live normal and not have to watch their backs twenty-four seven. Street life is no fun, take it from me." Jazz stared down MiMi's attempt at passing judgment.

MiMi raised both palms out. "I'll take your word for it. You're like the Mother Teresa of former gangstas."

Jazz let out a howl of outrage along with a string of cuss words. The musical chimes sounded, a signal someone was at the front door. MiMi laughed all the way through the house to answer. She peeped outside to see a short brown woman. A tall uniformed policewoman was beside her. Not good news from the stone-faced expression they wore. She swung open the door.

"Can I help you?"

"Good afternoon. I'm Mrs. Ola Young with the Louisiana Department of Children and Families. Ms. MiMi Landry?" The woman gazed at MiMi.

"Yes." MiMi glanced from her to the police officer.

The woman flashed a plastic card with a bad picture on it. "Here is my identification. And my card. May we come in?"

MiMi stared at the identification. Then she took the card. "Wait a minute. You're with the agency that licenses day care centers. Is Sage alright?"

"Nothing happened at the day care center, and your daughter is safe. May we come in?" Mrs. Young's tone sounded less like a question than an order.

"Okay, but I expect answers and fast."

MiMi swung the heavy door wide. She examined the two women as they walked by her. Once she pushed the door closed, MiMi led them deeper inside the house. The policewoman's gaze seemed to take in the foyer and living room with professional efficiency. Most likely the officer would have been able to describe every significant detail she noticed.

"What is this concerning since my daughter isn't involved?" MiMi glanced from the policewoman to the social worker.

"I said your daughter is safe, but this is about a report we received about her care." Mrs. Young faced MiMi.

"I've never had a complaint about her day care center or noticed anything wrong. I checked them out before she enrolled." MiMI frowned at them.

"The report was about how you care for your daughter, Ms. Landry. Maybe we should sit down. I can-_"

"Wait a minute," MiMi cut her off. She noticed the policewoman position herself in a defensive position. "What about how I care for Sage?"

Mrs. Young seemed unfazed by her reaction. "We have a report that you've been neglecting her medical care and she's showing signs of emotional abuse. Apparently you've been involved in alleged illegal drug activity, a murder investigation and left the child alone while out with... several male friends."

MiMi tried to talk but couldn't for a few seconds.

The word abuse had slammed into her chest and she felt breathless. "Lies, those are all lies."

"One of the daycare attendants reports that Sage has been crying a lot and seems to startle easily. She also has a bruise on her left thigh," Mrs. Young said.

"She's still unsteady on her little feet, like most toddlers. Sage tried to climb down from her booster seat and hit her leg. She didn't even cry when it happened. I can't believe this." MiMi pressed a hand to her forehead. "You can't take my baby."

"Ms. Landry, we're only investigating at this point. Tell me about the accident that caused the injury," Mrs. Young said.

"There is no *injury*. I know every inch of my child's body, and she has a bruise that's almost gone. And I haven't been charged, let alone convicted of a crime. I don't see how you can come into my house accusing me of not taking care of my baby." MiMi's voice rose with each word.

"What the hell is goin' on up in here?" Jazz said. She stopped short when the policewoman walked in front of her.

"I'm Officer Wells, ma'am. Mrs. Young is trying to get the facts for her report. I'm sure this will be cleared up soon. If you'll just give us a minute."

"No, I want a witness," MiMi said firmly. "Jazz don't leave."

"Staying put," Jazz said with attitude. She returned the policewoman's gaze. They looked at each other as if agreeing neither would move.

MiMi spun around to face Mrs. Young again. "Tell me who called in this fake report."

"We don't reveal the source of a complaint, Ms. Landry. Listen, no one says youphysically harmed your child on purpose. If I can get exactly what happened, in particular about three weeks ago when you left your child alone---"

"I've never left Sage alone, and whoever says I did is lying," MiMi shouted. Her voice broke. Tears threatened, but for a very different reason than moments before.

Mrs. Young consulted a small note pad she took from her pocket. "You were with a man on a date on April tenth, according to the report."

"Sage was with my sister. You can confirm with her. This is ridiculous." MiMi's mood took a sharp right turn from fear to anger.

"So your sister kept the child while you spent the night with this gentleman. The bruise is from an accident when you weren't looking at the baby perched on the chair." Mrs. Young took notes, a slight frown of concentration on her face.

"You're making me sound like a neglectful slut who'd rather have sex than take care of my daughter. I thought you people were supposed to be objective. I want to know who fed you this garbage." MiMi felt her body shudder with rage.

"Ms. Landry, I'm here to get your explanation in answer to these allegations. I assure you that we haven't drawn any conclusions based on the report. You'll be able to tell your side in court," Mrs. Young said in a calm, steady voice.

"What do you mean in court?" MiMi took a step back. Before the social worker could answer, the chimes sounded again.

"I'll go." Jazz left and returned with a man.

"MiMi Landry?" the man glanced around.

"Yes." MiMi blinked at him.

"This is for you." The man extended something to her.

MiMi took the folded paper. The man nodded and left. As she read, the letters on the beige legal-sized document blurred and ran together. Her body went numb as the world seemed to shatter. She heard voices, but they sounded muffled. Then the lights went out.

****

MiMi spent almost three days in a fog of depression. Fortunately, she had her friends. If Willa's mother knew anything, it was how to respond in a domestic crisis. MiMi had fainted once she read the summons. Her sister had filed a petition to get custody of Sage.

Mama Ruby went into action like an Army general marshaling the troops. Willa was dispatched to pick up Sage from the daycare center. She'd had to assure MiMi that the child welfare worker had no grounds to place the child in foster care immediately. A court order would have been required, and a judge would only grant an order if she was in immediate danger. Jazz called Elle to explain the situation. For four days Elle covered for MiMi at the office. She even made it appear that MiMi kept sending emails. Willa's twin brothers checked to make sure no odd jobs were needed at the house. With their support, MiMi's world didn't fall part while she moved around in a daze. All she wanted to do was hold Sage and cry. Finally after two days, Jazz cut through the gentle talk.

"Look, girl. You have to keep sending Sage to daycare. You got to keep your job. And you can't let this house go to hell. You'll just give your sister more dirt to report to the judge. Now get your ass out of that robe."

Slowly MiMi let go of the self-pity. She got equal doses of tender and tough love. By the following weekend, MiMi had strength to start planning. Sunday morning they'd gone to church. Willa's Aunt Ametrine beamed when they entered the doors of Saintsville Church of God. The choir rocked the house with gospel songs. Reverend L.C. Grimes preached a powerful sermon, and MiMi felt renewed. Two hours later they went to Mama Ruby's house for Sunday dinner. The smell of baked chicken, scalloped potatoes, green beans and buttered yeast rolls filled the kitchen.

"Ruby, you should have been there. Rev. Grimes showed out. Praise His Holy name," Aunt Ametrine announced as she strode ahead of Willa, MiMi and the children through the kitchen door.

"Yeah, and he showed out for a loooong time," said her husband as he peeled off his suit jacket.

"Uncle Preston, you're so crazy," Willa said with a laugh.

"My pastor prayed, sung and preached up a mighty storm," Aunt Ametrine continued. She spared only a second to shoot her better half a heated sideways glance.

"He could have done it in half the time and been just as powerful," Uncle Preston wisecracked.

"At Glen Oaks Methodist we're in and out in an hour, brother-in-law. Thank you, Lord!" Papa Elton shared a hearty laugh with Uncle Preston. The two middle-aged mischief makers slapped palms and shook hands.

"Y'all need to quit. Ametrine is going to start splashing some of that anointed oil to drive the demons out of you," Mama Ruby joked.

"See that's what's wrong with the world. Y'all playing with the Lord's business, and on his day to boot. Umph, umph, umph." Aunt Ametrine took off her church hat and marched off. "I'm going to wash up before I help set the table."

"We have everything just about ready, Ametrine," Mama Ruby called after her.

"Always more to be done," she echoed back down the hall.

"Which means things done the way *she* thinks they should be," Willa said aside to MiMi.

"Ametrine ain't takin' over my kitchen or my dining room. So she just might as well set her holy roller butt down and eat," Mama Ruby replied tartly.

"Thanks for inviting me to your big Sunday dinner." MiMi smiled when Sage gurgled as if in agreement.

"Don't be silly. You're always invited. Do what the rest of town does, just stop by and fill a plate." Willa grinned at her.

The toddler seemed to enjoy all the action around them. Willa's kids, Anthony and Mikayla came in to greet their sibling. Papa Elton and Uncle Preston got into a spirited discussion of sports with Anthony. True to her word, Mama Ruby fended off her sister's attempts to order and re-order things.

MiMi sneaked a dinner roll when Mama Ruby turned her back. "Your uncle was right. Girl, I'm so hungry. You should have warned me those folks stay in church forever."

Willa burst out laughing. "Why do you think Jazz told her thanks, but no thanks when she invited us?"

"I figured she was being her usual heathen self, as your aunt would say." MiMi grinned back.

"Come on, Sage. Let's play with our cousins." Mikayla swooped the child out of MiMi's arms and was gone in seconds. In the background, more children added to the joyful noise.

Jazz strolled in dressed in a denim jacket over a maxi skirt. "Hey everybody." A chorus answered her. "Damn it's loud up in here."

"Hey, girl. I'm glad you came." Willa hugged her.

"Yeah, whatever." Jazz looked pleased despite her response. Then she glanced at MiMi. "You lookin' a lot better."

"On the surface. I just can't believe Adrienne went so far." MiMi started to say more, but Willa waved at her to stop.

"Let's go where we can talk."

Willa pointed to the kitchen door leading into the house. MiMi and Jazz followed her. They went down a hallway past the living room where several adults held a loud discussion. Farther along, the children played in the family room, or what Papa Elton called his "man cave".

"You gotta be kidding," Jazz retorted. "This house is stuffed with chattering kinfolks."

"Yeah, but they're staying close to the food," Willa replied.

They ended up on the large screened in porch. A covered patio extended beyond the enclosed area. Papa Elton's prized grill sat there with another table and chairs. MiMi and Willa sat at a round glass table with five matching chairs. Jazz went to a swing sofa.

Mama Ruby appeared in the doorway. "We're going to be eating soon, so don't get into any trouble."

"Who us?" Jazz affected a wide-eyed look.

"No rushing off to start some confusion. This is

Sunday family time and..."

"Relax, Miss Ruby. Rev. Grimes stirred up the spirit of starvation with that long sermon. I'm not going anywhere," MiMi quipped.

"I hear ya. The man can beat a point to death. Ten minutes or I'm coming back to get you."

"Yes, ma'am," MiMi replied.

"We promise," Willa added. Mama Ruby left.

"That food is smelling good," Jazz said. She turned to MiMi. "I can talk some sense to your sister if you want."

"Jazz, don't even joke about going after Adrienne." Willa lay back in her chair and propped her feet on a second one.

"Ignore her, MiMi. Listen, I can be *real* persuasive." Jazz gave MiMi a wink.

"I'm going to ignore *you* instead," Willa said in a dry voice. She looked at MiMi. "Courts don't like to separate kids from their biological parent. The judge will want something pretty substantial to prove Sage should go to your sister."

"How about her mama has no job, went to prison in a foreign country for weed and is a murder suspect. Sounds substantial enough to me." MiMi swallowed hard. She resisted the urge to run inside and grab Sage for a tight hug.

"You really think your sister will get that down and dirty?" Willa asked.

MiMi stood and made a circle around the seating area. "Oh yes. I should have seen this coming. She kept offering to keep Sage longer than necessary. How she took over buying her clothes. She even decorated a bedroom at her house for Sage like she'd be living there. I'm such an idiot."

"I don't get it. Why doesn't she just try for another baby to complete her trophy family?" Willa looked at MiMi.

"Adrienne had problems conceiving the first time, something to do with fibroid tumors. Her first pregnancy was close to a miracle. Mama told me her doctor says she really should have a hysterectomy." MiMi stared across the green lawn of the backyard.

"So she decides to take her niece. Damn, talk about gangsta." Jazz shook her head.

"She doesn't care if she breaks your heart and destroys your reputation." Willa frowned. "I mean you're family."

"Adrienne will do what it takes to get what she wants. She and daddy are a lot alike."

"Of course Mrs. Got Rocks will show up and represent like her family is picture perfect. Too bad you can't sling some dirt on her." Jazz grunted.

"Custody cases can get pretty nasty." Willa bit her lower lip.

The three friends sat silent for several minutes. Their somber moods descended like a cloud. No one smiled. Sunshine outside and laugher coming from inside the house didn't even seem to help. Finally, Willa sighed and stood. She walked to the screen door, but didn't go through it to the open patio.

"Mama Ruby's flowers are going to bloom pretty all summer. She's got a green thumb. The woman loves digging in the dirt." Willa smiled.

"Dirt!" MiMi blurted out and slapped her hands together. Willa and Jazz jumped at the same time.

Jazz looked at Willa. "I think she's snapped."

"No, no. You both said dirt. Don't you see?" MiMi spread her arms. She glanced from Willa to Jazz and back again.

"Um, not really." Willa cast a side-eye at her sister.

"I'm not losing my mind. You said custody cases get nasty." MiMi pointed at Willa. Then she pointed at Jazz. "You said we should sling dirt at Adrienne."

"Okay." Jazz raised her eyebrows.

"Adrienne's marriage isn't perfect. Yes, a scandal is what we need. I can go hard, too." MiMi wore a wicked grin.

"Your thinking up evil stuff. I *like* it," Jazz said and matched MiMi's wicked grin with one of her own.

"Are you sure those civilized society folks will act a fool?" Willa wore a skeptical frown. "Adrienne knows about the mistress, and you said Chris won't leave his trophy family."

"Most mistresses are lying when they claim they don't care if he stays with the wife. Plus if Chris and Adrienne have one skeleton tucked away, then they have more. Let's find that walk-in closet and take a look around. Shall we?" MiMi crossed her arms. Willa's frown eased into a smile, and Jazz nodded with glee.

Chapter 14

Monday morning MiMi dove into work with more energy. Her outlook had changed. She no longer felt pressed down by the weight of certain doom ahead. When Kerry called, MiMi brightly reported progress on her projects. Kerry implied MiMi wasn't telling the truth. Even that didn't provoke MiMi the way it might have a few days before.

An hour later, Elle arrived at her house with fabric samples. Not even pictures would do, since texture and feel would help MiMi make buying decisions for the fall line. She pulled a rolling cart with samples and parked it by the sofa. Then she dropped a large white bag on the coffee table.

"I brought some famous Mickey's donuts. I hope you have coffee made," Elle said. She glanced around. "Nice home office you got set up."

"Thanks, but I'm not hungry. Has marketing set up the fall catalog yet? I need to finalize what we'll offer so they can fill in the clothes section. Julie in New York already has the accessories section done." MiMi dove into the samples and started scribbling notes.

"We've got time. It's only April. The final copy isn't

due until mid June." Elle dug into the bag and pulled out a glazed donut. "Coffee?"

"In the kitchen. I want the cosmetics line to coordinate with this season's hot colors, you know eye shadows and lip sticks. Then we want to make sure that new line of fashion jewelry complements the sweaters and skirts." MiMi spoke loud enough for Elle to hear her.

"Uh-huh," Elle called back. When she returned, she brought two cups on a tray. "You've been working since six o'clock this morning."

"How would you know that?" MiMi didn't look up from the fabrics. She fingered the textures. "This one seems a bit thin."

"Because you sent me emails, that's how. At least you took a break to take Sage to daycare." Elle put the tray down with a sigh. She walked over and picked up the textile sample in question. "They're going to line it with a poly rayon blend. It'll be fine for the career jackets we selected. Remember, these will be sold in the south where it doesn't get all that cold. The heavier fabrics will be sold in the Midwest and Northeast stores."

"I'll call Julie to see if she's seen these colors. She should have emailed the pictures of the jewelry by now." MiMi reached for her phone.

Elle blocked her by moving the cordless handset. "It's nine thirty, coffee and chat time."

"You do know my boss and her minion are plotting to get me fired, right? I have to score big this time around or I'm out." MiMi tried to push Elle's hand away. She sighed when her friend grabbed up the phone. "Elle, c'mon. You're supposed to be on my side."

"Your clothes look loose. Have you just been

feeding Sage and not eating?" Elle gave her a critical complete body examination.

"I may need a new career as a model or pole dancer. So I could stand to lose a few pounds. Now give me the phone." MiMi gave her pal a mock scowl.

"You need to keep up your strength. I'm cooking you a healthy breakfast of oatmeal with fresh apples, cinnamon and milk. I found bacon in the fridge to go with it." Elle smacked her lips. "Umm, good."

"Cut it out." MiMi turned back to looking at sample magazine pages. "I like these sweaters and skirts. Do these slacks for women look a bit too masculine to you?"

"I'll think about it while I'm stirring the oatmeal." Elle spun around and went back to the kitchen. Seconds later, the smell of fresh coffee mixed with bacon.

"I don't have time to eat," MiMi complained. But the smells coming from the kitchen made her stomach growl. She looked down at her midsection. "Shut up you traitor."

"You're going to eat," Elle yelled back as if she had communicated with MiMi's appetite already.

The chimes in the hallway signaled another unwanted intrusion. MiMi marched past the kitchen and breakfast alcove across the open floor plan. She ignored Elle. "If those Jehovah Witnesses are on my doorstep, they're about to learn some new words."

Instead her mother stood outside scanning the neighborhood as though assessing it for approval. Her mother looked at least ten years younger than her fifty-nine years. Her short modified long bob haircut suited her heart-shaped face. She wore a turquoise pullover t-shirt with white yoga style pants. Floral sandals and a taupe purse completed the outfit. When she turned to the door with an impatient frown, MiMi jumped as if caught doing something wrong. Pauline Mims Landry had always inspired anxiety.

MiMi undid the locks and swung the door open quickly. "Good morning, mother. What a pleasant surprise."

Pauline gave her a smile that lacked warmth. She brushed by MiMi without waiting for an invitation to come in. "Hello, dear. I apologize for not calling, but frankly I wasn't sure you'd answer. Caller ID is a gift and a curse these days. Interesting choices for the foyer."

"Thanks," MiMi said, ignoring the fact that her mother's comment wasn't a compliment. "I'm about to have breakfast. You're welcome to join me."

"You hired a cook?" Pauline's shapely eyebrows went up. Her hazel eyes seemed to question how MiMi could afford such a luxury.

"A friend is cooking for me. We're working on projects for store catalogs." MiMi closed the door. She hesitated as she faced her mother in the foyer.

Pauline took control as usual. "The living room is fine. I'll had breakfast, yogurt with fruit and organic cranberry juice. Bacon? I don't think that's the best choice, especially not for Sage."

"It's turkey bacon," MiMi replied crisply, though she wasn't sure. She frowned trying to remember what kind she'd bought on her last trip to the store.

"Hmm." Pauline sat on the sofa. She lifted her eyebrow again at MiMi until she sat as well. "I might as well address the elephant in the room, this thing between you and Adrienne."

"Adrienne plans to tell a judge I'm a drug using ex-con who puts men and street life before my baby." MiMi's temper flared. "That's more than 'a thing'. She's declared all out war."

"She's honestly concerned about Sage, and she's very attached to her. There's no need for our family business to be aired like one of those grimy reality shows. Your father and I talked to Adrienne." Pauline set her purse on the cocktail table.

"Mother--"

"And she's seriously considering what we think is a sensible solution. You're going through a rough time with no job and the police question your every move."

"I still have my job," MiMi clipped.

"For now. I understand there are difficulties with your supervisor," Pauline replied.

"The police aren't 'questioning my every move'. They've only talked to me once. I'm not a suspect."

"Yet..." Pauline let the rest of her thought hang in the air.

"What's your point," MiMi said through clenched teeth.

"Dear, I'm not trying to make you feel bad, but face the facts. Taking care of an active toddler is added stress. Adrienne can take temporary physical custody, not guardianship," Pauline added quickly when MiMi's mouth flew open.

"No."

"I'm not talking about a permanent arrangement. Adrienne can satisfy her need to mother a small child. While you'll be able to resolve all of these troubling issues you're having." Pauline nodded at her own reasoning.

MiMi pushed against rising panic in her chest. She'd always had trouble standing up to her mother. But not when it came to her daughter. "I said no."

"You're being stubborn. Adrienne is doing you a

huge favor, though frankly I don't know why. You've spoiled Sage terribly. She's as unruly as you were at that age. But there, Adrienne is determined to help you..."

"No, Adrienne can't have another baby so she's decided to steal mine," MiMi cut in sharply.

"Listen, I think she should have discussed this arrangement with you. I told her going to court was extreme."

MiMi stood. "So you knew. Adrienne discussed attacking me, taking my child and you simply went along with it. What kind of mother are you?"

Pauline sighed. She picked up her purse and took out a tissue. "Good Lord, both you girls are so theatrical. I just said I didn't agree with her approach."

"But you agree that she should take Sage away from me?" MiMi balled both hands into fists. She took a step closer to Pauline.

Elle stood in the archway that opened from the foyer to the living. "Um, is everything okay?"

"We're having a private family discussion, so please excuse us. Now MiMi, I--"

"I don't care if the whole city hears my answer," MiMi cut her off a second time.

Pauline's eyes narrowed to slits as she stood to face MiMi. "Watch your tone, Miliana Elise Landry. You wouldn't have this house, a very nice car and more if not for *us*. Your life has become as chaotic as those friends of yours."

"What are you saying?" MiMi's voice pitched higher with fury.

Her mother seemed not to notice she'd pressed her luck one step too far. She drew herself up. "I mean you've forgotten where you came from. Our families have never been connected to crime. They certainly have never been arrested."

"Only because they either didn't get caught or bought their way out of being prosecuted. You don't think I remember Uncle Jonathan's 'difficulties' in nineteen-ninety eight? Or what about the rumors that Daddy's father took money for his votes as city councilman?" MiMi drilled her gaze into Pauline as she spoke.

"How dare you repeat those lies in front of a stranger." Pauline's eyes flashed fire. "You're testing me, MiMi. That's never a good idea. I'm trying to help keep all of the unsavory details of your private life from spilling out in open court."

"If Adrienne wants a fight, she's damn sure going to get one. So if you came over here thinking you could bully me into handing her over, think again." MiMi stared her mother down.

Pauline's expression softened. "I'm not doing a good job of keeping the peace in our family. Let Adrienne look after Sage like she did when you were in that prison. She adores the child."

"Elle, does the word 'no' sound ambiguous to you, like I'm open to negotiation?" MiMi glanced at Elle for a second, but faced her mother again without waiting for an answer.

"Only a few weeks, a month at most. I'll remind Adrienne that it's just temporary until you can get your footing again." Pauline's conciliatory expression barely covered the irritation just beneath the surface. Her attempt at a warm smile failed miserably.

"Hell no."

"You wait a minute, talking to me like this," Pauline snapped, her voice rising.

"Goodbye, Mother. I have work to do, and a

lawyer to consult."

MiMi spun around and headed through the archway and into the foyer. She stood waiting for Pauline. Her mother huffed in outrage, but picked up her purse after a few seconds. Elle backed away when Pauline got closer.

"You're making a big mistake," Pauline said tightly.

"Not nearly as big as the one Adrienne made. I'll fight to the death for my daughter. Something I could never count on from *you*."

Pauline blinked as though the words had hit her in the face. She opened her mouth, but no words came out. Instead she threw a look of contempt at Elle like she was at fault. Then her mother lifted her nose in the air, walked to the door and yanked it open. MiMi pushed the door shut the second Pauline's rear end cleared the threshold.

"Whoa," Elle breathed out after a few seconds of charged silence. "Are you okay?"

MiMi inhaled and exhaled five times to calm the rage boiling inside. She resisted the urge to throw the front door open and scream insults at her mother's retreating back. Then a kind of determined calm took over. She turned around slowly to face her friend.

"No, but I'm not going to let them bulldoze over me. I have a plan that involves a nasty, cheap underhanded move. I'm talking about something that not even those reality show housewives would stoop to. Things are going to get messy," MiMi said, her voice knife-edged sharp.

Elle blinked at her for a second before a smile tugged her full ruby red lips up. "Please let me watch or at least get video."

MiMi smiled back at her. "Game on."

****

"What do they want?" Willa muttered for the third time.

After only one day of feeling back in control, MiMi walked around the conference table at her lawyer's office waiting for the police. Detective Drake didn't tell Edselle anything beyond they had additional questions for MiMi. Willa agreed to come for moral support.

"Making us wait is part of their strategy I'll bet," MiMi said.

She went to the window looking out on the historic downtown neighborhood. The three-story home was built around 1896. A mature magnolia tree bloomed in the backyard. The rooms had polished pine and oak furniture. Pictures on the walls depicted scenes from Baton Rouge in the late nineteenth century. Some were ink drawings, but there were vintage photos as well.

"These guys must make good fees. This is expensive real estate so close to the Capitol Building."

"This was Brad's great-grandfather's house. Or maybe it was his great uncle. Anyway, his family goes way back to almost when the neighborhood was founded, before even." Willa swiped a finger across the screen of her smart phone. Bradford Craft was the senior and founding partner of Craft, Mouton and Laplace. Willa had worked for the firm as a paralegal before she became her own boss.

"He can trace his family to before 1803? My parents would be so jealous." MiMi gave a sharp laugh. Her mother especially relished talking about her great-great-greats.

"Speaking of family, how..."

"I haven't spoken to any of them, and that's fine with me," MiMi cut in.

"You really think Adrienne is trying to take Sage permanently? Sounds pretty cold," Willa drawled.

"Adrienne could keep frozen food in her panties," MiMi retorted. "At least your monster mother lives a few hundred miles away in Houston. I keep hoping my parents will retire out of the country. I even brought them brochures about how cheaply they could live in a Latin American country." MiMi grinned at the look Willa gave her.

"Shame on you," Willa said. "Hmm, they could give Vivienne a ride."

They were still laughing when Edselle came in through the double doors followed by Detective Drake. They all exchanged good mornings. Detective Drake accepted a cup of coffee. Edselle poured, offered him sugar and cream, and sat down.

"Thanks, I take it black. And I need it with the schedule I've had lately." Drake took a sip. Then he put the paper cup down and glanced from MiMi to Willa. Then his gaze settled on MiMi. "I suppose you're going to let Mr. Underwood answer the questions."

"Ms. Landry is willing to help in any way she can, within reason of course," Edselle replied.

Detective Drake gave a grunt and nodded. He took out his smart phone. After a few minutes of browsing, he cleared his throat. "Your client stated that she had no business relationship with Roderick Jefferson, just a personal one. Correct?"

When Edselle gestured for her to answer MiMi said, "That's right."

"Yet you went with him to the Dominican Republic where he had business," Drake looked up from the notes on his phone.

"Our trip was primarily for pleasure, a getaway. He may have made a few phone calls, but I don't know who he talked to or why." MiMi shrugged. "Roderick worked constantly. He was always on his phone."

"A representative of a DR business group visited your home. Was her visit connected to the victim?" Detective Drake's gaze drifted to Edselle as if he expected him to object.

Edselle held up a hand when MiMi started to speak. "Ms. Villa's visit had nothing to do with Roderick Jefferson."

"Are you sure?" Detective Drake stared at MiMi.

MiMi looked at Willa, who was furiously tapping on her smart phone. When Willa didn't look up, MiMi turned back to the detective. "If Roderick knew these people it's news to me."

"Detective Estrada in the DR seems to think the murder of this Benito Herrera is somehow connected to our case. How well did you know Mr. Herrera?" Detective Drake raised an eyebrow at MiMi.

MiMi crossed her arms. Then she thought better of the defensive posture and relaxed. "I didn't know him at all."

"So the court records in the DR said," Detective Drake replied in a dry tone.

"Excuse me, but what aren't you telling us?" Edselle broke in before Detective Drake could form a follow-up question.

"He wasn't a street dealer at all but an employee working for this DR group. We have information that Ms. Landry not only knew Mr. Herrera, but she had a part in whatever business arrangement Mr. Jefferson got himself tied up in."

MiMi's eyes narrowed to slits. "That's a load of--"

Edselle cut her off by raising a palm. "Are you suggesting that Mr. Jefferson was involved in something illegal?"

"We're unraveling the details now. Those guys in the DR might be 'businessmen', but they've got shady reputations. The DR National Police suspect they're laundering money, some of it might even be for terrorists groups in the Philippines and Peru."

"What?" MiMi jumped to her feet.

"Ms. Landry has no information about illegal money transactions or terrorists groups," Edselle spoke up quickly as he stood. He placed a hand on MiMi's arm. "Keep calm. Detective Drake is only gathering information."

"Counselor, we'll need a DNA sample and fingerprint impressions from Ms. Landry," Detective Drake said.

"I dated him, of course you'll find my fingerprints and DNA in his condo," MiMi blurted out.

"So then you shouldn't mind providing them." Detective Drake gazed at her steadily.

"Fine." MiMi sat down.

"You can come to our headquarters tomorrow. Nine o'clock?" Drake took out his smart phone, but held his finger poised over it.

MiMi glanced at Edselle, who nodded slowly. "Tomorrow at nine works for me."

"You'll be in and out in less than an hour. I appreciate your cooperation." Detective Drake stood and shook hands with Edselle, smiled at Mimi and Willa.

"Thank you, Detective. My client is happy to help in any way possible," Edselle replied.

He opened the conference room door and

followed Detective Drake. He gave MiMi and Willa a quick glance before he left. They heard their voices fade away. MiMi chewed a fingernail. Willa got up and went to the window. When Edselle came back moments later, they started talking at the same time.

"We need to find out what he's up to," Willa said.

"I swear I didn't know anything about Roderick being in business with that weed guy." MiMi threw up both hands.

"Okay, okay, let's regroup." Edselle grabbed the carafe and poured three cups. He passed them around. "Obviously Detective Drake is trying to throw us off balance."

"Humph, then score one for him because he sure as hell succeeded," Willa retorted. She walked to the conference table but didn't sit. She picked up a cup. "I texted Cedric what Drake said, shorthand of course. He's working on it. You think this Nairoby Villa is his source?"

MiMi frowned. "She didn't say anything about Roderick. Nairoby came about Jack."

"Yeah, she would have said something about Roderick. I don't know." Willa sipped coffee. "I doubt coffee will calm my..." MiMi sipped. "Hey, that is delicious."

Willa sat back. "We need to find out where Roderick met these people and what they were up to."

"We should ask Ms. Got-Herself-Some-Nerve," MiMi snapped angrily.

"One, you should stay away from her. And two, you don't know where she is." Willa looked at MiMi.

"You have resources, investigate and *find* her," MiMi shot back.

"No need to spend time calling all over town.

Edselle can ask for another conference call and tell her bosses she needs to be there," Willa said.

"Great idea. I'll check my schedule." Edselle strode out, coffee cup in on hand.

"All I did was date a guy and now I'm a suspect." MiMi pinched the bridge of her nose. "I've got to figure out who put a voodoo curse on me."

Willa grunted. "No, you need to pick better dates and put a whipping on your sister."

"I'm taking a long break from dating. But that second suggestion? Yeah, kicking her scheming, backstabbing butt is at the top of my to-do list." MiMi indulged in the fantasy of slapping her sister silly.

Chapter 15

At eight o'clock that night Jazz and MiMi cruised by the Hotel Indigo in MiMi's SUV. The Lexus fit right in with the upscale feel outside the expensive hotel. Police officers on bicycles cruised by. One of them flashed a smile at MiMi. She waved back. A limo pulled up to deposit passengers. Then a BMW arrived, and the valet moved quickly to help a well-dressed blonde from the passenger side. MiMi turned on Lafayette Street.

"I'm going to make the block and let the valets park my car," MiMi said as she pulled up to a stop sign.

"Are you nuts? Find parking on the street. We'll walk." Jazz glanced around. "We can't be flagging down a valet if trouble breaks out."

"Don't be so paranoid. Besides, do you see any close parking? No. I can't walk in these shoes," MiMi said.

"You should have worn different shoes," Jazz shot back.

"Calm down. We're going to find out what we need, put a scare into this witch and get out." MiMi wheeled the SUV up to a red light.

"Sorry I even told you where she was," Jazz

muttered. "Dumb idea. Your lawyer was going to arrange a meeting with her."

"They've been putting him off, which confirms they're bluffing. I don't want to wait another day to find out the real story. You were smarter than any of us to have your guys follow her." MiMi pulled away when the light turned green. "Now relax."

"I don't relax when I'm walkin' into a situation and don't know what might come at me. Neither should you. Remember she's got a bodyguard." Jazz gave their surroundings a 360 degree scan.

"Yes, but so do we." MiMi winked at her.

"Bullets go through bodyguards, too." Jazz sucked in a breath and let it out when MiMi pulled up to the hotel.

MiMi released her seatbelt but didn't open the door. "And she'll be thinking the same. Besides, we have an advantage."

"Which is?" Jazz gave her a skeptical frown.

"We know her back is against the wall with her 'partners'," MiMi said.

She flashed a smile at the waiting valet. She swung open the door and exited gracefully. Another valet opened the passenger door for Jazz. They'd agreed to leave their larger purses at home. MiMi wore a small yet fashionable shiny silver cross body bag. It was only big enough to hold a few bills, her driver's license and one credit card. Jazz carried her essentials in the pocket of her red leather crop jacket.

"Good evening, ma'am."

"Hello. Charge our room, 588. Thank you so much," MiMi said without hesitation.

"Girl..." Jazz said as she walked beside her into the hotel.

"Yeah, let that heffa pay for our parking. Look for that big guy she had with her the other night." MiMi strode in like her mother would, nose in the air like she owned the place.

"He's at one of the casinos. But Nairoby is upstairs. I made sure." Jazz continued to scan their surroundings as they approached the elevator.

"How?"

"Told the front desk to leave her a voice mail message her crew would be calling tonight around eight or either-thirty local time." Jazz nodded at a sexy man and he nodded back.

"I see you've got things covered. I'm sticking up for you the next time Willa throws shade at your choice of friends on the street," MiMi whispered just before a group of middle-aged men and women joined them on the elevator.

"Let's see if you say that once the shooting starts," Jazz wisecracked. When a white-haired matron gasped, Jazz smiled. "Don't worry, ma'am. I'm a movie director. My employees are filming a night scene outside. I'm just making sure this minor actress remembers her lines from the script."

"How exciting," a tall silver-haired man said. He stood next to a heavily made-up blonde on the south side of thirty-five at least.

His blue eyes twinkled as he gazed at Jazz's form fitting dark blue leggings and MiMi's black leggings beneath a mini skirt. Jazz wore fancy platform-styled sneakers. MiMi had on three inch tan leather sandals. He didn't seem to notice the woman glaring at him in disapproval.

"Oh it is. Now if you hear what sounds like gunshots, ignore it. All make believe," Jazz said in a cool voice. She winked at him.

When the elevator stopped at the third floor, the woman grabbed his arm and pulled him through the open doors. She threw one last hostile glance at Jazz to make her point. The rest of the riders got off on the fourth floor.

MiMi sighed when the doors slid shut. "Don't start no ish before we even get to the woman's room."

"Take a breath and settle your nerves. Here we go."

Jazz stepped from the elevator first. Then she gestured for MiMi to follow. They followed signs pointing the way to Nairoby's room number. Moments later Jazz knocked. A muffled voice came through the door.

"What do you want?"

"She ain't surprised to see us. That tells me something," Jazz said softly close to MiMi's ear. "We've got a proposition for you, to help get you out of trouble with your bosses. We hear they're fairly unforgiving."

"Your bodyguard is on their payroll. Which means his loyalty isn't to you. I don't think you want him to join us," MiMi added.

"Damn, player. Jail and trouble agrees with you." Jazz gave MiMi a look of surprise.

Metal clicked and the door swung open before MiMi could reply. Nairoby stood eyeing them with suspicion. Dressed in black, both jeans and a sweater, she said nothing for several seconds.

"Why should I let you two in here? You might have a gun or something." Nairoby looked ready to slam the door again.

MiMi held up both hands. "We're not armed. See? No purses. I'd suggest we meet down in the lobby, but there are too many people. Same for the hotel bar and restaurant."

Jazz glanced around. "You don't want the bodyguard, what's-his-name, to see us talking. We're going to attract attention hanging out here in the hall. Big dude might show up."

"Maybe that would be a good thing." Nairoby didn't sound convincing. Her gaze shifted away from them briefly and back.

"So you're paying him?" MiMi raised both eyebrows at her.

"Come in, but this will be a short visit. You have nothing I want." Nairoby backed into the room.

She motioned to them to move away from the door. Then she kicked it closed with one foot. She held a cell phone in one hand by her side. Her other hand was behind her back. They stood in a small seating area. A few feet away, a big screen television played on mute. The queen-sized bed was unmade. A room service meal sat on a small round table under stainless steel covers. Jazz walked over and lifted one.

"You livin' it up on their money, huh? Shrimp cocktail appetizer, steak and lobster dinner, nice room." Jazz nodded in appreciation.

"Talk, be brief, and leave," Nairoby clipped.

"I hope you're not holding a weapon behind you. That would be downright unfriendly," Jazz said calmly. Her taut expression implied she could strike out defensively in a blink.

MiMi noticed a knife wasn't among the silverware on the table with the dishes. "We're not here to harm you. The police say you and you're partners were involved in some kind of deal with Roderick Jefferson."

"Who is that?" Nairoby glanced at Jazz as if

checking on her position, then back to MiMi.

"A local businessman found murdered a couple of weeks ago. Here's a picture of him." MiMi reached inside her purse. She held up one hand when Nairoby tensed into a fighting stance. She slowly pulled the phone out, opened the images app and held it up. "Do you recognize him?"

Nairoby's gaze flickered at the screen. "No. Now get out."

"Ah hell naw. You know she's lyin'." Jazz gave a snort. Then she snagged a plump shrimp and popped it into her mouth. "Hmm."

"I was wrong, I don't like you. How crude. Or do you still say ghetto here?" Nairoby flashed a scornful look at Jazz.

"I'm 'urban', and there's nothing wrong with my fashion sense," Jazz replied coolly. "You're still lyin'."

Nairoby ignored her and looked at MiMi. "I suppose that this man was your lover, since you have a photo of him on your phone. And I have no reason to lie. I've never met him."

MiMi studied her for a few seconds. "But you know who he is."

"If you leave quickly I won't call security or the police." Nairoby brought her hand from behind her back. She held a long tapered steak knife like she knew how to use it.

"You don't want the police involved," MiMi said carefully. "Let me repeat. They've made a connection between you and a dead man. They're doing research on your partners. Since the FBI is in town I bet they already know everything about you. Right down to when you last had your last pedicure."

"So what? Ramon and I will be gone before they

can do anything," Nairboy replied. The slight quiver in her voice betrayed her lack of confidence.

"Honey, this ain't the Dominican Republic. When the law in the USA decides to snatch your ass, you won't get far. You better listen to what MiMi has to say." Jazz stared at the shrimp as if deciding whether to eat another one.

"You don't know what you're talking about."

"Your partners can kill two birds with one neat stone; get the heat of a murder investigation off them and deliver some pay back. You make a mighty nice murder suspect." MiMi watched fear turn her pretty brown skin pale.

"Yeah, it's sinkin' in finally, MiMi." Jazz gave a short laugh, decided and ate a second shrimp.

"Tell me about your business with Roderick," MiMi pressed before they lost the advantage and Nairoby had time to think.

"Those greedy idiots," Nairoby burst out. "I told them..."

"Men rarely listen to us, especially when it comes to business," MiMi replied.

"Not all men, one woman other than me," Nairoby said. She nodded. "My partners are sharks. Oh they're polished, civilized on the surface. But make no mistake, these are dangerous people."

"How many?" MiMi frowned.

"Four, including Ava Torres. Well there were four until Benito..." Nairoby's voice trailed off. She blinked hard but then put on a blank expression.

Jazz studied her. "He was a friend of yours?"

"Don't look for things you won't want to find. I didn't kill your lover, so if you came here for revenge." Nairoby assumed a rigid fight stance once more.

"Don't be silly. People saw us come up here," MiMi snapped. "Look, is there any possibility your friends killed Roderick for any reason?"

Nairoby wore a stunned look for a few seconds. She dropped her hand, but she looked wary. "Why should I tell you anything?"

"I'm a suspect, too," MiMi said after weighing her options for a few seconds. "I figure your partners--"

"Sounds more to me like they're her bosses," Jazz interjected. She grinned when Nairoby glared at her.

"They'll decide that letting one of us be charged is to their advantage. You could be more vulnerable than me," MiMi continued.

Nairoby stared at MiMi, eyes wide. "How do you mean?"

"You came over here, met with Roderick and the discussion turned violent. You and your bodyguard killed him. Your partners will cut you loose to face the consequence. There's a reason you're looking so scared right now," MiMi said carefully.

"Jefferson met one of my *associates*..." Nairoby paused to shoot Jazz a heated look before she resumed. "At a trade conference sponsored by the New Orleans World Trade Center. They involved in an arrangement to import and export mineral or gravel products. Big industry in my country. I wasn't in on the deal." She waved a hand.

"Your interest being textiles mainly," MiMi said sourly. Jack Crown, another dearly departed traitorous lover. She was building quite a collection of that particular animal.

"Yes." Nairoby seemed not to notice MiMi's sarcasm. She frowned. "Jefferson bought up minerals, perlite I think at first for construction products.

Something about starting to offer those products for wholesale and using them for his own building projects. Very high profit potential, and everybody was pleased. Then something went wrong. I believe he cut them out of a lucrative contract, went straight to one of their suppliers."

"So they had a reason to be very unhappy with Roderick. But I don't think they'd kill him because he cut through the middlemen. I mean the streets would be littered with dead businessmen, and women." MiMi shook her head.

"There's more. I overheard Arturo, one of the partners, shouting once when I went to his office to deliver papers. It was about eight months ago I think. He said Jefferson threatened them if they tried to retaliate," Nairoby said.

"Threatened them how?" MiMi sat down on the arm of a large chair.

"My partners... engage in high stakes transactions at times with unsavory people." Nairoby shrugged. "Nothing different from any sharp business group in the global market. And no, I won't say more."

MiMi huffed in frustration. "You don't owe them loyalty."

Nairoby shook her head. "I would not live very long if I disclosed too much."

Jazz looked at MiMi. "Roderick might have known too damn much for his own good. AKA motive for them to shut him up."

"You cannot tell anyone we've spoken. Ramon would..." Nairoby's voice trailed off and she flinched at the unfinished thought.

"Don't sweat." Jazz wiped her hands on the cloth napkin.

"Of course. Make yourself at home," Nairoby muttered. She leaned against the wall, but still watched them closely.

Jazz gave a short laugh. She took her cell phone from the pocket of her jacket. She read the screen, and tapped a text. "Yeah, the big dude is still at the Hollywood Casino. He's occupied romancing a good looking lady."

"You're following him?" Nairoby's eyes went wide.

"*Ms. Villa*, I'm not going to be arrested for murder just so you can feel safe," MiMi said coldly. "I'm not totally heartless. We have a cover story to make it less likely your bosses will suspect we got information from you."

"My sister has a private security company. We'll say that's how we found out about Roderick and his deals with them. Plus the FBI and the police could find out just as well." Jazz didn't look up from her phone.

"Tell them the FBI is watching me and you couldn't risk being seen with me," MiMi added.

Nairoby sat without answering for a few moments, and then she nodded. "That could work, but only for a while. Ramon said as much once, that we best let things cool off. But if you tell the FBI about my partners they won't let us go home."

"The police can't stop you from leaving unless they have enough to arrest you," MiMi replied.

"Ha, American laws make life so easy," Nairoby said with a smirk. Then her expression turned grim. "My life is in your hands. If you slip, my partners will make me pay."

MiMi felt a chill spread over her body. "Like Herrera?"

"I believe he may have helped Jefferson cut out my

partners," Nairoby said in a somber tone. She glanced from MiMi to Jazz and back again. "Do you understand?"

"Yeah. They don't play." Jazz dropped the phone in her jacket pocket and zipped it closed. She walked over to MiMi and dropped her voice low. "My friend can't keep Ramon distracted much longer. He's wanting more than conversation."

"You mean..." MiMi gaped at her. Then she recovered from the shock and turned to Nairoby. "Tell them--"

"Yes, yes. I don't need coaching. I'll handle my partners." Nairoby stood straight again.

MiMi started to probe more about Ramon, but decided against it. "Okay."

"We'll need time, eight hours." Nairoby moved sideways to the door without turning her back on them.

"Fine." MiMi glanced at Jazz and gestured they should leave.

As if on cue and eager for them to be gone, Nairoby opened the door. Jazz led the way. She gave Nairoby a head to toe look as she walked by. The woman backed up. Her gaze darted from Jazz to MiMi until both were in the hallway. Then she shut the door hard.

"Well that was interesting," Jazz murmured.

They didn't speak again as they entered the elevator and rode down. MiMi felt exposed as they exited on the lobby level. Waiting out on the street for the valet to bring the SUV made her nervous. MiMi let go of the breath she'd held when her vehicle appeared. She quickly gave the young man a tip and got in.

"Call the cops and spill what you just found out," Jazz said when they pulled away into traffic. She lit up on of her smokes.

"I agreed to give her eight hours," MiMi replied. "And roll down your window. I don't want my baby breathing second hand smoke."

"Hell, so damn picky," Jazz muttered. Still she complied. She blew smoke out of the passenger window. "You need to offer up some suspects ASAP to get your ass off the hot seat."

"You heard what she said. I don't want her blood on my hands." MiMi turned onto Florida Boulevard taking the direction toward Jazz's club.

"Nairoby is street all the way, a true survivor. Besides, you can't believe everything she said. For all we know she could have her own dangerous crew. We just have her word for it that Ramon isn't one of her boys." Jazz sucked in more smoke and streamed it through the window.

"She looked genuinely scared, but you're right," MiMi replied with a frown.

"That girl's a player. She knows how to think fast and put on an act. Her back up is a cash reserve only she knows about and an exit plan."

MiMi stopped as a traffic light turned yellow then red. She glanced at Jazz. "Takes one to know one, huh?"

"Exactly, cause that's what I'd do in her shoes. She's kinda cool. So Jack and her..." Jazz made a crude gesture and indicated the sex act.

MiMi hissed just as the light turned green. She hit the accelerator pedal too hard and the SUV shot off. "That no-good--"

"Careful, no cuss word. You'll get in the habit and slip up in front of Sage." Jazz giggled when MiMi let loose with expletives anyway.

"You know what he did? Pumped me for

information on the textiles business to help him do deals with *her*. I earned any money he made."

"Gotta admire a smooth operator." Jazz pressed against the passenger door when MiMi growled. "Hey, I'm just sayin'."

"Why should I give her any damn time," MiMi muttered. She started the speed dial feature connected to her cell phone on the steering wheel, then hung up. "No. I can't do it even to her. I'll call Edselle and fill him in. Then ask him to call Detective Drake or his partner in the morning."

"Okay, but waiting might not make a difference. Sounds like Nairoby's pals back home are done with her already." Jazz shrugged. She tossed away the cigarillo when MiMi pulled up to another red light.

"Overnight won't hurt. How did you arranged for a woman to hook up with Ramon at the casino?" MiMi grinned at Jazz.

"So you know my guys followed them. They saw the big dude hitting on good-looking women in the hotel bar and a couple of Third Street nightclubs. He likes blondes. I called my friend Sandy. We worked at the same gentlemen's club in Houston back in the day. She owes me big time, so she took the job." Jazz breathed in the night air.

"But what if Ramon had tried something?" MiMi drove on through the green traffic signal.

"One of the guys stuck with 'em. He would have pulled the jealous boyfriend routine at her signal. Now the best part is she might have learned something, but I doubt it. The dude may be muscle, but I don't think he's stupid." Jazz smiled at MiMi. "Speaking of smart, you played a nice hand with Nairoby. I was like, damn. Look at my girl."

MiMi shook her head. "Yeah, all of this mess has changed me. I'm not sure it's in a good way, not for my little girl's sake."

"In other words you're scared of turning into *me*" Jazz quipped.

"I've seen your soft side." MiMi grinned at her.

"Hey, keep that to yourself. I've got a reputation to protect." Jazz slapped her on the shoulder playfully. "I could tell Don what we found out. I didn't promise that heffa a damn thing."

MiMi shook her head. "No, don't do anything. I've involved you and Willa in my crazy drama too much as it is. But thanks. You both are now officially my blood sisters."

"Sisters," Jazz repeated with a wink.

"Since I may dodge being charged with murder, all I have to do is save my house and find our money." MiMi frowned into the night ahead as she drove. Jazz seemed content to remain silent and let her think through her next moves.

Chapter 16

The next morning MiMi went to Edselle's office and they made a call to Detectives Drake and Forrester. She let the attorney do the talking. The detectives took turns asking questions, but they didn't say much. Edselle told them what MiMi had learned from Nairoby first. Then he described MiMi's volatile encounter with Yvette Theirry. Drake remarked dryly that they had suspects up to their eyeballs. When the call ended the lawyer wore a wide smile.

"Following up on those juicy leads will keep them busy for a while. And the fact that we haven't heard from the FBI could be an encouraging sign. I think they overplayed their hand hoping you'd panic and lead them to Mr. Crown's money." Edselle rocked back in his chair.

MiMi sighed. "If only. We haven't been able to find a scrap of paper that even hints he had an offshore account, much less where. So far Willa's only hit dead ends."

"I've dealt with hidden assets with previous clients. People who were, um, very creative when it came to burying cash, art, even real estate they didn't want found. I may be able to point Cedric in promising directions he may not have considered." Edselle sat forward and tapped on the keyboard of his desktop.

"That would be lovely. Now I'm off to a brunch."

MiMi looped her designer purse into the crook of her arm as she stood. She smoothed down the skirt she wore. A chevron pattern in black and white, it accentuated the curves of her hips. She wore a red belt along with a white blouse tucked in. Red pumps and her red purse matched her ruby red lipstick.

"Good, enjoy yourself. You've been through a lot lately." Edselle stood and came around his desk.

"Thanks, but I'm looking for fun."

"Ah, a business mixer dressed up as a brunch." Edselle opened the door for her.

"No, my mission is very personal. But I mean *serious* business." MiMi smiled at his puzzled expression. She slipped on her sunglasses and waved goodbye to him.

****

MiMi sipped a mimosa as she made her way around the room. She smiled at a group of matronly socialites as if her life was not in turmoil. One of three Baton Rouge Links, Incorporated chapters sponsored the brunch as one of their annual charity events. The new Marriott Hotel looked elegant. Decorating committee members had gone all out as usual. Fresh flowers graced each round table. A raised dais held a podium and microphone, but the speeches were over. Attendees engaged in power networking, check writing and gossiping. MiMi figured she was the subject of more than one hushed discussion. Of course no one would be uncouth enough to be obvious. Still she didn't miss the furtive glances her way. She even raised her glass to a couple of prominent ladies staring at her. They blushed, gave her twin nervous smiles and hastily look away.

"Hi MiMi, how are you holding up?" Brianna Draper strolled over. A state senator's daughter and former college classmate, she was also a Links member. She wore a faux sympathetic expression.

"I'm good. How've you been, Bree? I read you're running for the school board seat in district two. Good luck."

"Thanks. The children of our community deserve the best public education can offer. As a parent I know how vital the right decisions can be," Bree said, easily switching into campaign mode. "We can make the schools excellent for my children and your little girl."

"Hmm." MiMi sipped from her glass to keep from saying. Brianna's kids had been in private school until recently. Even then she got them into the best magnet schools in town. Not to mention Brianna, like MiMi, had attended only private schools herself.

"Anyway, it's so tragic what happened to Roderick. Crime is linked to a poor education system, you know. Just one more reason we all should be concerned about our public schools. Probably some young person or persons who meant to rob him. Right?" Brianna leaned closer to MiMi she hoped for inside scoop.

"The only thing I know is I didn't kill him."

MiMi's blunt reply made Brianna jump, but she recovered fast. "Well, um, of course not. Though Roderick wasn't the type to have enemies, not of that sort."

"What sort?" MiMi raised an eyebrow at her.

"You know; the violent criminal kind. Not in our circles for sure." Brianna nodded as though her logic was obvious.

"You never know. I heard Roddy didn't always make friends when he did business. The police are keeping an open mind." MiMi gasped when she spotted Yvette Theirry across the room. She didn't act as if she'd seen MiMi yet.

Sharp-eyed Brianna noticed and followed her gaze. "I know her, though not well. I understand she and Roderick... dated."

"Yes, they *dated*," MiMi said and gave Bree a wink. "Of course the way I found out was a shock, but I got over it. Men."

Brianna let out a soft sigh as if she understood. "Yes."

MiMi kept a close watch on the object of their discussion. After five minutes, Yvette went around shaking hands and then left. MiMi felt a wave of relief. The last thing she needed was a dramatic scene with psycho girl. MiMi's real goal lay elsewhere. When finally saw her true object, she turned her back and focused her full attention on Brianna.

"Well, that was close. Can you believe Yvette Theirry got in my face about Roderick? I told her she was a side piece. Roderick was going to give me the ring. The 'other woman' always gets it wrong."

"They don't last either." Brianna took a deep gulp from her wine glass. Her voice had turned throaty with emotion, as if she knew from experience.

"Yes." MiMi switched her attention to Brianna. "What counts is who gets the assets. The wife wins big every time, if she's smart and patient."

"Like Adrienne. She..." She put a hand to her

mouth. "I'm so sorry to gossip about your sister."

"Chris might play, but he's going nowhere honey." MiMi waved a hand dismissing Brianna's phony concern. Brianna's acting skills could use some work.

"You must be furious," Brianna said.

"He hasn't done anything to Adrienne. Like you said, she's one of the smart wives." MiMi let out a short laugh.

"She's standing right across the room," Brianna whispered.

"Who? Where?" MiMi started to turn around, but Brianna pulled her back.

"Nedra," Brianna whispered through tight lips.

MiMi managed to turn to the side and look without being obvious. She sipped more of her mimosa. "So, Nedra Xavier is his latest play thing. I hope she realizes it's temporary."

"Maybe she does, and maybe she doesn't." Brianna drank more of her red wine. "I heard Nedra is very much in love with your brother-in-law."

"Chris understands the concepts of community property. He's heard of a little thing called alimony, too." MiMi giggled and Brianna joined her.

"You know what happens when a woman falls in love. The 'other woman' starts saying she doesn't care if he stays with the wife. Some of them might even convince themselves they believe it. But eventually there's the ultimatum." Brianna really seemed to speak with authority.

"MiMi's curiosity about Brianna went up, but she couldn't be distracted. Instead she nodded with compassion. "I know, girl. Jack and I got together when he was separated. My friends told me not to do it, but I was caught up."

Brianna gulped more wine. "I dated a professor in the astronomy department when we were in college. Dr. Federspiel was so... everything."

"Blonde, tall guy from Sweden, the hunky Dr. Fed?" MiMi didn't have to pretend shock at this revelation. She almost dropped her glass. "He was married to that professor in the physics department."

"Three perfect blonde kids, a cocker spaniel and tenure. He couldn't give all that up." Brianna cleared her throat and brushed a hand over her eyes. "Anyway, I got some sense, and my Ph.D." Brianna gave MiMi a grin at the old joke. She'd married Payton Draper, a doctoral student in chemical engineering.

"Snatched that prize right from under three sorority girls' noses. I salute your awesomeness." MiMi raised her glass. When Brianna frowned at her empty glass, MiMi got another full one from a server passing by. She needed to keep Brianna's lips lubricated.

"If Nedra thinks Chris is going to leave Adrienne she's got a long wait. They'll have grandchildren and still be married." MiMi shook her head.

"She's looking this way," Brianna whispered. "Oh my God, she's actually headed over here."

Nedra made her way through the crowd. She stood tall, at least five feet nine, with naturally auburn hair and brown freckles sprayed attractively across her brown sugar skin. MiMi blinked several times. The closer she got, the more MiMi noticed how much Nedra reminded her of Adrienne.

Brianna looked nervous for the first time. "I hope she doesn't cause a scene. Don't say anything to Adrienne."

"Relax, Bree. I know how to handle this situation." MiMi faced her brother-in-law's mistress wearing a wide smile.

****

Detectives Drake and Forrester sat across the table in the interview room wearing twin blank expressions. Forrester's pen remained poised over the legal pad on the gray metal surface. Edselle Underwood wore the smug look of a defense attorney who'd just beat the system on his client's behalf.

"It's raining suspects up in here," Drake said breaking the silence. "You got anymore names of folks who had a beef with Roderick Jefferson? Hell, I wouldn't be shocked if you handed me the phone book."

Detective Forrester, good cop, cleared his throat. "Ms. Landry, let me make sure I have this correctly. Yvette Theirry is the woman who had an ongoing affair with your boyfriend. She's jealous, possessive and threatened you."

MiMi nodded. "She's been following me, too. She went ballistic when I reminded her Roderick had proposed. She said he wasn't going to go through with it, even though he'd given me the ring."

"You rubbed her nose in it, didn't you?" Detective Drake raised one dark eyebrow.

"I told her the truth. Roderick had his faults, but he was practical. Our families have known each other for years. His father and mine do business on occasion." MiMi shrugged.

"Right." Detective Drake looked at his partner.

"Motive, detectives," Edselle put in.

Forrester didn't look at him or respond to the comment. "Then you say the victim did business with this Dominican group. Their legitimate cover hides some kind of criminal activity. Jefferson stiffed them on a juicy deal."

"According to Ms. Villa, yes. She came here as their representative. I think they wanted him to compensate them for the loss. I had no idea Roderick traveled in such shifty company." MiMi shook her head slowly as if disappointed. "Still, he didn't deserve to be killed, not in such a brutal way."

"Was there another way you would have preferred?" Drake snapped.

"Your remark is out of line, detective," Edselle said quickly. "Ms. Landry has been cooperative during a very difficult time for her."

"It was worse for her boyfriend," Drake retorted and gave a louder grunt.

"Okay, okay." Forrester held up a hand before Edselle could reply. He shot his partner a look. Some message passed between them. Drake leaned back in his chair and crossed his arms.

"I suggest you lay all of these facts out to the district attorney. Let's save the tax payers money and valuable time for all of us. Not to mention the emotional toll this would further inflict on my client, a single mother who--"

"Yeah, yeah counselor. We get the point," Drake broke in. He pulled a large chocolate brown hand over his face. Then he cut another glance at his partner.

"I'm guessing that's the same speech you'd give the DA," Forrester said. He wore the faint outline of a grin.

"You'd be right, detective. I have another version for the grand jury, if the DA has time and money to burn calling one. I don't have to guess on that one. He doesn't." Edselle nodded to MiMi and she stood with him. He buttoned his suit jacket. Both detectives stood as well. "We'll wait for your call."

Detective Forrester let out a brief sigh. "Thanks for your cooperation."

"Yeah, always a pleasure." Drake gave a grunt.

"Thank *you*, detectives, for listening with an open mind." Edselle cupped a hand under MiMi's right elbow as he opened the door with his other one.

Outside the police station, they paused on the broad walkway a few yards from the entrance. People streamed by. Most wore impassive expressions. A few looked glum. Even fewer smiled and held conversations with companions. MiMi figured they must either be employees or people who weren't in trouble.

"They didn't seem all that thrilled to have leads to follow," MiMi said with a sour look. She put her sunglasses on.

Edselle squinted against the sunshine for a few seconds. He nodded to a couple, who said hello and scurried by. Then he carefully removed his own designer sunglasses from an inside jacket pocket. He gestured for them to walk along farther from the entrance instead of answering right away. They reached the edge of the shade before going into the full blast of hot late spring day.

"The police like cases to be simple. We just complicated their jobs. But at the end of the day, following all leads *is* their job."

"Excuse me if I don't feel bad for them. The easy way meant arresting me. No thanks. Let them be frustrated as hell for a little bit." MiMi slung the strap of her purse over one shoulder.

"They'll get over it, trust me. Those two love tracking down clues. I have no guarantees, but I don't think you have to worry about being a murder suspect. They'll probably tell the DA pretty much what I just told them. They're back to the starting line instead of closing their case." Edselle took out the keys to his BMW sedan.

"I'll be sobbing into my pillow all night about how hard I made their jobs," MiMi retorted.

Edselle laughed as he walked MiMi to her Lexus SUV.

****

That evening MiMi was stunned to find her father standing at her front door. He'd been the last person she expected to see when the chimes sounded and she peeked outside. Even in early May the light lingered until after seven o'clock in the evening. Drexel James Landry, Jr. stood looking quite handsome for man closing in on sixty-two. He wore his expensive tan cotton knit shirt and slacks well. Only a slight bulge at the waist hinted that he was getting the typical older man gut. He played golf and tennis to keep fit.

"This is a surprise. How are you?" MiMi said and waved him inside with her free hand. Sage perched on her opposite hip.

Her father pecked the toddler on one velvet cheek as he passed by. "My baby girl is pretty as spring day." Without waiting he headed into the kitchen.

"Yeah, make yourself at home," MiMi whispered softly as she followed him. Sage replied with baby chatter, reminding MiMi that she'd be talking soon. She'd have to get in the habit of watching what she said.

"You've redecorated. The place looks wonderful." He sat down on a comfortable stool at the breakfast bar. He smoothed a hand over the granite counter surface. Then he looked across the open floor plan at the den. "Very tasteful. Did Adrienne help you decorate?"

"Believe it or not I was able to create my own interior without Adrienne. In fact I live day to day without asking anyone to hold my hand."

"Don't be so touchy, I only meant your sister has a knack for decorating. That's all." Drexel spread his hand out.

"Yes, she's sheer perfection. Did you come over to sing her praises, or is there another point to this visit?" MiMi made sure Sage's favorite toys were within her easy reach before she faced him.

"I came to see how you're holding up, and check on my grandchild. I fail to see why that's such a surprise," her father replied in a mild tone. "Yes, a cup of coffee would be great. Thanks."

MiMi bit back another tart comment as guilt pricked her. "Sorry. Fixing a pot won't take long."

Neither of them spoke for a few minutes as MiMi poured filtered water into the well of the fancy coffee maker. Her father picked up the remote and turned on the television across the room on the wall. He watched with the sound low while MiMi finished. Seconds later the smell of a gourmet Louisiana blend floated around them. The faint scent of cinnamon, the remains of dinner, and coffee brewing created a feeling of warmth. Sage continued baby speak across the room as she played. Drexel crossed over and patted her head. His granddaughter looked up at him briefly, and continued to play.

"I think she has my mother's eyes. At least I think so," he said with satisfaction and sat down again. He muted the television. "So the police have other leads. I'm glad you won't have to deal with their questions."

"How do you... Right, never mind." MiMi didn't need to ask since her father 'knew people'. "Of course you have the latest on the investigation."

"Nothing the police won't release if reporters ask. You've had excellent legal advice obviously." Drexel fingered the television remote.

MiMi set up the creamer, sugar and a cup on the counter. "Yes, and help from my friends."

"Hmm. Though I wish you'd consulted me before talking to those detectives. I'm sure Roderick's business dealings had nothing to do with his murder. I could have told you as much." Drexel looked at MiMi.

"Then the police will find out when they investigate. In the meantime they're not warming up a cell for me," MiMi replied evenly.

"Of course I'm happy you've been eliminated as a suspect. I'm just concerned about how they'll treat our colleagues in the DR. Business culture is different in other countries. What we might think of as... out of the ordinary is just a different way of doing things. You see what I mean?" Drexel rested his elbows on the counter.

"No, I don't. You're going to have to be a tiny bit more direct, Daddy." MiMi poured coffee for him.

Her father fastidiously poured cream until the coffee turned a rich mocha color. He stirred once with a spoon, sipped and put the cup down. "Quentin and I are working with them on a deal that could be very lucrative."

"Roddy's father is still willing to cut deals with them? These people are suspects in his death. Unless you haven't told him," MiMi added.

"Roderick may have made a mistake in that

mineral import arrangement. And believe me his father let him know it." Drexel shook a forefinger in the air. "I put it down to being rash, not thinking in the long term. Black business owners are shut out of the competition in subtle ways. I've always told you that."

"Yes." MiMi hoped he wasn't about to go off on one of his favorite rants again. She knew it well. "I don't see what that has to do with Roddy's murder."

"Black entrepreneurs with foresight, the ones who've done their homework, are thinking global. We're leveraging overseas partnerships with people who look like *us*. We're on the verge of making a break through to leverage international partnerships. We've built solid relationships and established credibility as serious contenders with the right resources."

"So Mr. Jefferson agrees with you," MiMi said, pressing the point.

He picked up his cup again. "He'll come around. Naturally he's grieving now. The point is, before you make another move, check with me."

"You come into my house for the first time and..."

Drexel glanced around and then looked at MiMi. "You moved in here like a kept woman. At least your sister found *her own* husband. You ran around with Jack Crown of all people. His father is a fool. Another Black politician who got caught red handed. Your mother can't stand the wife either."

"Jack was good to me. By the way, the Landry family can't throw stones, Daddy," MiMi clipped.

"At least he had more brains than his father. Humph, must have skipped a generation. You didn't even wait until the man was actually divorced. Use your head next time," Drexel replied.

"Like with Roddy? As I recall you and Mother

thought he was the perfect catch." MiMi gave a snort.

"He had his faults, but he knew his family business well. More importantly, Roderick was willing to overlook your past."

"You... I can't believe this." MiMi bit off the stream of cuss words that almost came out. "Roddy is the reason I ended up in prison."

Her father seemed to ignore the truth. "Roderick would have talked you both out of the situation, but as usual you acted on impulse." Drexel heaved a sigh. "I don't want to fight with you, MiMi. What we built, the effort we made for over a year has the potential to make our company a lot of money, not just in the immediate future. I'm looking ahead. These men have access to more mining firms, imports goods. No more begging for minority set asides or taking insults that the only reason we have business is because of affirmative action. Damn bigots."

"You, you, you. Adrienne didn't fall far from the tree. You probably could care less if I end up in prison. Just like you don't care that Adrienne is trying to destroy my family." MiMi's voice trembled despite her efforts to not get emotional.

"You benefit very much from what I worked to provide young lady. As for Adrienne, your sister is trying to give your child a good life. You keep getting into scandals and sketchy situations with those so-called friends of yours. I mean Jack Crown's estranged wife and her jailbird stripper sister." Drexel pushed the coffee cup away as he gave a grunt of disgust.

MiMi came around the counter. "Get out of my house. Now."

"Think carefully before you burn this bridge. I helped maintain this house, make life very comfortable for you. Your *friends* can't bankroll a fancy lifestyle ," Drexel rumbled.

"I'll work three minimum wage jobs before I take another dirty dime from *you*," MiMi said, shaking with the effort not to scream and frighten Sage. "I mean it. Get the hell out of my house."

Drexel stood slowly. "I won't easily forgive you speaking to me like this, MiMi. I'm your father and I demand respect."

"You haven't earned it, not with money. Oh, and I'll tell the police anything they want to know. Goodbye." MiMi glared at him.

"Okay then. As of right now you're on your own."

Drexel went to Sage and patted her on the head. He frowned at MiMi once more before he strolled from the kitchen. MiMi followed him to the front door, fists balled tight at her side. Her father turned as if to say something, but stopped. Something in her eyes must have changed his mind. He undid the locks, pulled open the door and went to his shiny black Mercedes GL SUV. Once the door slammed shut, MiMi shook with the strength it took not to fall apart. Somehow she managed to play with Sage, give her a bath and put her to bed. Yet the toddler became fretful as though she'd picked up on the tension. When she finally tucked Sage in for the night, MiMi stumbled to her bedroom. She spent the night crying into her pillow.

Chapter 17

MiMi and Jazz sat on Willa's patio, the only space she'd let Jazz smoke. All three friends were dressed in T-shirts, Capri slacks and sandals. The kids were busily working off the hot dogs and chips they'd wolfed down. Sage romped around with Mikayla on the back lawn. After a time they settled on the grass to make a flower necklace. In a rare concession to family time for a teenager, Anthony was at home. He was playing a pick-up basketball game with a couple of friends on the wide driveway. No doubt generous helpings of food had played a part in his decision. The sounds of the bouncing ball could be heard on the other side of the wooden fence. Willa returned from the kitchen with refills of her special strawberry lemonade. The lovely spring Saturday afternoon should have been a happy time.

Jazz sucked on her cigarillo and blew smoke above her head. "I still say you should let me whip Adrienne's ass. Add your daddy to the list."

"Nah. Besides, daddy might be old, but he's tough as a pitbull." MiMi tried to make a joke of it and failed. Miserably. She wanted to cry because after all those years he could still hurt her.

"Nobody is whipping anybody's," Willa snapped. Still holding the tray with tall glasses, she stared down at Jazz. "Especially not anybody's daddy."

"I'm just kiddin' around." Jazz shrugged.

"Uh-huh, make sure you keep it that way." Willa put the tray on the round table and sat down.

"Your family is bat shit crazy," Jazz muttered.

"Watch your language. The kids might hear you," Willa said as if by reflex.

"Not way over there. Relax your butt muscles."

"They reached a new level of low down," MiMi said, for once not noticing Jazz's language. "Crazy is only half of it."

"The best thing we can do is make sure our kids don't go through the same kind of craziness," Willa said.

"I'll drink to that," MiMi replied.

The three women raised their glass, tapped them in a toast, and drank in unison. For a few moments they sat in silence watching and listening to the children at play. The cool morning had given way to warm weather in the upper seventies. The birds flew against the clear blue skies and a few white clouds. Giggling, Sage jumped up to run around holding a long string of flowers with Mikayla in hot pursuit.

"I won't let my parents make Sage feel like a second hand dress. And Adrienne? She mostly wants to take something from me. Having a pretty little girl to create her 'picture perfect' family is a bonus." MiMi picked up her lemonade glass, suddenly wishing she could swig something a lot stronger.

"Hey, you've pulled the teeth out of her custody case. You're not a suspect for Roderick's murder, well not their best one anyway," Jazz said.

MiMi sighed. "Adrienne has plenty of ammunition left. I'm still connected to two murders. As for my job? Let's just say I'm hanging onto it by a thin thread. Kelly would love nothing more than to cut me loose."

Willa shook her head. "Hey, you have to look at the positives. Edselle says mud slinging won't hold up in court. He's got the transcripts from the Dominican court, which shows you didn't even know about the drug deal. You fully cooperated with the Baton Rouge detectives, which resulted in a promising lead to real suspects."

"Now if we could just take some shine off your sister's solid citizen, loving wife and mama image..." Jazz squinted as if coming up with ideas.

"I didn't find anything," Willa said.

MiMi gasped. "You looked for dirt on my sister?"

"Sorry, I should have asked you first." Willa wore a sheepish expression. "I went over the line."

"No, you did what a real friend would do." MiMi got up, hugged Willa and sat back down. She dabbed at her eyes with a napkin.

"Our background checks from usual data sources turned up zero." Willa crossed her legs.

MiMi leaned back in her chair and took a nice long sip of the lemonade. "I rattled one particular skeleton. As your Aunt Ametrine would say in her church lady voice, I think them dry bones are about to fall out into the light."

Willa frowned. "What does that mean?"

For the first time, MiMi didn't have to force the smile she wore. "Adrienne probably doesn't even remember telling me about her hubby's mistress."

Jazz waved a hand. "Girl, please. Everybody has a side piece these days, wives and husbands. Naw, you need something juicy. You know, pictures of him goin' into a seedy massage parlor or with a street prostitute. Maybe a few pictures of him dressed in a diaper getting a spanking. Yeah, I'm liking these ideas more and more."

"Oh hell no!" Willa blurted out loudly. When Mikayla's head snapped around, Willa waved at her. "Just saying hello to you guys. Let me know if you want more lemonade."

MiMi laughed. "Thanks for the creative solutions, but let's save the scorched earth approach as a last resort."

"Okay, but remember I've got the resources." Jazz gazed back at Willa, undaunted by her scowl of disapproval.

Willa hissed, but turned her attention back to MiMi. "Okay, now give us the delicious details. This sounds really good."

"I did a little investigating on my own with some friends, and friends of friends. Chris is sleeping with a divorced ex-debutante in their social circle. Nedra is a bit needy, and she's hoping he'll leave Adrienne." MiMi paused to sip more lemonade.

"Amazing how women believe married men when they say that stuff," Willa said.

"Apparently she's counting on it. Nedra attended a big charity event put on by Baton Rouge Links, Inc. I've skipped the last two or three, but not this year." MiMi grinned widely. "I might have dropped a few hints about the happy couple, how they're going at it hot and heavy to have a baby; how Chris just adores his trophy family."

Jazz shrugged. "So what? Side-line women expect their married guys to put on a front."

"I have to agree, MiMi. Plus I don't get how dropping that knowledge on her will help the custody case." Willa blinked in confusion as though trying to figure it out.

MiMi rested her head against the chair. Her plan had sounded so smart a few days before. Describing it to her pals made it sound flimsy, and very uncertain. Still, she had hope. "We'll see. I need insurance even with things looking a bit better."

"Hey, mama, we got *company*. Anthony gave a short jerk of his thumb over one shoulder when the women looked around.

Don strolled in ahead of Detectives Drake and Forrester. His expression was unreadable behind the dark sunglasses he wore. The two detectives walked onto the patio wearing mirror frowns.

"Afternoon, ladies," Don said, speaking up first. "My colleagues wanted to talk with y'all again. They agreed to let me tag along."

"Coming was all your idea," Drake retorted. "Not that it's going to help your little friends here."

"Ladies." Forrester gave them all a curt nod. "We're having a problem finding Miss Nairoby Villa."

"Mostly because you gave her the heads up and time to run," Drake put in, pointing a meaty forefinger at MiMi.

MiMi shrunk back into the canvas of the chaise lounge in the face of his fierce gaze. "I... I don't know what you mean."

"You visited Ms. Villa on April twenty-seventh. Two hours later she checked out of her room. Coincidence?" Detective Forrester took off his sunglasses and shoved them into a shirt pocket.

"I wanted to talk to her, sure. She claims I owe her

and her business partners a lot of money. My lawyer has been discussing that claim with them, but I wanted more information." MiMi glanced at Willa for a signal.

Drake moved forward as if he'd seen the non-verbal cues bouncing between the women. "You told us you and Mr. Jefferson weren't in business together."

MiMi resisted the urge to look at Willa or Jazz. Instead she lifted her chin to gaze back at Drake. "The supposed business was with my deceased fiancé a couple of years ago. Jack Crown."

"Damn, how many murdered ex-boyfriends does this woman have?" Drake gave a grunt and looked at his partner. "Some bad mojo getting romantically involved with you, girl."

"So you come in here insulting me and expect cooperation? Well let me tell you a few things, detective." MiMi sat up straight.

"No, we'll do the talking for a little longer, and then you'll cooperate," Forrester said in a tone that sliced through the atmosphere like a steak knife. His measured, reasonable persona dropped, he crossed to sit in the empty chair near MiMi.

"Look guys, these ladies are good people. MiMi might be fumbling around playing amateur detective, but..."

Drake held up a palm. "Addison, we agreed to let you come on one condition. So stay outta the way and keep it shut."

"Hey, don't you talk to him like that," Jazz said jumping to her feet. She put both hands on her hips. "Don's a decorated and very respected cop. He wouldn't put his career on the line even for *me*."

Drake shot his partner a look. Then he glanced from Don to Jazz and back again. "Oh, so that explains why you wanted to come today. Seems we're out of the loop on station house gossip."

"Put your smart remarks on hold, Greg, or else..." Don spoke in deceptively even tone.

"Or else I'll let the boss know you're interfering with our investigation to protect your lady friend," Drake replied.

"Detective Addison, my partner has a point. Let us ask the questions and let Ms. Landry do the answering," Forrester broke in. He raised a palm to his partner as if telling him to back down. Drake huffed, but said nothing. "Ms. Landry, we only have your word that you and Ms. Villa aren't associates of some kind."

"I didn't help her go back to the Dominican Republic," MiMi blurted out.

"Ms. Villa found out from you we're looking for her. Now why would you warn a suspect?" Drake crossed his arms.

"I didn't *warn* her. I only wanted to get more information before she left. I mean once she was out of the country learning more would have been impossible." MiMi didn't flinch when his dark eyes narrowed to slits.

"Except she's not out of the country," Forrester said.

"But she..." MiMi stopped at a hiss from Jazz.

Drake gave a short humorless laugh that was more a growl. "Surprise."

"Your behavior implies that you know more than you've told us. Interfering with a police investigation is a crime," Forrester said and glanced at Don as if warning him to keep quiet.

"Might make us think you helped these folks kill Jefferson, maybe some sweet payback for him slipping around behind your back. Let's go." Drake jerked his head toward the door leading into the house.

Don took off his sunglasses as he stepped forward. "Hey, wait up guys. You didn't say anything about taking her in for questioning."

"I'm not going anywhere today. My little girl is here. I'll set up an appointment for Monday." MiMi glared back at Drake.

"You'll come now, Ms. Landry. We have a warrant for your arrest based on forensics from the crime scene, your actions with Ms. Villa and circumstantial evidence." Forrester placed a hand on Don's chest. "Stand down, Addison. Our case. The boss was clear. You want to call him?"

"Look man, I know these are friends of yours. But getting in the middle now is a bad idea," Drake said quietly.

Willa went to MiMi and put an arm around her shoulders. "Don't worry, we'll take care of Sage and make sure she doesn't get upset."

MiMi stood. "At least let me go tell my baby goodbye. Willa, call my lawyer."

****

Two hours later MiMi was at home. She wouldn't answer questions without Edselle Cunningham. Once he got there, they had to let MiMi go. At home with Sage, MiMi tried to relax. She moved around doing chores with Sage perched on one hip. She put clothes in the washer and started. Next Sage's dinner went in the warmer and her own leftovers warming in the oven. MiMi worked on making their Saturday evening normal. When she yelped at the front doorbell, MiMi realized she wasn't doing a very good job. Sage blinked at her with a baby frown as if deciding whether to cry.

"Calm down, baby girl. Mama's just being silly." MiMi laughed and made a funny face. When her little frown eased into a smile, MiMi sighed with relief. "Now let's see who's at the front door. But we won't open it unless it's somebody nice to us, will we?"

"Baba," Sage replied.

MiMi placed her on the living room floor and piled up toys. She went to the front door. "I'll just take a look and see who we're going to ignore tonight."

"It's me, open up," Willa called out. She stood back to make sure MiMi could get a good look under the lights on either side of the door."

Once she'd undone the locks, MiMi glanced around. "What are you doing here?"

"Checking on you, and finding out what happened." Willa didn't wait for more of an invitation. She walked past MiMi. Hearing Sage's baby talk, she continued into the living room. "Hello sweet pea."

"My nerves are on edge," MiMi said.

Willa picked up an over-sized stuffed pink horse. When she squeezed it a children's tune played. Sage bounced to the beat with a laugh of delight. "No kidding. Lucky Sage is too young to understand all this craziness right now."

"She'll be telling a therapist about me by the time she's twenty-one."

"Umm, are we still talking about Sage?" Willa raised an eyebrow at MiMi.

"There's nothing wrong with seeing a therapist," MiMi shot back. "The world wouldn't be so screwed up if more people got help with their issues."

"What I meant was... I didn't say... Stop tripping,"

Willa said finally.

MiMi blew out a long breath. "Sorry, like I said--"

"On edge is an understatement. Sheesh. What have you got to eat?" Willa picked up Sage along with the pink horse and headed for the kitchen.

"I've got enough Greek takeout left for three people. My appetite has been off lately. Have a seat and I'll fix dinner for all of us."

Willa placed Sage in her high chair and continued to entertain her. MiMi checked the double warmer that held Sage's toddler dishes of mashed potatoes, green peas and sliced wieners. Then she tested the food in the oven. Since it still wasn't hot, she decided to feed Sage. Once she placed the food on a plate, Willa took it.

"I'll do this. Kinda nice, reminds me of when my two were small." Willa fastened the bib around Sage's neck.

With a nod of thanks, MiMi went to the laundry room. She emptied the washer and loaded the wet clothes in the dryer. Then she returned to the kitchen just in time to see Sage happily slurping a spoonful of mashed potatoes.

"She loves that stuff. And she'd eat green peas every day if I fixed them," MiMi said with a laugh.

"Yeah, well I'm getting the vegetable in her before she starts in on the meat," Willa said as she wiped Sage's already food smeared cheeks.

"You know a lot about being a good mother. I'm obviously making a mess of it." MiMi sat down hard across from them.

"Don't even start with that crap. I know you're not saying Adrienne could do it better," Willa said.

"Hell no," MiMi blurted out. When Sage's big brown eyes widened at her, MiMi hissed. "Sorry, little miss. Mama will wash her mouth out with soap and be more careful."

Willa smiled at MiMi before giving Sage another serving of mashed green peas. "I'm pretty sure she'll be okay."

"I have a confession." MiMi twisted part of the hem of the too big t-shirt into a ball.

"Good thing the police or FBI aren't around," Willa quipped.

"You think they've planted listening devices in here?" MiMi sat straight and scanned the room.

"I need to stop kidding around and watch what I say to you right now." Willa put the plate down when Sage refused potatoes or more peas. She gave Sage a slice of wiener. Then Willa placed two soft squeeze toys within her reach. "Okay, you ate most of it, so here you go."

"Hmmm." Sage happily gnawed on the meat clutched in a tiny fist.

"Now, what's the confession?" Willa wiped her hands on a dish towel.

"Being a mother scared the crap out of me. I didn't exactly have the best role model. Sometimes I have to stop myself from dressing Sage up like a mini sorority debutante. I catch myself sounding like my..." MiMi gave a shudder, shoulders shaking. "I sound like my mother when I fuss at her about something."

"You're not your mother," Willa said firmly.

"I can't be sure. What if I slip into being rigid and judgmental? I can be a bit calculating you know." MiMi chewed her lower lip.

"Tell me something I *don't* know. You were my late husband's mistress and had the nerve to sashay in my office trying to find out about his will." Willa laughed at the grimace that twisted MiMi's face.

"For the one-hundredth time, Jack was almost your *ex*-husband. You'd been separated for a year," MiMi snapped.

"Okay, okay, I'll stop for real, but that was too good to pass up." Willa grinned at her. "Seriously, everything you do is to for Sage, to make her life better. You're a good mama."

"That means so much coming from you." MiMi blinked away sudden tears.

"How you go about it needs some work." Willa went to the oven. She used pot holders to remove the hot food. Moments later she'd heaped rice pilaf and roasted lamb on two plates.

"Yeah, like picking Roderick as her new daddy." MiMi frowned.

"Don't forget going asking about laundered money in the Dominican Republic," Willa added over her shoulder.

"My choices may help Adrienne put together her perfect family. One boy, one girl and a handsome, successful husband."

"So your plan to get the side piece stirred up hasn't worked out?" Willa came back to the table with their food.

"Nothing, not one peep. Add one more bad idea to the other stupid moves I've made."

"Hey, I didn't come here to have pity party. Besides, it was a pretty clever idea. Might still work. Now let's eat before this little dynamo gets restless and wants to get down. I'm hungry." Willa stabbed a piece of lamb with her fork. She tasted it and made happy sounds.

"Enjoy. Ali Baba's has some of the best

Mediterranean food in town."

MiMi smiled at Willa with affection. Then she popped out of her seat and got a damp dish cloth. She cleaned up the mess Sage had made while eating. Clumps of cold mash potatoes were on the floor as well as the high chair.

"Sit down and eat. You'll lose those curves you used to lure so many men into your clutches."

"Right, and look how well *that* has turned out so far. Keeping busy helps settle my nerves," MiMi said as she scrubbed the kitchen table around Willa's plate.

"At least let me eat in peace," Willa protested.

"Alright, alright. Just don't make a mess." MiMi scuttled beyond her reach with a laugh when Willa pretended to jab at her with the knife.

In a few minutes, MiMi had cleaned up most of the dishes, emptied the trash can and took clothes out of the dryer. When she returned to the kitchen, Willa had Sage in her lap. She gently rocked the contented toddler.

"You're a natural with kids," MiMi said.

"I had practice with my younger siblings before I had mine," Willa said quietly. "In a minute this one will be sleepy. Get her cleaned now because the bath will wake her up."

"Right. Up we go boo-baby." MiMi lifted Sage into her arms. She breathed in the sweet smell of her. "Mama's good girl."

"Mah-mah," Sage said. She clapped a palm on MiMi's right cheek.

Willa followed upstairs and watched MiMi bathe Sage. They swapped mother to mother chatter as Sage enjoyed the warm sudsy water. Bright yellow rubber ducks and a tiny swan floated around her. The toddler squealed with joy when ripples made them bounce. By the time they got her into the pink onesie, Sage showed no signs of being sleepy. In fact she chattered baby talk and played as if bedtime was not on her agenda.

"Dang, she's wide awake again. You know what that means." Willa shook her head.

"Maybe sitting in the rocker will help." MiMi picked Sage up. Once she settled into the rocking chair, Sage promptly whined and twisted to get out of her lap. "Lord, another bedtime battle."

"Humph, been there and done that too many times. Screaming baby is my cue to go home." Willa waved.

"Aw c'mon. At least keep me company during the struggle, girl," MiMi quipped.

"Nah, I'm out for the terrible toddler blues. Sung my own twice," Willa retorted.

"You ain't right." MiMi started to say more when the house phone rang. She picked up the cordless handset on a small table in Sage's room. "Hello."

"I'll lock up on my way out," Willa whispered.

MiMi covered the phone with one hand. "Don't leave," she whispered. Then she spoke into the phone again. "Hi Nairoby. I thought you were getting out of town ASAP."

"What?" Willa mouthed and then hissed her displeasure.

"Yeah, so why didn't you follow the plan? Oh. Huh? No, I can't help you with... Listen to me, the police are anxious to talk to you and Ramon. Trust me, it won't take them long to track you down and..."

MiMi gave Willa a series of hand signals. Sage blinked at her as if wondering if mama had lost her mind. When Willa shrugged and wore a baffled expression, MiMi waved again. Willa mouthed at her to hang up three times and huffed in frustration when MiMi pretended she didn't notice.

"Wait, you what? Okay, so maybe going back to the DR is a bad idea right now, but I don't see how..." MiMi listened to the rising panic in the woman's rapid explanation. "Oh shit."

"Language in front of the baby," Willa said sharply.

"No, I'm alone. That's the television." MiMi frowned at Willa as she flailed a hand at her to keep quiet. "Talking to the police is unavoidable. I mean they'll find you. No, you have to show ID at hotels these days and... Uh, I see."

Willa shook her head slowly. She whispered, "I don't like the sound of this conversation."

"Right. What? You've got to be kidding me. Ramon left you? I told you he was loyal to them. I didn't get you into anything, Nairoby. I..." MiMi paced with the phone as she listened. "Let me call you back in fifteen minutes. No, I'm not telling you now. Give me the number or work it out by yourself. Decide."

As Willa again shook her head and huffed with a frown, MiMi rushed out of the bedroom. "What the?"

Moments later MiMi came back with a slip of paper. She dropped the handset into the charger again. "Her number. She wants an answer."

"Easy, the answer is hell no," Willa muttered low. She darted a look at Sage who played nearby.

"You haven't heard what she said yet." MiMi stared at the small square of note paper in her hand.

"Oh I can tell you what she said. I want to pull you into deep sh... trouble and make your life even more messy than it already is." Willa went over to where Sage sat on the carpet and picked her up. "You were nuts to give her this number."

"I didn't give it to her, but these days of no privacy she could have gotten it anywhere. On the internet in some search database. But that's not what matters. She said..." MiMi waved her arms.

"I don't care what she said, and neither should *you*. Put your baby to bed. Drink some chamomile tea, and forget her."

"Just listen to me," MiMi insisted.

"What part of 'No' is confusing you, MiMi? She's in trouble with her gangster friends or partners. Her problem, not ours, and let's make sure it stays that way."

Willa tried to put Sage in her bed. The toddler squealed in protest and twisted until Willa put her down again. She made a dash for a pile of toys instead.

"Yes, but you don't--"

"I don't care what she said. Nothing is going to change my mind. We've had like way too many close calls with American thugs. I'm not looking to expand internationally. She's running from them, which means we should stay out of her problems." Willa faced MiMi with her arms crossed.

"But--"

"I'm not hearing it," Willa turned her back.

"Nairoby says Jack transferred up to four hundred thousand dollars out of the US," MiMi blurted out fast and loud.

Willa gasped and froze in place. "Did you just say..."

MiMi nodded. "Maybe more."

Chapter 18

Two hours later they had dropped Sage off at Mama Ruby's house. Papa Elton scowled at Willa and MiMi seconds after they walked through his front door. Mama Ruby went off to put a half asleep Sage into a comfy bed. Papa Elton took that time to deliver a firm lecture. Not that it did any good. After the lecture, a round of goodbye kisses to the kids and half-truths they left. Willa didn't say anything for the first ten minutes. When they stopped at a red light in a section of Baton Rouge called Easy Town, Willa heaved a sigh.

"Crazy; we're all bat shit out of our minds," Willa muttered. "And why do I let you suck me into crazy right along with you? If it's not you, it's my sister. Not only that, I'm dumb enough to be driving my SUV. It's only a year old."

"Jazz said driving my Lexus is a bad idea, let alone parking it." MiMi barely listened as she stared out of the window at the passing houses.

"Humph, they'd just think we were drug dealers." Willa took off when the light winked green.

"Drug dealers don't drive Lexus SUVs. They prefer

Range Rovers," MiMi replied absently.

"You're suddenly an expert on drug dealers and they're preferences. Impressive," Willa drawled.

"Jazz told me. Most dealers are low level. They don't make much money anyway. They drive old cars they fix up with those fancy wheels and stuff." MiMi kept thinking.

"Right, fascinating. Now we're going off to learn about foreign gangstas. We could write a book, maybe get a movie deal. If we survive," Willa grumbled.

"Hmmm." MiMi flipped a hand as her only response.

Willa mumbled barely above a whisper as they continued on. MiMi didn't pay much attention to her sour commentary and foul mood. In spite of her bad attitude, Willa came along. No matter what she said or how many times she rolled her eyes, Willa had MiMi's back. More and more MiMi considered Willa's extended family as her own. So a few minutes later when they pulled beneath the flashy red electric sign with Candy Girls in bold letters, MiMi felt right at home.

"Jazz was supposed to change the name of this place and move to another location," Willa griped.

"Don't pick a fight with her. Just don't," MiMi clipped. Before Willa could reply she hopped out of the front passenger seat and got into the back.

Jazz strode out dressed in a tight dark top with matching knit pants. She wore a pair of sneakers. She climbed into the passenger seat MiMi had vacated. "Hey y'all. So, Willa, you had enough time to get out all the bitchin' on the way over here? Or do we need to drive around a few more minutes, give you more time?"

Willa shot a heated glance at Jazz. "Blow it out your..."

"We don't have time to fight each other. We have to focus on the business at hand," MiMi said to head off a fiery exchange. "Nairoby says Ramon is gone, but she could have lied. Or she might have more hired help."

"Yeah," Jazz agreed. A frown replaced the smirk on her face.

"So let's get our game on. I don't want to be surprised." MiMi tightened the band that held her thick hair back into a ponytail.

They rode in tense silence for the next few minutes as Willa negotiated heavy Baton Rouge traffic. The volume of cars and trucks became thicker when they got on Interstate 10 toward New Orleans. Once they crossed the East Baton Rouge Parish line and into Ascension Parish, MiMi allowed herself to relax a bit.

"We should have taken time to let Don check if Ramon really is gone," MiMi said.

"Don would have asked why and seen through any lie we told. Plus I won't get him involved. This is the best plan on short notice anyway," Jazz replied.

"What if Nairoby hired local dudes?" Willa chewed on her bottom lip.

"I checked around and didn't hear anything, but with it being so last minute..." Jazz shrugged. She glanced out the windows as the SUV rolled down dark streets.

"Just great. We're going in blind, deaf and dumb; emphasis on the dumb," Willa retorted.

"Look, Nairoby has no ties in Louisiana, not to mention she's in a hotel in Kenner. She'd be crazy to trust gangsters she's never met before. Let's all just calm down. We'll be on our way home in no time." MiMi forced cheer into her tone.

"Yeah." Jazz sat on the edge of the seat. Her gaze

darted between both of the outside rearview mirrors.

"I don't believe her story. That's why I think it's got to be a trap." Willa frowned as she glanced briefly at MiMi in the interior rearview mirror.

"She knows Jack moved money," MiMi replied.

"But that can't be. Banks have to report transfers over ten thousand dollars. There would be a paper trail and we've found nothing. And Cedric and my team are good at skip tracing." Willa rubbed her forehead as if that might help her understand.

"Nairoby says she'll tell me the details. There's a legal way we can get the money," MiMi said.

"Uh-uh, not possible. She's lying. And what was all that about some guy named Ramon?"

"Ramon is the muscle that came with her. Turns out he was sent to keep an eye on her. He took off, left her on her own." MiMi squinted. "Anyway, she's scared of what he might tell the others."

"Yeah, which is a very good reason to stay far away from her. They could be sending a hit team on her. I say we avoid getting caught in the crossfire," Willa said firmly.

"I don't think it's that simple, Willa. They already know about us so we have to take action," MiMi said.

"What you mean 'us' and 'we'? Sweetie, *you* and Jack, and then Roderick got yourselves mixed up in gangsta drama. Tell the police and FBI what she said, turn it over to them and leave it alone. We can still turn around and go home," Willa said.

"Ramon or those dudes in the DR can't set up any kind of hit on Nairoby long distance," MiMi argued.

Willa heaved a deep sigh and let it out. "She told you they've done business here before. They could hire somebody local. You have no clue how many thugs they're connected to in Baton Rouge."

"Jazz checked, and she didn't."

"No, Jazz did a rush job and isn't sure," Willa said with force.

"If we hurry we can talk to her, get the story and then talk to the cops." MiMi nodded eagerly.

MiMi ignored Willa's eye roll and loud grunt. Jazz remained quietly vigilant. For the next hour the air inside the SUV remained charged. MiMi's attempts at small talk fell flat. Finally she gave up and found a smooth jazz station. They rode in silence with music playing softly. When the large green exit sign loomed up ahead, MiMi pointed.

"Exit 223 A-B, that's it," she said.

"I see it," Willa clipped back and smoothly changed lanes.

Ten minutes later she turned on Airline Highway. The Days Inn sign glowed high up lighting the way. She maneuvered the Honda Pilot onto the driveway and into a parking space between two minivans.

Willa turned off the engine. "Okay let's go over it one more time."

"Aw hell Willa, stop being so OCD," Jazz blurted out and fell against the seat back with a huff of annoyance.

"Excuse me Miss Action Figure, but this isn't a video game. We're not going to go busting up in there. Now tell me again what she said. Go on MiMi."

"Oh Lord, if it will make you feel better. Jack somehow got a lot of money out of the country. The money was in the Dominican Republic first, maybe seven years ago. That was just when the DR government tightened up banking laws under pressure from the United States." MiMi tapped on the dashboard clock as a prompt they needed to move.

Willa ignored the hint. "Sounds really thin to me."

"Then we'll fill in the blanks after I talk to her," MiMi snapped, her patience at an end. She pulled on the door handle. Locked.

Jazz tried to open her door as well. "You've got to be joking. Open these damn doors."

"I was hoping you'd both get some sense during the ride here. Look, we're pretty sure this Villa woman is too scared to leave. We can make sure by sitting on her until then. We can call Don..."

"No," MiMi broke in.

"And he'll get in touch with the local police and those FBI agents will get here in no time," Willa continued.

"Drake and Forrester will say Don knew all along. They might even accuse him of being dirty. Is that what you want you? We don't repay our friends by getting them in trouble?" Jazz snapped.

"Jazz is right, Willa. I don't see a way of involving him at this stage. Unlock the doors." MiMi rattled the handle.

"Call the FBI guy, you've got his card. Tell him you're scared and want to talk. Then he can make the decision to call Drake and Forrester. That leaves Don out of it," Willa argued.

"Open the fuckin' damn doors, Willa," Jazz hissed at her. She reached across Willa for the lock switch.

Willa blocked the move and pushed Jazz back. "Get off. Look, Nairoby can talk when the FBI or police are interviewing her."

"Now who's crazy? We've got almost a million in cash on the line. The feds will swoop down and get our money before she finishes her last sentence." Jazz's eyes narrowed to slits as she stared down her sister.

"You don't have a claim to any money," Willa shot back.

"I think some of Felipe's stash ended up in Jack's hot, greedy hands. So yeah, I've got a stake in this," Jazz replied. She tried to reach across Willa again but got shoved for her trouble. "I'm going to--"

"I wish you would," Willa replied with deadly calm.

Jazz reached out as if to try for the master lock again, but instead pinned one of Willa's arms. Meantime MiMi tried to take advantage of the distraction to stretch from the backseat and get at the switch. Willa managed to twist her body until her butt covered it.

"Get the hell off me," Willa shouted.

"You've finally lost your damn mind." Jazz panted the words between tussling with Willa.

MiMi tried to help Jazz pull Willa away their target. The Pilot rocked as all three grunted, cursed and got twisted into a human pretzel. Seconds later a loud tapping on the window startled them. They froze.

"Somebody's out there," Willa gasped.

"Step out of the vehicle," a female voice ordered.

"You were supposed to make sure we weren't followed," MiMi whispered harshly at Jazz.

"I did," Jazz whispered back. "Can't see, the windows fogged up."

"Step out with your hands first please. Everybody exit on the driver's side. Now!" A male voice shouted.

"Shit, now you've done it, Willa. Thanks for getting us arrested." Jazz mumbled a few cuss words. Then she spoke loud. "Y'all keep calm, we're coming out."

Willa clicked the locks open. One by one, with Jazz going first, they slowly opened each door and stuck their hands up. When they all stood on the pavement they stared at an older white couple. Dressed in khaki shorts and a plaid shirt, the man stood with spindly legs spread apart. The woman with him wore a matching outfit, except her sandals were bright pink.

"What the hell?" Jazz lowered her arms.

A tall black man strode up dressed in a dark uniform. The short woman behind him wore a white shirt with the hotel logo embroidered on it. She stood well to the side as if ready to let him take any bullets.

"Hotel security. What's going on out here?" the man barked. He glanced from the white couple to MiMi and company.

"I'm Fred Watkins and this is my wife Irma. We're retired sheriff's deputies Hancock County Indiana. We're here on vacation," the man said in an officious and brisk tone.

"Yes, sir. We observed these three acting suspicious. Then they started a ruckus in this vehicle, maybe arguing over drugs," Irma said with a sharp nod of her head. "NOPD should probably bring a drug dog out."

"Don't listen to Homer and Marge Simpson," Jazz spat as she jerked a thumb at the couple. "We're minding our own business, visiting a friend in town."

"That's right, sir. She's registered at this hotel. Check it out." Willa put in.

"They were fighting in there, officer. Or doing something else. Look to see if a man is in there pulling up his pants," Irma said with a raised eyebrow.

"Hey, we're not prostitutes. You've got a lot of nerve, and by the way you're not even cops anymore. Mind your own business," MiMi yelled.

"Even if you were, you're out of your jurisdiction," Willa added.

"Everybody just calm down. Lana, go check on this guest they claim to be visiting. Name of..." The guard looked at Willa.

"Her name is Nairoby Villa," Willa said calmly.

"I'll send Ray out here just in case," Lana said to the guard before hurrying to the lobby entrance.

"What's your name, sir?" Jazz smiled at him.

"Terrell Jackson. Move away from the vehicle everybody." Terrell held up a hand when Fred took a step to follow him. "Everybody includes you, too."

"Sure. Just trying to help," Fred said with a nod. He went back to stand next to his wife. Still both of them craned their necks to watch him.

The security guard shined a flashlight around the interior of Willa's Pilot. He sniffed a few times. When a second man walked up, the guard nodded at him. The man nodded back. Terrell then climbed into the Pilot for a closer look. A few minutes later he climbed out.

"You should call the NOPD," Erma said again.

"Ma'am, we're in Kenner, not New Orleans. Did these ladies try to steal from y'all, or approached you aggressively?" Terrell looked from Irma to Henry.

"Well, no," Henry admitted and frowned. "But..."

"So they were in their SUV and you didn't like how they behaved," Terrell pressed on.

"They were acting suspicious, like they were in a fight or something," Erma put in. She glared at Willa, Jazz and MiMi in turn.

"So you didn't really know what they were doing when you ordered them out of their vehicle?" Terrell planted his beefy fists on his waist.

"We got into a bit of an argument," Willa said quickly before Erma or Henry could speak.

"Yeah," Jazz added. "MiMi wanted to drive, but

she's had a few drinks. She gets a little hard to deal with. She grabbed the keys out of the ignition, and I grabbed them back. Then she tried to get them again."

Lana returned. "Ms. Villa checked in two days ago. I asked was she expecting anyone and she said yes, a business associate."

The guard turned back to Willa, MiMi and Jazz. "You said y'all were friends."

"We became friends after doing business together, sir," MiMi replied. She blinked as if genuinely confused. "Is that a crime?"

"Sounds fishy, like they're thinking up a story on the fly, officer," Henry piped up as Erma bobbed her head in agreement.

"I'm not an *officer*. Hotel security doesn't have rank, mister," Terrell said. "Look, bottom line is these ladies didn't do anything wrong."

"Sounds like some party girls out for a good time," Ray replied with a grin at them.

"Too bad you're working, Ray," Jazz said and winked at him.

"If there's nothing going on, then you should get back to the desk," Lana said sharply as she glared at him.

"Sure. Call me if you need anything at all," Ray said, his gaze on Jazz's full breasts outlined by the knit shirt that clung to her figure.

Terrell let out a sigh as he watched the slender young man stroll off. "Look folks, they didn't do anything to y'all, and neither of you saw them do anything that might be illegal."

"Coming to a hotel isn't against the law in Louisiana. Maybe they do things different in Hicksville

County Indiana," Jazz drawled and leaned against the Pilot.

"Yes, we were minding our own business. You might want to try it," MiMi quipped.

Irma squinted at Jazz, and then swept a critical glance at MiMi and Willa. "You're going to find yourselves in trouble real soon. I can tell."

Terrell held up a palm. "Okay, okay, let's all try to get along. Ladies, be careful and have a good night. Mr. and Mrs. Watkins, anything else I can do for y'all?"

Henry wore a frown for a few seconds before he shook his head once. "No, guess not."

"Good deal. Now you folks enjoy your stay. I'll be glad to suggest some fine places to eat. You going to the French Quarter this evening?" Terrell transformed from a stern security professional to a friendly local.

"We have reservations at The Bombay Club," Fred replied. He continued to eye Jazz, MiMi and Willa with skepticism stamped on his pugnacious features.

"That's a fine jazz club. Y'all have a great evening, okay?" Terrell managed to herd them away. They ended up at a large RV parked at the other end of the lot.

Lana cocked her head to one side. "Well? Your friend is waiting."

"Hmm, right. I'll go up and get her. Y'all wait down here," MiMi said.

"Okay." Willa studied the hotel windows facing the parking lot where they stood.

Jazz stared at Lana. "I think we can take it from here. We don't need an escort."

The hotel manager gave them all a look of suspicion, but said nothing. She left, but not without glancing back at them and the security guard. Terrell still stood with Henry and Erma. MiMi suspected he was arguing that he had no grounds to call the police. Once Lana entered the automatic glass doors to the hotel, MiMi spun to face Willa and Jazz.

"I think we're in luck. The hotel manager didn't mention how many of us were here, just asked if Nairoby was expecting company. Y'all stay put." MiMi took only a couple of steps when Willa jerked her back.

"She's not stupid, MiMi. She's going to figure you didn't come alone," Willa said.

"Yeah, but her back is against the wall. So she's got no choice," Jazz replied.

"Exactly, we're all she's got at the moment. At this point, I'll bet she doesn't care. Nairoby hopes I help her dodge a police interview. If she tells me about missing money, the FBI and Baton Rouge detectives will forget about her." MiMi nodded eagerly to convince Willa.

"You want us to wind up being suspects with the feds and the local police over some money?" Willa blurted out.

"Half a million? Hell yes. I've talked my way out of bigger jams for nothing," Jazz joked with a laugh.

"Willa, the police are building evidence against me while we stand here arguing. Let's at least find out about the over *four hundred thousand dollars* Jack finessed out of the country. I may need it to fund my defense team," MiMi said, struggling to keep from shouting or shaking her stubborn pal.

"Okay, fine. Dial my number and keep your cell phone on speaker. I'll mute mine so background noises won't come through on your end. The minute I hear something funny, we're coming in." Willa pulled out her phone.

"Great idea. See, you were right to come along with me." MiMi did as instructed and dropped the phone in the pocked of her hoodie pullover. "Okay, ready."

MiMi crossed the parking lot. Despite her show of bravery, her stomach knotted the closer she got to the hotel entrance. Lana and Ray stood at the desk, both watching as she entered. MiMi gave them what she hoped was a carefree smile. Lana simply raised a dark eyebrow in response, but Ray winked at her.

"Room 302," he said with a grin.

"Thanks."

Once she got past them, MiMi glanced around to get familiar with the layout. A hallway lead branched off from the lobby to another glass door to the parking. A sign said it was locked at night for the safety of guests.

"Hey y'all, come to the north side of the building. You'll see a big green exit sign. I'll let you in," MiMi said quietly into the phone.

Five minutes later Willa and Jazz appeared at the door. MiMi let them in, careful to open the door slowly in case it made noise. She eased it closed again. The click seemed as loud as July fourth fireworks. All three scurried to conceal themselves around another corner, but no one came to investigate.

"We'll take the stairs and wait on the landing. That way we'll be close if something goes wrong," Jazz said.

"Right." Willa nodded though her expression implied she wished they were far away.

"You act like you've done this before," MiMi said as she texted Nairoby she'd be at the door soon.

"I refuse to answer on the grounds it may incriminate me," Jazz murmured rapidly and gave them a crooked grin. "Now go before Nairoby gets too jumpy."

MiMi read Nairoby's cryptic "I'm here" reply then

dropped the phone back into her pocket and zipped it shut. She gave them a thumbs up signal and went back down the hall to the elevators. Lana appeared when MiMi rounded the corner leading to the elevators. She frowned, suspicion.

"I thought you'd gone up already." The manager studied MiMi.

"I took a wrong turn, and then I answered a text," MiMi answered smoothly. The soft ping announced the arrival of the elevator.

She disappeared inside and pressed the button to close the doors. All the while she prayed Lana wouldn't get on with her at the last minute. MiMi let out a long sigh of relief once the doors slid together and she was alone. Seconds later she arrived on the third floor. The thump of loud music came from one of the rooms. The Days Inn had seen better days. Maybe Nairoby had chosen it because it was cheap. Still it appeared clean. A burst of raucous laughter made MiMi jump. She increased her pace to find the stairwell exit. After a whispered confirmation that Willa and Jazz were on the fifth floor, MiMi again concealed the cell phone. She found room 502. At first she knocked discreetly. The noise forced her to try again, this time banging hard.

Nairoby jerked the door open. "You want to make more noise. Maybe the entire world didn't hear you."

"You picked a..." MiMi didn't finish because Nairoby yanked her inside and shut the door.

"Were you followed?" Nairoby dragged MiMi with her to the window and looked out.

"You lost your mind?" MiMi twisted her wrist until she had freed her arm. Then she stepped back.

"I know you brought your little ghetto friend, whats-her-name, and her gang. Am I right?" Nairoby moved from the window quickly and into a defensive stance to face MiMi.

"We're not the ones you have to worry about. We need each other." MiMi hoped she sounded as cool and confident as Jazz would be.

"Yes, little spoiled American princess. You want the money." Nairoby's worried expression eased into a smirk.

"Get to the point so I can help you get back to the DR even faster," MiMi snapped. "Or maybe you don't want to go home."

"Where I go is none of your concern, princess," Nairoby shot back. Yet the smirk melted from her pretty brown face.

"Fine, tell me about Jack's money and if you know anymore about Roderick," MiMi said. She was as eager to be rid of the troublesome woman as Nairoby was to leave.

"First things first. What have you told the police and FBI about me?" Nairoby backed up to the window while keeping her gaze on MiMi. Barely moving the drab tan curtains, she darted another quick glance outside.

"I told them you thought Jack cut you out of a big money deal and you came here to get it back," MiMi started.

"You mean Jack stole from me," Nairoby spat like the words were bitter on her tongue.

"Yes, darlin'. Your one true love jacked you big time," MiMi replied, this time with her own smirk.

"You..." Nairoby glared at her for a few seconds. "What else?"

"I told them you didn't know anything about Roderick's business, that he only met with your bosses.

You're only a step above their secretary." MiMi took pleasure at the scowl her last words brought.

"That's bullshit. They wouldn't have made any connections here without me. I put money in their pockets. If they were so much smarter than me, then they wouldn't have trusted Jefferson so easily. I know men, I would have seen through him." Nairoby waved a hand in the air.

"So what happened with Jack? You didn't see through him obviously." MiMi held up a palm. "Look, let's not waste energy fighting about him. Jack had skills in and out of the bedroom. His charm was almost supernatural."

Nairoby gazed at her for a few seconds before she nodded. "Those eyes like smoky topaz, and the scent he wore. And his hands, his mouth--"

"Whoa, whoa, I don't need the details. Like I said, he was good." MiMi studied Nairoby. Despite the hard exterior, the woman seemed to have had a worse case of Jack Crown than MiMi or Willa.

"You couldn't have kept Jack satisfied. You were just a tool." Nairoby tossed her long black hair over one shoulder.

MiMi gave a grunt. "Don't be so smug, honey. He used *you*, too. Jack planned to have help moving his money out of reach of the IRS and banking laws. He saw you coming a mile away."

"What we had was business and pleasure, a lot of pleasure." Nairoby's Dominican accent made the word sound even more erotic.

"Look, I didn't come here to talk about your sex life. All I want to hear about is the money." MiMi crossed her arms.

"So, you can't stand the thought of how much Jack

craved every inch of me. Believe me, I loved every *inch* of him." Nairoby's full mouth lifted at one corner into a leering expression.

"In other words you don't know anything. You're stalling for time. I'll just go talk to the FBI and the police. Girl, bye," MiMi said and flipped a hand at Nairoby.

MiMi kept Nairoby in sight, careful not to turn her back. Just as she started to leave, a side door connected to another room clicked open. A woman stepped through. Her long hair had reddish blonde highlights. She wore a shiny burnt orange sateen jacket belted over paisley leggings and oversized hoop earrings. Her other fashion accessory was a small black handgun. She wore a nasty smile as she gazed at MiMi with hatred.

"Nice to see you again, Ms. Landry."

Chapter 19

Nairoby stepped around MiMi. She threw clothes and toiletries into a carryon suitcase. "What the hell took you so long? She could have shot me or something."

The woman's laugh came out like a high pitched fingernail scraping chalk board. MiMi stared at her hard. Her face seemed both real and unreal, the voice familiar. The woman removed the clip-on hair extensions. Next she peeled off the nose like it was a second skin. She gave MiMi a smile that sent a chill through her.

Yvette Theirry removed the wig cap and fluffed out her natural hair. "Not the prissy sorority sister here. She might sound tough, but all she's got is big talk. You, sit down."

MiMi gazed at the gun. Size didn't mean anything, especially at such close range. Still MiMi felt more anger than fear. "No, say what you've got to say so I can leave."

"Leave? You're not going anywhere until I'm ready. I said sit your ass down," Yvette hissed.

"I'm not sitting down." MiMi crossed her arms. "Shoot and people will come running."

"Not with the noise from the neighbors they won't," Yvette said with smile of confidence.

"The music has stopped." MiMi's gaze darted around for any kind of escape route.

"They're just taking a short break. I had beer and pints of malt liquor sent to them with a note that it's a tourist promotion gift." Yvette's smile widened when the music pumped up again two seconds after she stopped talking.

"I still won't sit." MiMi swallowed hard.

"Stop the pissing contest. Who cares if she sits, stands or does a back flip. Get on with it so I can get out of here. I've been trapped in this dump long enough." Nairoby crossed to the window and barely twitched the curtain so she could look out. "Her friends will start to wonder why she hasn't come back down."

"There's no one waiting in the SUV and or the lobby waiting. She bluffed you." Yvette's full mouth, twisted with distaste the longer she gazed at MiMi.

"Did you ask what's his name, the desk clerk?" Nairoby looked away from the window.

"The bitch manager came back and started looking me up and down. I couldn't draw attention to myself. She got busy with a crowd of people checking in, and the desk phone started ringing. I took that chance to slip on the elevator with some of those drunk ass kids."

"But she said..."

"I said I looked around, didn't I?" Yvette shot an irritated glance at Nairoby.

"Excuse me for interrupting your performance of who's the biggest moron, but neither of you seems to have thought this through." MiMi moved but went still when Yvette leveled the gun at her chest. "Witnesses know I'm in Nairoby's room, and no doubt security cameras will show you coming in. So if anything happens to me..."

Yvette grunted a brusque laugh. "Watch her while I clean up."

"Okay, but make it quick. I want to get out of this crazy state." Nairoby hurried to the chair and took another gun from beneath the seat cushion.

MiMi blinked at her. "You must know this won't work."

"I'll be long gone. All your police will have is speculation. Even you said they can't charge me with anything. No evidence," Nairoby said. The shrill note in her voice implied she needed to convince herself more than MiMi.

"They'll connect you to her. How..."

MiMi stopped when Yvette appeared. She looked totally different, or at least different enough not to be recognized. She nodded slowly as she gazed back at MiMi.

"They might have this girl on camera, but not me." Yvette shook the fake hair and giggled.

"I have to repeat myself. Why am I here?" MiMi hoped Willa and Jazz had called the police. She just had to avoid getting killed before they arrived.

Yvette pointed her gun at MiMi again. She sat on the arm of the large chair. Though she seemed relaxed, she held the gun like a pro. "Well, I'll tell you. Roderick, the no-good shit turd, stole from me and his Dominican business partners. The law firm I work for represents several corporations looking for the mineral products Roderick would sell. He got the whole idea from me."

"You invested, and disclosed client information,"

MiMi said with a frown.

"Roderick talked as if he'd confided in you, his trophy fiancé. So you're going to tell us where to find the money. It's not in the US." Yvette raised an eyebrow at MiMi.

"Roderick didn't tell me anything."

MiMi stopped. She knew which banks in the DR Roderick had visited. Then she remembered Roderick's belongings still at the house, and in her home safe; items she'd never bother to look at because she was busy. Roderick locked up his grandfather's antique white gold cuff links and watch, at least that's what he'd told her. MiMi tried to remember if he'd taken them out before they broke up.

Yvette studied MiMi. "I'm a lawyer, trained to know when a witness isn't telling the truth, the whole truth and nothing but the truth."

"You knew more about his business dealings than I did. All he did was romance me and give me gifts." MiMi kept her voice steady. Or at lease she prayed she did.

Yvette's eyes narrowed until her gaze seemed like a gun laser. "Bullshit. You know something."

"Like you said, Roderick thought of me as his empty-headed trophy. I was for show," MiMi replied. "He didn't tell me anything he thought was important. Maybe his father knows, but not me."

"Yeah, for show, like the jewelry he bought for you worth a few thousand dollars," Yvette said, her mouth twisted until her features seemed distorted. "He used me and then bragged about how clever he was to outsmart the Domincans. I wasn't good enough to marry, just hook up with every now and then for a quick freak."

"He... he lied to me, too. Roderick only cared about

my family connections." MiMi's heart pounded at the wide look in Yvette's eyes.

"I don't give a damn who this guy wanted to marry or screw, find out where the money is so I can go home. I'll pay off my partners with it," Nairoby said, her voice squeaking. "You two are still competing for a dead man who obviously cared only about himself."

"Shut up. What do you know about it?" Yvette snarled. Then she looked daggers at MiMi "Roderick wouldn't have turned on me if she hadn't come between us. Maybe you suggested he stab me in the back."

MiMi took a step back when Yvette stood suddenly. The irrational turn of the woman's conclusions ratcheted up the danger level. "You're wrong, Yvette. I didn't know about any of it..."

"Look, just tell Yvette what she wants to know," Nairoby blurted out as she wrung her hands. She darted a look at her conspirator.

MiMi needed to play for more time. She sent a mental message to her pals and the cops to speed it up. "If you want money, then talk to Narioby. She already knows where close to half a million is stashed. You can get back your investment. I'm telling you, Roderick kept a lot of stuff from me. I don't know anything."

"He treated you like a queen; *his* queen. You had a lot of fun rubbing my nose in it, remember? He wanted to build a life with you, not me." Yvette's breathing grew heavy as she spoke. "I saw you two together. That huge diamond ring he gave you. He took you to the Dominican Republic with him. Is that where you two hatched up a plan to cut me out? Yeah, Roderick told you about all his big plans."

"Keep cool, girl," Nairoby said. Her eyes were wide

with fear as she looked at Yvette. "As scared as she is, she would have told you everything by now. Let's just get far away from here before we have more trouble. You can sue Jefferson's father to get your investment back, and at least I'll recover enough to satisfy my partners."

Yvette continued to stare at MiMi for a few moments in silence. "Don't be stupid. I can't sue his old man. If what I've done comes out, I'll be disbarred or go to prison. Probably both. Besides, you forget our little witness here."

Nairoby blinked hard. "She won't talk. I can prove she helped Jack Crown hide money offshore. The FBI would take everything she owns, and arrest her."

"She's right. I can't afford to say anything. The FBI will take everything I own. Just leave and get the money." MiMi talked fast as if that would help convince Yvette. Her heart dropped when Yvette shook her head slowly.

"Not until you tell me where Roderick hid my money. I'm sure you wouldn't want anything unpleasant to happen to sweet baby Sage, now would you?" Yvette said as she took a step toward MiMi.

Nairoby walked between them and spoke low to Yvette. "Hey, don't overdo the threats or she'll freeze up. Talk about hurting her child is a bit much."

"Who says I'm just talking? The bitch took everything from me. I don't care if she and her little bastard get dumped in a deep hole." Yvette spoke matter-of-factly.

"Listen, I can understand how you feel with the guy dumping you and all, but... I didn't sign up for doing no murders," Nairoby said.

She lapsed into rapid fire Spanish. MiMi blinked in

shock when Yvette answered her fluently. The women went back and forth for a time. Nairoby's tone went from pleading to desperate and terrified. Though MiMi couldn't follow every word, Yvette made her intention clear.

"I'm calling this whole thing off. Now put away the gun," Nairoby said in heavily accented English. "I came to get paid, not to end up rotting in a US prison because of a mujer loca."

"Why are you worried, my sister? American prisons are paradise compared to lock up in the DR. I've visited both enough to know." Yvette gave MiMi a brief smile. "Ah, you didn't know my father is Dominican."

"I'm not kidding with you, Yvette. Put down your gun," Nairoby raised her pistol.

"Or you'll shoot me? Ha. I unloaded the gun two days ago. But I can assure you mine has lots of nice bullets. Now get over there with the princess." Yvette gestured with her pistol. She frowned at Nairoby. "Move."

Nairoby backed up so fast she almost knocked MiMi over. Instead MiMi grabbed onto the dresser. Once steady, she snatched the revolver from Nairoby and popped out the cylinder. The little Colt special had no bullets.

"First you talk, and then I'll take care of you both," Yvette said.

"If I'm dead I definitely won't be talking," MiMi replied. Her heart hammered so, she thought it might drown out the pounding music still coming from the party people.

"No, no, no. Stop this talk of killing people. Chica, listen to me, I can get you all kinds of money," Nairoby gasped. Then she spun around to face MiMi. "Don't be a little fool. Tell her everything."

At that moment the music stopped. MiMi breathed hard. "No. She won't risk people hearing the shots."

Yvette's expression didn't change. When the music pumped up again, she smiled and shot Nairoby in the right thigh. The pounding hip-hop music down the hall drowned out the loud pop. Nairoby screamed once then crumbled to the floor.

"Silencer. I came prepared. Now tell me where I can find the money and little Sage will grow up healthy," Yvette said quietly.

MiMi felt all feeling drain from her legs. "You're totally insane."

"No, just pissed off and determined to get back what's mine," Yvette replied with a sideways smirk.

"You killed Roderick," MiMi said, horror moving through her like an electric shock.

Nairoby stopped rocking abruptly and gaped at Yvette. "What? What did she say?"

"No, the police will have evidence enough to get a nice neat conviction against you. At least they will by the time I'm through." Yvette smiled for a few seconds. Then her features twisted into a mask of fury. "Roderick played with my emotions, then stole from me."

"How could you kill the man you claimed to love so much?" MiMi managed to say though her throat had gone dry with fear.

Yvette blinked hard, her eyes glassy with unshed tears. "I poured my heart out to Roderick, told him things I'd never confided in anyone. Did things for him I wouldn't have done for anyone else. I even tolerated him screwing you. Roderick swore he had no intention of marrying you. Once he had access to your father's deep pocket connections, he'd dump you. That was a lie, and he enjoyed telling me so. The bastard laughed at me. At *me*, after I set him up to make millions. I risked my career and criminal charges for him, and he laughed."

"Oh my God. I thought..." Nairoby clamped a hand over her mouth.

"That your buddies back home had Roderick taken out? Exactly what I wanted you and everyone else to believe." Yvette's grin looked like a death mask.

Nairoby groaned. "Oh Dios, I need a doctor. Please help me."

"Oh shut the hell up. It's the blood that's scaring you more than anything. The pain will come later," Yvette retorted.

"The safe, in my house. Roderick put something in there, but I haven't looked," MiMi blurted out when Yvette aimed the gun at Nairoby again.

"Good. Now you'll tell me the security code so your alarm system won't go off." Yvette nodded at MiMi to speak up.

"It's 669327." MiMi squatted next to Nairoby and placed a hand on her forehead. "She's going into shock I think. You've got what you need, so go. Nairoby can't walk, and I sure can't carry her. I swear we won't follow you."

"But she can still talk, and so can you," Yvette said.

"You can't explain two dead women." MiMi frantically scanned the room for even a slight hope of escape.

"I won't have to. You came there to meet up with your dead lover's shady business partner. You two planned to split stolen money, but got into an argument and shot each other. Before Nairoby could get treatment, she bled out. Wow, you nicked an artery.

Nice aim." Yvette smiled down at them both. She shrugged when the music stopped. "I can wait."

"New Orleans PD. Open the door. We've had a complaint about a disturbance," a female voice ordered, and pounding on the door followed a few seconds later.

Yvette jumped but held the gun steady. "Get away from the window," she hissed.

"What are you going to do, jump? We're up three floors and there's no balcony." MiMi stood. "You need better put down that gun. If they see you holding it---"

"Nobody's going to see anything. Shut your mouth. If you cooperate maybe I won't kill your kid once I take care of you." Yvette moved to the door.

She pointed at MiMi to cover Nairoby's mouth to muffle her soft whimpers. Then she went to the closet and grabbed a robe. Yvette covered her clothes and tousled her hair. Then she opened the door a crack.

"Sorry, I'm just out of the shower and not dressed. I called about those rowdy thugs and..."

Yvette grunted as the door slammed open. The force caused her to fly back and MiMi swung out without hesitation. Before Yvette could aim, MiMi kneed her in the back hard. Then she grabbed her wrist and twisted. Yvette held onto the gun as she tried to twist around. Jazz barreled into the room and slapped Nairoby as she tried to make a run for it. Willa scooped up the gun Nairoby had dropped.

Dazed, yet still enraged, Yvette tried to defend herself. MiMi jammed her against the sharp edge of the dresser. Music thumped louder as the gun popped twice when Yvette struggled to regain her footing and aim at the newcomers. MiMi ducked, landed a kick on Yvette's left knee and shouted "She's got a gun" in blur of action. MiMi shoved Yvettte to the floor. The woman screamed a gutteral sound when MiMi stomped on her back and then wrist using her full weight.

A tall young blonde guy stumbled through the open door holding a beer bottle. "Hell, there's a better party in here."

The loopy grin froze on his face when he took in the scene. Nairoby lay slumped on the floor on the blood soaked carpet and two women holding her down. MiMi and Yvette still fought for control of the gun. He bounced from one foot to the other, no help at all.

"Oh, shit. Oh shit. Oh shit. Somebody call the cops."

MiMi got her hands on the cheap hotel flower vase and broke it over Yvette's head. The blow stunned the crazed woman. Willa took the chance to stomp on Yvette's wrist, and the blow got Jazz's arm in the process. Both women screeched in pain. The gun went off a fourth time. Willa kicked hard and it flew across the shabby carpet. The blonde drunk peed his jean shorts, and the police finally showed up.

****

Three weeks later MiMi, Jazz, and Willa lounged around their private resort patio. Two days of soaking up the St. Lucia sun proved to be excellent therapy. Cedric swam his third short lap, blue-green water splashing with each stroke. Willa and Cedric were booked in a cottage with their own private pool. MiMi and Jazz had adjoining cottages on the other side of the resort with ocean views. The women had spent the first day sleeping. The events of the post Yvette and her gun had been bad enough. Meeting with various law enforcement agencies had left even Jazz with frazzled nerves. Willa's parents and aunts had taken the children on an island tour. The entire family enjoyed much needed holiday, and what a spectacular setting the Ti Kaye Resort and Spa offered.

All four lounged around the private pool as a waiter made the rounds refreshing their drinks. He smiled at them cordially, no doubt expecting a nice tip in a few days when the rich Americans checked out. Edselle frowned at them from the video call app on MiMi's android tablet. They'd propped it up TV style on the patio table. The image came through clearly as did his disapproval.

"You ladies were extremely lucky."

Jazz accepted a drink from the poolside waiter. "Yeah, yeah."

"Be polite," Willa mumbled. "This man has been on our side through a lot of crap."

"Thank you," Edselle replied. He grinned when Willa blushed at being heard.

"Hmm, you're welcome," she said and pressed her lips together.

Jazz swung her legs out of the pool, stood and strolled over so he could see her. "I agree. You did your job, Mr. Lawyer." She winked at him, raised her glass and sipped.

"And, uh, thank you, too." Edselle blinked as Jazz strolled off giving him a nice view of her curvy butt covered in the turquoise bikini bottom.

"I'm sorry we put you through so much, Ed." Willa shot MiMi a sharp glance.

"What? I'm the victim here. None of this was my fault," MiMi protested from behind her Louis Vuitton amber sunglasses.

"At any rate the police have plenty enough to

charge Yvette Theirry with murder thanks to your friend Nairoby Villa," Edselle said. "She's healing nicely by the way. Thank goodness that gunshot was just a flesh would after all."

"She's *not* my friend. The only reason she talked is because I threatened to tell her 'business partners' she tried to scam them," MiMi said. "Trust me, if nailing my rear end to the wall had helped her, Nairoby would have been happy to do it."

"Well she told the truth about Jack's hidden money." Willa switched her attention to the sight of Cedric's long, muscular frame emerging from the pool.

"She thought I was going to jail for murder and she'd get to keep it all. She's lucky I'm generous and won't snitch to those snakes back in the DR. They all deserve each other," MiMi retorted.

The mention of money caused Jazz to put down her tall glass. "So the cash is clean? That's for sure?"

Edselle wore a pensive frown. "The FBI can't definitively link the money in the Scotia Bank account to a criminal enterprise, or that Mr. Crown did anything against the law. The DR business group may be shifty, but they're very smart. They use legitimate business ventures as a cover. So far they haven't been caught. It's complicated, but proving they did anything illegal would be long and involved. And the feds probably still wouldn't win that battle."

"Besides, they moved that money around in through at least a dozen companies and through four countries. Most of those four foreign governments drag their feet on request from US law enforcement," Cedric put in as he dried himself with a large towel.

"Which leads to the happy bottom line; the money is all mine." MiMi beamed.

"Oh?" Willa removed her tortoise shell sunglasses.

Jazz walked behind MiMi's chair and placed a hand on both her shoulders. "Really?"

"Ahem, y'all know I was just kidding around." MiMi gave a playful laugh and patted Jazz's hands.

"Uh-huh," Jazz grunted. She plopped down on the chaise lounge next to MiMi.

"Yvette is safely locked up. Nairoby is talking her head off, and we're over eight hundred thousand dollars richer. There could even be more. As Willa's Aunt Ametrine would say, won't He fix it?" MiMi grinned at the word.

"Oo-wee, Aunt Ametrine thinks we're all godless heathens," Jazz wisecracked. "I wouldn't be surprised if she showed up with a jumbo spray bottle of holy water to wash our sins away." They all had a good laugh, though Cedric glanced at the door leading from the cottage.

"Well you may be having a vacation, but I've got work to do. Have fun, and do me the huge favor of staying out of trouble. Please," Edselle said pointedly and without smiling.

"We'll give it our best shot." MiMi lifted her glass of frozen mango daiquiri to him as a salute. Edselle heaved a deep sigh as his only response and signed off.

They sat in companionable silence for a few minutes. Jazz kicked her legs in the pool. Willa and Cedric took turns massaging sunscreen on each other. MiMi stared out at the azure water of the Caribbean Sea.

"You know, we could turn this whole mad drama into a business. I mean might as well put our skills to use and earn high fees in the process," MiMi said thoughtfully.

"Let's see. Get shot at, thrown in jail and accused of murder. I don't find that business plan attractive at all." Willa gave a grunt.

"I mean tracking down the hidden assets. Wealthy men are always pulling a switch to keep from paying high alimony or child support. We'd strike a blow for justice, and charge a nice percentage based on the amount we find." MiMi glanced between her friends.

"Why be sexist? Rich women do the same thing ya know," Jazz put in.

"Excellent point my friend." MiMi grinned at her.

"High end law firms hire investigators for that purpose. The pay can be in the six figures depending on the size of the stash and what you uncover." Cedric shrugged when Willa scowled at him as if betrayed. "I'm just saying."

"We'd only take cases that involved assets or cash of three hundred thousand or more. Then we could take on lower income clients for free. Give back to the community," MiMi replied.

Willa swatted him on the shoulder. "*No.*"

"Yeah, that would be nice. We can start up with minimal cost because we already have the resources, know- how and manpower," Jazz agreed. She giggled at the deadly look from Willa.

"Good. Let's start working on it when we get home." MiMi gave them a crisp business-like nod.

"Domestic battles can get dirty and deadly," Willa insisted. "Hell. No."

None of them answered her. Cedric lapsed into thoughtful silence nodding to himself. He seemed to be devising their first moves. Jazz grinned and raised her glass to toast exciting profitable adventures. They appeared not to notice when Willa fell back against her chaise lounge with a dramatic groan. MiMi smiled with pleasure as she gazed into blues skies and a profitable future.

"Hell yes. I'll be the CEO. Landry and Associates Asset Recovery, LLC. Has a sweet ring to it," MiMi said.

If you enjoyed Pretty Dangerous please leave a review.
Thanks and happy reading!

Enjoy the rest of the Triple Trouble Mysteries

Best Enemies

Devilish Details

Visit www.lynnemery.com
See book videos
&
subscribe to my newsletter

About Lynn Emery

Mix knowledge of voodoo, Louisiana politics and forensic social work with the dedication to write fiction while working each day as a clinical social worker, and you get a snapshot of author Lynn Emery. Lynn has been a contributing consultant to the magazine Today's Black Woman for three articles about contemporary relationships between black men and women. She sold her first novel in 1995 to Kensington publishing for their groundbreaking Arabesque line. **NIGHT MAGIC** went on to be recognized for Excellence in Romance Fiction by *Romantic Times Magazine*. Her third novel, **AFTER ALL**, became a movie produced by BET. Holly Robinson Peete stars as Michelle Toussaint, an investigative television reporter. In 2004 Lynn won three coveted Emma Awards. She was chosen Author of the Year and her novel **KISS LONELY GOODBYE** won Best Novel and Favorite Hero. **GOOD WOMAN BLUES** was nominated for the Romantic Times Best Mainstream Multicultural of 2005

Lynn's current titles include a paranormal mystery series set in Vermilion Parish, Louisiana featuring psychic LaShaun Rousselle and Deputy Chase Broussard, the latest release being Only By Moonlight. Pretty Dangerous is the third book in her Triple Trouble Mystery Series featuring a trio of female amateur sleuths.